P9-DXZ-195

The Rainy Spell
and Other Korean Stories

The Rainy Spell
and Other Korean Stories

Translated, with a Preface,
by Suh Ji-moon

onyx press

Onyx Press Ltd
86 Lauriston Road
London E9 7HA

ISBN 0 906383 24 2

© translation by Suh Ji-moon 1983
First published 1983

UNESCO COLLECTION OF REPRESENTATIVE WORKS
Korean Series

This book has been accepted in the Korean
Series of the Translations Collection of the
United Nations Educational, Scientific and
Cultural Organisation (UNESCO).

Set in Century
Typeset by Heather Hems, Chilmark, Wilts.
Printed in Great Britain by
Redwood Burn Ltd., Trowbridge, Wiltshire and
bound by Pegasus Bookbinding, Melksham, Wiltshire.

CONTENTS

For my mother, Mrs Duk Hee K. Suh

Preface

The work which eventually resulted in this book began as far back as ten years ago, shortly after my return from my first study trip abroad. It was not until I began my advanced study in English literature in America that I felt an intense yearning to know what the literature of my own country was like. Once abroad, I realised with shame that I was very ignorant of my own country's literature, having always taken it, like many other things Korean, for granted. But there was something much stronger than shame or curiosity or sentimentalism in my interest in Korean literature. It was like a thirst, and I think it came with my full awakening to the fact that only literature bears the full and true record of a nation's life.

Thus, when I returned to Korea with my MA in English literature, I began avidly reading in Korean literature. The reading enthralled me for many reasons. One delightful characteristic that I found running through almost all works of Korean literature was artlessness. Artlessness, of course, is a doubtful virtue in literature, inasmuch as literature is an art before it is anything else. And it is true that this artlessness not infrequently results in a lack of refinement in expression and in looseness of structure. But it also produces, more remarkably, a truly refreshing sense of immediacy and candour. This was the more delightful to me as it seemed a reflection of the unsophisticated Korean character, and it had a poignant beauty all its own.

This artlessness may seem surprising, in view of the fact

that most modern Korean men of letters, especially of the earlier era, have initiated or participated in some literary movement or other, have chosen literary careers when such activities were regarded as the surest road to poverty, and were very conscious of their literary aims and mission. But I think there may be an explanation here, too, in that for Korean men of letters their literary aims and mission meant mainly fulfilling the role of enlighteners, chastisers and champions of the people, and their self-definition as literary craftsmen was not very strong.

Modern Korean literature had a difficult birth amid harsh circumstances. It did not grow out of a native tradition. There was, of course, a literary tradition in pre-modern Korea, but it was not the kind of literature we know today, with professional writers and a ready reading public. For the upper-class man, literature was a gentlemanly tool and accomplishment, through which he absorbed all the philosophy and culture of his predecessors and in which he left what cultural contribution he had to make. It was also his pastime and emotional outlet, and as such was shared with high-born ladies or low-born entertaining women, the evidence of which we have in many gems of short formal verses.

For the populace, such literary and pseudo-literary media as prose fiction, mask dance dramas and puppet shows were entertainment and also served as outlets for their pent-up resentments against the ruling class, which they satirised and showed as ridiculous and contemptibly hypocritical. Some of the satire was, of course, directed at themselves—at their own servility, venality, and helplessness. Most of the popular literature output is anonymous, a fact from which many inferences can be drawn.

Koreans having suffered many abuses at the hands of fate and the social structure, the dominant mood of their verse literature was regret and longing. Some verses also show pungent wit and sarcasm, but these also had at the basis thwarted idealism and betrayed affection. In verse all emotions were lyricised, which enabled aesthetic distancing and purification. Prose literature always contained explicit didactic lessons; but the didactic aim was almost overbalanced by earthy humour, frank eroticism and uncouth satire. It is noteworthy that, while personal literature of the upper classes predominantly struck the chord of grief, the literature of the populace, while giving vent to their many grievances, celebrated life with its abundant energy.

As noted earlier, modern Korean literature did not grow out of this native tradition. It is not far wrong to say that modern literature, at least in its formal aspect, was born fully grown out of the heads of a few modernists early in this century.

The last years of the nineteenth century and the early years of the twentieth century were a period of turbulent unrest in Korea. Having long insisted on national isolation and rejection of foreign culture, Korea was still maintaining an agricultural economy and authoritarian political system that had become corrupt to the core. The masses having been exploited for centuries by the feudal bureaucracy, Korea was sick and impoverished internally and was defenceless against the foreign powers which tried to force open her doors.

Korea was on the brink of complete subjugation to Japan when Yi Kwang-soo (1892–?) and Choi Nam-sun (1890–1957) began their youth club and published the club's magazine, the first literary monthly in Korea, in 1908. Japan had forced a protective treaty upon Korea in 1905 and was soon to colonise it completely by annexation in 1910. Yi Kwang-soo and Choi Nam-sun shared a fervent zeal for national modernisation, and they had set for themselves the objective of awakening the nation to the past evils resulting from a Confucian political and social structure, and the new possibilities of a more democratic society and harmonious human relationships. And they adopted literature as their chosen tool.

Yi Kwang-soo established his position as a writer and humanitarian teacher very soon. Hard upon his heels came Kim Dong-in, who was his antithesis in literary creed and personal lifestyle. Kim Dong-in rebelled against Yi Kwang-soo's didactic aim and proclaimed an "art-for-art's-sake" literature. This is not, however, to be taken as a declaration for conscious and conscientious literary craftsmanship; it was an announcement that he would write what he liked in the way he liked, without any pragmatic aim. Kim Dong-in was a powerful writer who often wrote beautifully, hauntingly, but his arrogance and egotism prevented his attaining the self-discipline and full maturity of vision necessary for making him a great master.

After these two early giants came a great many writers, most of whom made significant contributions to the establishment and enrichment of the tradition of modern literature in Korea. Naturally reflecting the circumstances of the nation, a majority of the literary output of Korea in colonial times dealt with the suffering and sorrows of the Korean people, and comprises a chronicle of a nation's survival.

Thus it is only in recent times that beauty of form, both of words and of structure, began to be consciously cultivated by Korean authors. The beauty of the prose of Korean literature in the early years of its modernity, therefore, has the freshness of accidental achievement, and seems truly appropriate to the subject matter and viewpoint.

A greater and deeper delight was the life and character of the Korean people that Korean literature revealed. I had always assumed that I knew my people—their tragic past as victims of invading foreign powers and the feudal social system, their long and ceaseless struggle against poverty, and their dominant attitudes of withdrawal, resignation and passivity. It was not until I began reading deeply in Korean literature that I realised the full extent of the tragic implications of being born a Korean. To be born a Korean meant to be a victim of fate's caprice. There simply was no guarantee for the basic sanctities of life or the right of survival. Of course the villains of this violation could be traced—unjust or deceived rulers, the hierarchical and sexist social structure, the invading foreign enemy or the dire poverty which was the heritage of Koreans for centuries upon centuries. In almost every case, the victimisers were powers too huge to be fought individually, and thus the victimisation seemed, and was conveniently treated as, a wrong inflicted by fate. More frequently than not, Koreans reacted to the wrongs that fell their lot with tears and sighs rather than with vengeance and revolt.

These were the Korean characteristics until modern institutions of democracy and capitalism, and the newly opened possibilities of wealth attendant on industrialisation, turned many of us into aggressive pursuers of gain. All these factors were known to me more or less, and to most Koreans. What I did not suspect until I read deeply in Korean literature was that such passivity, such apparent lack of determined efforts for improvement of their conditions, were in fact wisdom gained through generations of experience of life in this land. I had not known until I met my fellow Koreans in literature that they *had to* become submissive and yielding *in order to survive*. It was the Koreans' way of living with their fate, without battering themselves against the huge, inhuman forces that wronged them, and without consuming themselves with indignation and resentment. I understood for the first time that lack of self-assertiveness can sometimes be a strength, and more often than not wisdom. It was truly moving to discover how my compatriots, with their simplicity and humility, have borne and made liveable inhuman conditions of life, and have managed to preserve their capacity for joy and affection.

I think it was this realisation, this discovery, that moved me so strongly to take up the task of introducing Korean literature abroad. I wanted to share these moving chronicles with more people, with people who have hitherto had no chance of meeting the real Koreans—the Korean people.

I did not know at the time how poorly qualified I was for such a task, both in my understanding of literature and life and in my skill with the English language. Even after painstaking revisions over many years I cannot claim to have done anything like justice to these moving stories I have dared to transcribe into what is an acquired language for me.

As I was moved to the task of translation by my love of the individual works, I did not really "select" the stories according to a set standard. The stories in this collection are simply my favourites. But I think my intuition guided me to some extent in choosing stories centring around typically Korean situations and sentiments, as stories that can most readily engage the interest of foreign readers. I have no intention of claiming that these works represent the finest achievements in Korean literature; there are many others that I respect equally or even more highly, but these have had the strongest appeal to me, and I hope and believe they will exert a similar appeal on foreign readers.

As a translator I have been as faithful as possible to the original, the translations representing full texts. For Korean customs and traditions, I have supplied footnotes only where factual information seemed necessary for intelligibility, and have left it to the readers' imagination to recognise and understand unwritten codes of behaviour and etiquette from the moods and circumstances inherent in the stories themselves.

My greatest debt in preparation of this book I owe to Mr James Wade, composer and writer, for reading the translations through, most of them twice, to correct errors of grammar and to smooth out awkward renderings. Mr Wade contributed this service when there was no definite prospect of financial remuneration, and I am doubly grateful to him for this reason.

Mr Milton Rosenthal, Mr Lionel Izod and Mr M.L. Sedat Jobe of the UNESCO headquarters in Paris have kindly read this anthology through, granted it the UNESCO seal of approval, and recommended it to the present publisher. My gratitude to them is unbounded. Sincere gratitude is also due to Mrs Katherine El Salahi of Onyx Press for her competent and prompt work in bringing out this book.

To the original authors of the stories included here, I am grateful for their authorisation for this publication.

Finally, this book is dedicated to my mother, who watched the whole process with loving concern.

Suh Ji-moon,
July 1982, Seoul

Yi Kwang-soo

Today, Yi Kwang-soo's position as the virtual founding father of modern literature in Korea is impregnable. Like many others who followed him, he was a child prodigy. Born in 1892, he was orphaned at the age of ten and went to Japan at twelve as a scholarship student. At fifteen he organised a Korean students' club in Japan and published the club's magazine Youth, the first literary monthly in Korea, for which he wrote poems and criticism. He wrote his first short story, 'Heartlessness', at the age of eighteen. This was later expanded into a novel and marks the first real modern fiction in Korean literature.

Yi Kwang-soo had to struggle throughout his life with severe illnesses, and suffered imprisonment for his patriotic activities. Notwithstanding, he produced a great quantity of poetry, fiction and critical essays, most of them bearing on the theme of the need for democratic human rights, reform of the feudal social and familial systems, spread of education, and marriage based on love. He also organised a campaign for use of simpler, less mannered and more colloquial language in writing. He was abducted to North Korea in 1950 by the invading Communists, and there has been no news of him since.

Although today his works are criticised for excessive didacticism and idealised characterisation, his importance not only as a literary pioneer and humanist teacher but as one of the great masters of fiction remains unchallenged. 'Halmum', written in 1940, although a slight piece, is a good example of his easy style and unaffected humanism.

1

Halmum

Yi Kwang-soo

"Young missus, what's that sound?" asked the old woman servant who had been polishing brassware in the front yard for Chusok,[2] when they heard the keening of hired funeral palanquin bearers passing their house.

"That's a funeral procession," answered the young mistress, without raising her head. She was sitting sewing on the floor in the living room, rapidly moving her needle.

"Is that a dead man being carried away to the grave?" Halmum asked in her heavy accent.

"Yes."

Halmum moved her toothless mouth for a good while and then asked carefully, "Young missus, can I go out to take a look?"

The young mistress said, "Yes, of course," and kept on sewing. The old woman carefully put on the rubber shoes she had bought the day before for 85 cents and ran towards the middle gate like a child. The lugubrious keening of the coffin

1. Halmum is a familiar or condescending appellation for a woman old enough to be a grandmother. Old women who worked as domestic helpers were usually called 'Halmum', but it could also be an affectionate term when used by old husbands for their wives.
2. Chusok is the biggest holiday for Koreans next to the New Year. It is the Korean equivalent of Thanksgiving, and people celebrate the new harvest by visiting relatives' houses and ancestors' graves. Being 15th August by the lunar calendar, it usually falls in late September or early October, and marks therefore the beginning of cool, though not cold days.

bearers continued to float by.

After the Halmum's footsteps died away, the young mistress turned and called her husband, who was reading in the inner room.

"Yes?" the young man answered without raising his eyes from the book.

"Halmum's just like a child," the young mistress laughed and said, "She went to look at a funeral passing," and laughed again. The young man did not laugh but came out to the living room with a cigar and a match and an ashtray.

"She's got a lively curiosity, like anybody from the country," he said, striking a match and lighting the cigar. The young mistress ignored the generalisation and went on,

"Oh, listen to me. She went out to look at a funeral the day before yesterday and she said she lost her way in front of the police station. How could she have lost the way from here to the police station?"

The young man sat down on the edge of the floor and swung his legs,[3] and instead of concurring with his wife, queried, "Dear, isn't she a very good woman?"

"Oh yes, she is. The old woman's got a heart of gold. She's rather stupid, like many country people, but she's hard-working and she never cheats us. I don't feel like scolding her even when she breaks things. But she says she'll go home before Chusok. She says she'd die of cold if she stayed in Seoul after Chusok, so she'll go back to her home and stay in her warm room and mend her grandchildren's rags. She says she won't stay here even if we let her sleep in the inner room and give her thick covers. She says she has to go home before Chusok. She won't stay with us even if we raise her salary. She says she doesn't need money. Darling, why is she like that? If she stayed here she'd be well fed and she'd make money, too."

3. In a Korean house, rooms are built on an elevated plane above the ground, and one must step up from the yard to the rooms and step down to the yard from the rooms. The edge of the living-room floor is therefore frequently used as seats for momentary visitors or for brief rests between work in the yard, or for any casual relaxation. There are usually a few stone steps on which shoes are left, as Koreans do not wear shoes in the rooms.

The young mistress, as if worried about the old woman servant and her unreasonable obstinacy, stuck the needle in the collar of her blouse and turned to face her husband. The young man also looked interested and asked, "Is she going away?"

"Yes. From the first she said she'd go back by Chusok, and now she talks about going home every day. Yesterday she said she'd like to buy silver hair-slides for her daughter and daughter-in-law, so I took her to the night market. When she was told a silver one costs one won and eighty cents, she said if she bought two silver ones she wouldn't have the train fare home, and thought for a long time and said she couldn't buy them, and hurried out of the market. Isn't that funny? Maybe she thought silver hair-slides cost ten or twenty cents apiece."

She sat thinking for a while and then said in an impressed tone, "Isn't it nice of her, to work so hard to earn money and then think of buying presents for her daughter and daughter-in-law?"

"What does her son do?"

"Her son seems to be a real bad sort. He hates working, and he sells off anything in the house. So she says she didn't tell her son she was coming to Seoul when she left, but that she kept looking back for miles to see if her son was coming to ask her to go back. She said she was going to go back if the son came after her and insisted on her going back home. But he didn't show even the tip of his nose, so she cried. What a worthless son that is!"

"Then she doesn't have a house of her own?"

"She has a small house of her own. Her husband left money for her to buy one when he died. Well, maybe that son of hers has sold it by now."

"Her husband bought her one?" the young man asked.

"Yes. The old woman was widowed at thirty-five, and she didn't have any means of livelihood with her children, so she remarried. The second husband had sons and some property, too, and before he died he told his son to buy the old woman a house, so she has a small house of her own," the young mistress said, turning over her sewing. "She calls that husband's family the big house. I guess she was his 'small house'.[4] She says she goes to stay at the big house often even now. She says her husband's son is always inviting her to come to live with him and his family."

The older mistress of the house called "Halmum! Halmum!" from the back yard.

The young mistress laughed and shouted, "She's gone sightseeing."

"Sightseeing? What sight?" the older woman, who was still invisible, shouted back.

"She's gone to see a funeral procession," the young mistress answered, raising her voice again. The older mistress was slightly deaf.

At last she came out through the kitchen door with unsteady steps, saying, "Oh, she might lose her way again. Why is she so fond of looking at coffins? Has she been out long?" She stepped up into the living room.

The young mistress said, "Oh no she won't, mother,[5] not again."

Right then the old servant woman came in with slow steps.

The older mistress laughed and asked, "You didn't lose your way this time?"

"No. I was afraid of that, so I didn't follow it but looked at it standing right in front of this house," the old woman said, blinking her soft dim eyes. Everybody laughed aloud. Halmum, not knowing what it was about, followed suit. The older mistress lit her pipe at the brazier and asked,

"Well, was it an interesting sight?"

"What?" the old woman asked back, not understanding.

"Was the coffin palanquin colourful and nice to look at?"

---

4. To be the 'small house' of a man means to be his mistress, or extra wife. Such a relationship was usually permanent, and men entered into such relations as much for the purpose of procuring heirs or for other reasons of convenience as for amorous reasons. Women usually entered into such arrangements to secure means of support.

5. It is hard to tell from what is told in this story whether the mother here is the young wife's mother-in-law or own mother. It is unusual for the wife's mother to live with a married couple, and if such were the case, it would have been mentioned; on the other hand, the informality of the relationship here suggests it. The translator has assumed that it is a regular household, with an unusually fond mother-in-law and daughter-in-law.

"Oh no. There were only a few people following the coffin, and only the hired bearers were keening. It must have been a lonely man," the old woman answered and began scrubbing the bowls again.

"Then it couldn't have been nice to look at. Only sumptuous coffins with a lot of bereaved kinsfolk are good to look at," the older mistress said and glanced at the old woman. The old woman did not understand "sumptuous" and "bereaved" but said,

"Well, what's the difference? They'll all rot after they get buried," and scrubbed hard.

"But people don't look at it that way." The older mistress relighted her long pipe and went on, "They say death is as important as birth. So people prefer to be buried well. You and me, neither of us has long to live. Don't you think so? How old are you?"

The old woman said, "Sixty-five," without emotion, and scrubbed harder, as if she was out of temper.

"Sixty-five. . ." The older mistress exhaled smoke with a sigh and said, "Then, wouldn't you like to be carried to the grave in a big colourful coffin?"

"Why, of course I'd like to be." She was now beginning to clean the chamber pot, and said, "I'd like to be buried well, but I haven't got any money. The likes of me are lucky if we get buried in a proper coffin. These days I'd be happy if only my son would mind me a little."

Everybody laughed. Halmum laughed, too. The young mistress said comfortingly, "It doesn't matter how you get buried, as long as you go to a good place afterwards."

"I've done nothing good, so how can I go to a good place?" said Halmum, scooping cold water from the water jar and drinking it.

The older mistress was silent for a while and then, putting aside her pipe, recited, "Ohm Jirijiri Baura Badara Hohmbata," and fingered her prayer beads. The young mistress gazed at the toothless mouth of her mother-in-law and then signalled to her husband in the inner room to look at his mother. The young man looked at his mother's mouth. The old servant, with one hand in the chamber pot, also gazed at the older woman's mouth. A fly made as if to alight on Halmum's eyelash but changed its mind and flew away. The young mistress, unable to suppress her laughter, giggled. Halmum laughed and the young man also laughed. The older mistress, opening her eyes wide as if startled out of a revery, also laughed.

The young mistress squeezed her sides and mimicked, "Oh, mother, hahaha! Ohm Badara Hombatang."

The woman servant eagerly turned and said, "Missus, this Ohm Badara, would I go to a good place if I learned to say that?"

The old mistress turned to look at her and replied, "Who knows if there's anywhere for souls to go? They say chanting the scripture will do good for the soul, so. . ."

"Then can I learn, too? Oh, the likes of me have no memory. Ohm Badara Hambakdang." The old woman tried with her hardened tongue.

The young mistress corrected her, "No. Ohm Baura Badara Hohmbata. Now try."

The old woman tried, "Ohm Baura Hohmbatak." She had omitted "Badara".

This time the older mistress taught her, "Ohm Baura Badara Hohmbatang."

"Oh, I can't do it. I keep forgetting." She gave up and scrubbed the chamber pot hard.

"Halmum, don't go back to your home but stay with us. Then I'll teach you the scripture verses. Yes? Do stay," the older mistress earnestly pleaded with her.

"How can I, in the cold? I heard it's killing cold in winter in Seoul." She gave her usual excuse.

The young mistress joined in, "Look, Halmum, we'll give you clothes and covers. Don't go, Halmum. Will you stay, please?"

Halmum could not give a cold answer to such earnest pleas, so she hesitated for a while and said, "Well, I'll go back *after* Chusok, then." Before her dull eyes loomed her son and daughter and the countryside in which she had lived and toiled for nearly seventy years. Then Halmum said again as if she had made a big decision, "Yes. I'll go *after* Chusok, then."

Everyone became solemn. Nobody spoke. Seeing that the

shadow spread now over more than half the yard, Halmum went into the kitchen. The old woman who had borne many children and laboured hard all through the near-seventy years of her life fed logs into the stove without any sign of complaint on her face.

Kim Dong-in

Kim Dong-in was born in 1900 in Pyongyang into a family of great wealth. He studied in Japan after 1914, and engaged in literary activities from 1919 with other Korean students there who shared his vision of literature and with whom he founded a cotery magazine called Creation. *From the first, he had set before himself a distinctively artistic objective for his literature as opposed to Yi Kwang-soo's humanitarian and didactic aims.*

One of the many precocious literary geniuses of the early years of modern literature in Korea ('The Seaman's Chant' [1920] was written at twenty years of age), his overconfidence in himself led to a lack of discipline, both in his art and in his private life. His novels convey the force of his confidence in his vision, but his vision of humanity was not fully mature. It was unfortunate for him that he came so early in the modern period of Korean literature, and thus lacked a frame of achievement against which to measure himself. He neglected critical evaluation of himself as artist and thinker, and his works exhibit many flaws as a result of this neglect. However, his boldness in claiming for literature a territory all its own, independent of social and moral considerations (an audacious act indeed in the climate of the day), which is borne out by his own practice, greatly aided experimentation in, and diversification of, Korean literature. 'The Seaman's Chant' is an unashamed melodrama redeemed by its haunting remorse that exerts a strong appeal to our primal sympathy.

The Seaman's Chant

Kim Dong-in

That day it was heavenly weather.

It was heavenly weather, but not the kind where there is hardly a speck of cloud and the sky seems unapproachably high, as if it were looking down on men with contemptuous haughtiness. It was the kind of heavenly weather when the sky looks upon us through the pink blossoms of low clouds, like an earnest sympathiser with men, offering us friendship. It was a loving sky. I was lying relaxed on the greening grass at the foot of Peony Hill, facing the Taedong River that incessantly pours its blue waters into the Yellow Sea.

It was the third of March, the day boating parties began on the Taedong. On the river flowing far below, banquet boats were gliding and bobbing, breaking the water into a thousand gem-like glitters, and from the boats came poignant spring-intoxicated melodies, stirring the fragrant, velvety spring air. And the strains of Korean musical instruments, drifting up with the songs of the female entertainers—now slowly, now drawlingly, now volubly, now softly, now plaintively—sounded as if they would not leave you alone until they had blended everything into the sentiment of spring, nor cease before they built a bridge of melody between the dark waters of the Taedong River, and the green grass growing on its banks, and even the warm blood in the human heart pounding to the thrill of spring.

It made music, incomparably beautiful music, when the soft, light wind brushed past the dark Korean pine trees

13

and the sprouting grass.

Ah, the beauty of the green spring that intoxicates men! That spring could not fail to make a doubly strong impression on me, as I had lived in Tokyo since the age of fifteen, and had been denied the relish of this kind of spring for many years.

In the town of Pyongyang, one could perceive the arrival of spring by the new plants that sprouted through the chapped earth, and the young shoots on the willow trees. It was not fully spring in Pyongyang yet, but over this area around Peony Hill and in the Changrim plain that one could see across the Taedong River (a plain fertile as the land of Canaan), spring had poured profusely its affectionate caresses.

One could picture in the mind without actually seeing them the green fields adorned with the bluish-green ripening wheat and barley, and the figures of the farmers looking upon their fields with contented smiles.

The clouds seemed to be incessantly flying across the sky. The shadow of the clouds on the wheat field rushed far away now, and in their place spread green, as green as the green of the newly-created world. When there was a wind to stir it, the full-grown winter wheat bent low and straightened up in ranks like a wave, flashing now dark green, now light green. And hawks, floating high up in the sky as if in praise of the leisureliness of that spring, added to the happiness and beauty.

"I will rise, to the warm affection of spring,
   I will rise, to the affection of the warm spring."

I recited aloud the familiar lyric a couple of times and lit a cigarette. The smoke from the cigarette soared to the sky in wreaths.

Spring had come to the sky also. The sky was low. It looked as if, should you climb to the top of Peony Hill, you could touch it. The pinkish clouds, which seemed to be higher than the sky, were flying here and there, mingling and parting.

I cannot help thinking it is Utopia whenever I see the beautiful scenery in spring and hear the murmur of its fullness. What is our end in striving like this hour after hour? Isn't it for construction of a Utopia?

Whenever I think of Utopia, I cannot help but be reminded of that manliest of men, the one who enjoyed the greatness of manhood to the utmost, Shih Huang Ti of China.[1]

No matter how many thousands of historians abuse him, Shih Huang Ti, who sent off three hundred virgin boys abroad in search of the elixir of eternal life, and who built his palace of pleasure in all the perfection of luxury and beauty; and who enjoyed banqueting every day with thousands of his subjects, and who thus strove to construct a Utopia on this earth, was the truest of the true arbiters of pleasure, and the greatest man since the beginning of history. The history of the human world can boast of having had a great man, since it produced a man of such sheer courage, even if the world were to end now.

"A great man was he indeed," I said to myself and raised my head.

Just at that moment I heard a strange, sad sound coming from the direction of Kija's tomb,[2] stirring the spring air. I was listening to it even before I realised it. It was a seaman's chant, the Baetaragi of Yong-yu.[3] The singer was undoubtedly an expert, for the strain was divine—far above the artistry of any male professional singer or female entertainer.

"I pray, I pray to you, spirit
  Of the hills and the rivers, of the wind and the land,

1. Shih Huang Ti of China is of course the notorious Chinese tyrant of the third century B.C., whose cruelty and sensuous extravagance remain unsurpassed. He built the Great Wall of China and reputedly had three thousand concubines and committed other incredible deeds. The fact that he is here mentioned in glowing terms is proof enough of Kim Dong-in's amoral aestheticism and adolescent worship of power (he was twenty when he wrote this story).
2. Kija is the legendary refugee from China who reputedly founded Kija Chosun in prehistoric Korea. It is generally held today that Kija Chosun is a fiction created by the Chinese to justify their partial colonisation of Korea in the second century B.C. The tomb, therefore, is also regarded as a sham.
3. Yong-yu is a town in the Pyongan Namdo Province, now in north Korea.

Of the sun and the moon, the stars and planets,
And to God in Heaven above,
To spare our lives, fragile as a reed,
To grant us a span more of this life.
Oh, sad is this existence, this life on earth."

When the chanting had progressed thus far, the songs of the female entertainers, mingled with the music of the hourglass drum,[4] came up from the river below and the Baetaragi could be heard no more.

A couple of years ago I had spent a summer in Yong-yu. Whoever has spent a season in Yong-yu, the birthplace of the song called Baetaragi, cannot but feel the unassuageable sorrow of this melody.

Whoever has once looked upon the vast Yellow Sea from atop the nameless mountain of Yong-yu in the evening would be unable to forget the sight of the sun sinking below its waters. Looking at the sun, that great mass of flame, dancing on the surface of the overbrimming sea, threatening to sink into it or to soar above it the next moment, and hearing a plaintive strain coming intermittently from an invisible boat, I used to shed many tears of nameless sorrow, emotionally impressionable as I was. At moments like that, you do not feel like dismissing as fantastic the story of the magistrate's wife who left behind her wealth and dignity to go and live an aimless life on the waters with a seaman.

Even after my return from Yong-yu, the melody of the Baetaragi was engraved deep in my memory, never to be forgotten, and I have never ceased longing to go back to Yong-yu once again to hear the chant and to gaze on the entrancing sunset once more.

The singing of the female entertainers and the sound of the hourglass drum ceased, and only the mournful melody of the seaman's chant was heard drifting along the wind. Sometimes, because of the gusts of adverse wind, the chant ceased

4. The drum is shaped like an hourglass and its two ends are covered with skins of different thickness. It is struck with the palm or a stick, and is a very popular instrument for beating time. It can be slung from the shoulder of dancers, and the hourglass drum dance shows the female body line to advantage.

to be heard, but with the aid of my memory I could re-
construct the lyrics clearly in my mind.

"My beloved, meeting me walking on the riverbank,
  Didn't know if it was life or a dream;
  Ran up to me, and seizing me with her thin fingers,
  Said between sobs: 'Have you dropped from Heaven,
  'Sprung out of the earth, blown here on the wind,
  'Or been carried by the clouds?'
When thus we were bathed in tears, holding fast to one
    another,
All our folks and friends gathered to. . ."

Hearing this much, I could not stay still any more, but
sprang to my feet, put on the hat I had hung on a pine
bough, and went up to the top of Peony Hill to make out
the direction of the song. The sound could be heard more
clearly from the top of the hill. The singer sang the refrain
of the chant:

"Even if you had to go begging for food,
  Oh, never, never go to sea again.
  Oh, sad is this lot, this life on earth."

I stood still, desperately yearning to make out the direction
of the sound. "Where? Kija's tomb? The Moonlight Pavilion?"
But I could not stay still very long. I was going to find him
out at any cost, so I started off, determined to investigate
everywhere thereabouts.

The deep pine forest around Kija's tomb spread before me.
"Where?" I asked myself again.

At that moment he began the Baetaragi anew. The sound
came from left of me. Heartened, I searched among the pine
trees for a good while, feeling for the direction of the sound,
before I found him lounging alone in a sunny place near the
tomb that had a good view of the sky. His looks were as I had
imagined: angular face, nose, mouth, eyes, limbs. . . The
deeply grooved wrinkles on his forehead and his dark eyebrows bespoke his tortuous past, and also the simplicity of
his nature.

He sat up and ceased singing when he saw a man in gentlemanly attire looking at him.

"Oh, why don't you just go on?" So saying, I sat down beside him.

"Oh. . ." He barely answered and, raising his eyes, looked up at the clear sky. They were nice eyes. The greatness and vastness of the sea were well reflected in his eyes. He was a seaman, I guessed at once.

"Are you a native of Yong-yu?"

"Well, I was born there, but it's been nearly twenty years since I saw it last."

"Why have you neglected to visit your home town for so long?"

"Well, it's a man's fate. Things never go as one wants them to." So saying, he heaved a sigh. "It's destiny that's our master." His voice held a note of immitigable bitterness and regret.

"Oh, do you think so?" I could only look at him in interrogative silence.

After a considerable pause I spoke to him again. "Let me hear your past history, if it's not a jealously guarded secret."

"What secret could there be worth guarding in the history of one like me?"

"Well then, please let me hear it."

He looked up at the sky again. After a pause he said, "Very well," lighted a cigarette as I did, and began his story.

"It was on the eleventh of August, nineteen years back. . ." And he told me a story which went thus:

The town he lived in was a small village facing the sea, a few miles from Yong-yu. In the village of some thirty households he was a man of some consequence.

He had lost both his parents before he was fifteen, and the only remaining members of his family consisted of himself, his wife, and his younger brother and sister-in-law who lived next door to him. The two brothers were among the better-off villagers, and the most skilled in fishing. They had some learning as well, and excelled most in the chanting of Baetaragi. In other words, they were the most eminent family in the village.

The August Full Moon Day is a big holiday there as elsewhere. On the eleventh of August, he set off towards town to
do some shopping for the Full Moon Day feast, and also to
buy a mirror for his wife, which she had been yearning for
for a long time.

"Buy one bigger than Mrs. Kim's. You won't forget, will
you?" his wife asked him again and again, following him as
far as the entrance of the road to town to see him off.

"I won't," he promised, and left his village for the town,
the red sun showering rays upon him from the front.

He had doted on his wife (though such an admission
always makes a man look silly, he said). His wife had been a
delicate and pretty woman, such as is not frequently met
with in such country villages. "I don't think you can find
many like her, even if you go to the pleasure resorts of
Pyongyang," he said.

So they were a devoted couple, something which was rare
and regarded as ridiculous in villages like that. Aged people
often told him not to lose his head over his own wife.

Although they loved each other, or perhaps because they
did, he was very jealous about his wife. Not that she was
unfaithful or lewd, but she was of a gay temperament, made
friends easily with other people and was affectionate to
anybody.

In his village, young men used to gather in his house on
holidays or celebration days, on the pretext that his house
was the cleanest and most spacious.

All the young men called his wife "sister", and his wife
called them "brother" and chatted and laughed with them,
and her gay mouth at those times always wore an affectionate smile. At those times he would just keep glaring at her
with evil eyes from a corner, and after the young men left
he would jump on her without a word and kick and beat
her like mad, taking away from her all that he had given her
as presents before. Whenever there was a quarrel in his
house his brother and brother's wife next door would come
to appease them, and then he would always beat his brother
and sister-in-law, too.

There was a reason for his behaving in such a way towards
his brother. His brother was a well-built man with a dignity

unusual for a country youth, and was of fair complexion, although always buffeted by the sea wind. That might have been sufficient reason in itself for him to be jealous, but he just couldn't contain his fury since his wife was especially kind to his brother.

About half a year prior to his departure from Yong-yu— that is, about half a year before his trip to the town market to buy a mirror—he had celebrated his birthday. His wife had made many delicious dishes for him. One of his habits was to save his favourite foods for later. His wife couldn't be ignorant of his habit, but when his brother came about lunchtime she started to give his brother the food he was saving for later. He raised his eyebrows to signify that she should not give it to the brother, but his wife, whether she had noticed or not, went ahead and gave the dishes to his brother. He was very upset. He was going to make her pay for it, and he was looking for the merest excuse. His wife, coming away after setting the food table before her brother-in law, stepped on his foot by accident.

"You bitch!" He raised his foot high and kicked his wife with all his might. The woman fell across the table, and then painfully arose again.

"You bitch! How dare you step on your man!"

"Did it get broken or something?" the wife, blushing, wailed in a tearful voice.

"You bitch! How dare you cross words with your man?" He stood up and grasped her by the long braid of her hair.

"Brother, why do you treat her so harshly?" His younger brother stood up and held his arm.

"You shut up, you son of a bitch!" He pushed his brother away and showered kicks and blows on his wife.

"You dirty bitch! You get out of here or I'll kill you."

"Kill me if you want! I won't leave this house even if you kill me."

"You won't leave this house?"

"Never! This is my house!"

At that moment, he felt stabbed in the heart by his wife's protest that she would never leave his house. He did not feel like beating her any more. He stood there giving her a vicious look for some time and then ran outside, shouting, "You

God-damned bitch, then *I* will leave."

Without bothering to answer his brother, who came running after him and asked, "Where are you going, brother?" he went to a roadside tavern in the neighbouring village without one backward glance and sat down before a liquor table with a hostess.

Completely drunk, he went home that evening with a bundle of cakes for his wife.

Thus there was peace for some time. But the peace could not last forever. It was broken again because of his brother.

His brother, who used to go to town frequently, began to be absent from his home, staying in the town for days at a stretch from around the end of May. About the same time, the rumour that he had a mistress in town spread in the village. Hearing this rumour, the elder brother's wife hated her brother-in-law's trips to town more than insects, and when he returned after a few days' stay in town, she would go at once to the brother's house to argue with him. She even quarrelled with her sister-in-law for not preventing him from going to town.

Around the beginning of July, the brother returned from town after about ten days' stay there. His wife, as usual, quarrelled with her brother-in-law and his wife, and even came to him reviling him for not preventing his brother going down the path of evil. Having long been resentful of his wife's attitude, he began shouting at her at once.

"What business is that of yours? I don't want to hear it."

"You fool! You can't even keep your own younger brother from going to evil places!" his wife shouted back in anger.

"What did you say, you bitch?" He stood up.

"Fool!"

Before she could finish the word, she was pitched down on the floor with a scream.

"You bitch! Who taught you to talk like that to your man?"

"Then who taught you to beat your wife like this? Fool!" she wailed in a tearful voice.

"You low-down bitch, you! You get out of my house! Get out of my house this minute!" he yelled, while beating her with all his strength without pause. And he opened the door and threw her out.

"I won't go!" she screamed, and ran out, weeping.

"The God-damned bitch!" He vomited an oath and flopped down on the floor.

His wife did not return after the sun had set and darkness covered the village. Although he had thrown her out, he was waiting for her to return. In that darkness, without bothering to light the lamp, he waited for his wife to return, shaking with fury. But he could hear his wife's merry laughter from his brother's house next door all night. He spent the night sitting riveted on the floor, and at dawn he took the knife from the kitchen and flung open the gate, determined to kill both his wife and his brother.

Had his wife not been standing there outside the gate looking into the house with a worried face, he really would have killed them both. But the moment he saw her face, he felt love filling his heart. He flung away the knife, seized her by the hair and dragged her in, yelling, "You bitch!" Throwing her down on the floor, he bit her cheeks and fondled her in a frenzy.

There would be no end to it if he were to tell all the incidents of this kind, but in brief such had been the relationship between him, his wife and his brother.

To make a long story short, he had found a good mirror that day in the town market. Compared with mirrors of today, the thing enlarged or distorted a nose or a mouth, but a mirror at that time and in such a village was something as precious as a jewel. After he had bought the mirror and did all the other shopping, he headed for his house without even taking his usual refreshment at the roadside tavern, walking in the direction of the overbrimming sea, crimson-coloured with the evening sun, happy in the expectation of his wife's joy at the valuable present.

But he encountered a dumbfounding scene when he stepped into his house.

Spread in the middle of the room was a table laden with cakes, and his brother, whose hood was loosened and hanging down behind his neck, and the fastening of whose jacket was almost untied, was standing in a corner. His wife's hair was undone and the waist of her skirt had slid down to the hips.

His wife and brother, on seeing him, did not stir a step, as if they didn't know what to do.

The three just stood there like that for a while, lost. Then his brother at last managed to speak: "Where has that rat disappeared?"

"Oh, a rat! A magnificent rat you were catching!" He threw down his bundle, and even before he finished speaking, he grasped his brother by the collar.

"Brother! It was really a rat!"

"A rat! You low-life! What son of a bitch catches that kind of a rat with his sister-in-law?" He gave his brother a few hard slaps on the cheek and threw him out the door, pushing him from behind. Then he swooped down on his wife, who was standing trembling with fear.

"You bitch! What bitch on earth catches that kind of a rat with a brother-in-law?" He kicked his wife to the floor and showered blows upon her, not caring where they fell.

"It was a rat, really. Oh, you're killing me!"

"You say a rat, too, you bitch? Serves you right to die!" All four of his limbs fell on his wife indiscriminately.

"You're killing me! Really, I was just going to give your brother some cakes when. . ."

"None of your excuses! What excuse do you have, you bitch who slept with a brother-in-law?"

"No! No! I mean it. A big rat jumped out. . ."

"Still babbling about a rat?"

"We were trying to catch it!"

"You dirty bitch! Serves you right to die! Why don't you drown your dirty body in the water and go to hell!"

He beat his wife till he had no strength left, and then threw her out by pushing her from behind as he had his brother, shouting, "Go feed the fish!"

Although he had beaten her to his heart's content, his wrath was far from appeased. He went to a corner of the room, stood leaning against the wall like a man out of his wits, and kept gazing at the cakes on the table.

The village faced west toward the sea, so night came there later than in other places, but it became dark about eight o'clock. To light a lamp, he moved away from the wall and went around looking for a match. The matches were not in the usual place. He was feeling about here and there, and pushed his hand inside a heap of old clothes when there came a squeaking sound and something ran out from the heap and rapidly scurried away to the other side of the room.

"It really *was* a rat!" he muttered faintly, and dropped down there, all his strength drained out of him. The scene that took place in the room during his absence went through his head like a scene in a play: The brother came. His wife, who was always kind to her brother-in-law, prepared a cake table for him. Then out jumped a rat from nowhere. The two ran about, trying to catch the rat. The rat, which had teased them for a good while, suddenly disappeared into a corner. The two searched about, trying to find the rat. It was at that moment that he stepped in.

"The bitch. She'll come back all right. Where would she go, anyway?" He calmed himself with difficulty and lay down.

But his wife did not return, even when the night was spent and it was broad daylight again. By and by he got worried, so he set out in search of her.

She was not at his brother's house either. No one in the whole village had had a glimpse of her. Then at last about noon they found his wife on the seashore a few miles away from the village. But his wife was not the pretty, vivacious woman she used to be, but a dead woman swollen to twice her size with foam at her mouth, at the mouth that used to smile so prettily.

He was not conscious of what was happening while he was carrying his wife home on his back.

They buried her the next day without much ceremony. On the face of his brother who trod behind him on the way home from the grave there was a look of reproach, as if he wanted to say, "What have you done, brother?"

His brother disappeared from their small village the day after the funeral. A couple of days went by without people taking much notice of his absence, but five or six days passed and his brother still did not return. When he made inquiries, he learned that someone who fitted the description of his brother was seen several days before walking wearily towards the east, with a small cloth sack on his back and with the red rays of the evening sun shining on his back. Ten days, then twenty days went by, but his brother never again made an appearance, and his sister-in-law, left alone, sighed away her life.

He could not stand to see her thus. He was to blame for all the miseries. At last he became a seaman, and boarded a ship to be at least always near the sea that killed his wife, and to inquire about his brother wherever he went. Everywhere he made inquiries about his brother, giving out his name and a description, but he could find no information whatever about him.

Ten years went by like that, on land and on the waters. Then one autumn, nine years ago, his ship was wrecked by a storm while sailing through a thick fog on the sea off Yon-an, and some of his fellow seamen were drowned, but he floated on the water almost unconscious.

It was night when he regained consciousness. He found himself on land again, somehow, and illumined by the flames of the log fire burning beside him, he saw the face of his brother, who was tending him.

Strangely enough he was not even surprised, and slowly spoke to his brother: "Why, brother! How have you come here?"

His brother was silent, then answered at length: "Brother, it all is up to Fate."

He was about to fall asleep again from the warmth of the fire, but he woke up startled and exclaimed: "How pale you've become, brother, in these ten years!"

"I have indeed, but you have changed too, brother."

Hearing these words half asleep and half waking, he fell into a fast sleep again. Then after a few hours of delicious sleep, he woke up to find that the red fire was still burning, but that his brother was not to be seen. When he managed to question people about him, he was told that his brother had been sitting there looking into his face for a long time and had disappeared into the darkness without a word, walking tiredly, with the red flames illuminating his back.

However diligently he inquired after his brother the next day, he could not unearth the slightest information about him, so he set off on another journey by water on another

ship. When the ship reached Haeju, he thought he saw someone who looked like his brother in a shop while he was in
the town market making a purchase, so he ran over at once,
but the man had already disappeared. His ship did not
anchor in Haeju, so he had to continue his journey on the
sea, leaving his heart in Haeju.

Then for three years after that he caught not a glimpse of
his brother, though his journey took him far and wide.

After a lapse of three years, or six years ago, while his ship
was sailing fast by Kangwhado Island, he heard the strains of
Baetaragi floating towards the sea from the vicinity of a
steep hill near the shore. It was a Baetaragi he well knew
was his brother's, the lyrics and melody of it being modified
by his brother in a way no one but his brother knew how
to chant.

The ship did not stop at Kangwhado, so he had no choice
but to sail past the island, but as it was anchoring for about
ten days in nearby Inchon, he disembarked at once and went
to Kangwhado. He made inquiries all over the island, and at
last got information from a small streetside tavern that one
who bore his brother's name and who looked like his brother
had stayed there for some time, but had left for Inchon a
few days earlier. He sped back at once to Inchon and looked
for him, but could not find him even in that small town.

Thereafter six years passed, but he could not meet his
brother again, and did not even know whether he was still
alive or not.

When he finished his story, his eyes shone with tears in the
evening glow of the sun.

I asked after a pause: "What became of your sister-in-
law?"

"I don't know. I haven't gone back to Yong-yu for twenty
years now."

"Where will you be going from here?"

"That I don't know either. What destination could there
be for one like me? I will just be going where the wind will
carry me."

Then once more he sang a strain of Baetaragi for me.

Oh, the immitigable regret in that strain! The sorrowful

longing for the sea!

After he finished the song, he stood up and walked absently in the direction of the Moonlight Pavilion, with the scarlet evening sun pouring its rays on his back. Not knowing how to detain him, I just sat there, gazing at his back.

That night after I returned home I could not fall asleep, so vividly did the melody of his chant and the tale of his fateful life ring in my ears. The next day I rose up early, and without eating breakfast ran toward Kija's tomb and looked for him. The grass on which he had been sitting, flattened down, bespoke of his having been there, but he was not to be found anywhere in the vicinity.

But—but the strain of the Baetaragi seemed to be ringing from somewhere, as if it would not leave off until it had made all the pine trees there vibrate to its melody.

"It's from Peony Hill! He's on Peony Hill!" So exclaiming, I ran up to the top of Peony Hill at one stride. There was not a soul on the hill. I went to the tower but he was not there either.

"It's from the Moonlight Pavilion!" I said, and went to the Moonlight Pavilion. From the pavilion to the tower on top of Peony Hill, the needles of all the pine trees—grown densely, as if not to let even a drop of water seep through, as if their roots stretched to the very heart of Hell—were singing the tremulous strain of the Baetaragi, but he was nowhere in sight. The tens of millions of needles of the pine trees that stretched skyward from Kija's tomb, and the countless million blades of grass that spread thickly underneath the pines, all were singing a doleful strain of Baetaragi, but he could not be seen anywhere near this small Peony Hill.

When I inquired at the riverside, I heard that his ship had left that morning.

Thereafter, although summer, autumn, and indeed a full year has gone by, and it is now spring again, he who had passed through this city of Pyongyang and left behind that fateful tale and the sorrowful Baetaragi did not make an appearance again around this small Peony Hill.

Spring has come again to Peony Hill and Kija's tomb, and the grass he sat on last year has all grown straight again, and is about to bloom in purple blossoms; but he who made the confession of his undying regret with the doleful strains of Baetaragi was not to be seen again on this small hill near this small tomb. Only the leaves, all the small leaves, whisper the strain he has left behind, as if in commemoration, as if in consolation.

Yu Chin-o

Yu Chin-o, born in Seoul in 1906, is better known today as a scholar of law and educator than as an author. An outstanding student throughout his school life, Yu, like many other early giants of modern Korean literature, began writing in his teens. He organised a students' literary club in his student days and started a club magazine.

Having become a law student in 1926, he organised a student club which, with the addition of radical members the following year, turned leftist. From 1927 he began writing in earnest. At first his stories had a proletarian leaning, concerning themselves with the harsh lot of working-class people, but from 1935 there is less ideological content in his works.

'Clear Water Pavilion' (1940) has the fresh naiveté appropriate to a recollection of childhood. In his adult stories he shows great sensitivity to the nuance and tone of everyday occurrences, to subtle hints of words and gesture, psychological penetration, and an understanding of feminine psychological needs uncommon for a man of his times. However, literature was not his major occupation at any time, and he stopped writing after Korea's liberation when the country demanded his services as a scholar of law. He drafted the constitution of the new republic, and for many years was a professor of law and university president. After his retirement he went into politics briefly, became president of the New Democratic Party, and even ran for the presidency on the opposition ticket in 1967. He lives quietly in retirement now.

The Clear Water Pavilion

Yu Chin-o

1

"As soon as the sun sets, nostalgia soaks me through like salt water," sang Mr C., a poet friend of mine. It is true that the longing for home is a feeling poignant and sweet, beautiful and unsettling, joyful and sad, residing within us but undefinable; and yet when we are tired in mind and body from disappointment or frustration, it creeps into our hearts like salt water, to dye in pink shades the memories of the past, and makes us fret with yearning for the small pine hill behind our boyhood country house and those childhood friends who used to go to the village school with us and carry out raids together on neighbourhood chickens on winter days. It is a sentiment that has such strange power.

But nostalgia is not something that always unsettles the mind; if we have room in our hearts for it, it can gently smooth our coarsened emotions, and collect into a single thread our torn and tangled thoughts. Let us imagine that here is a man who had come to live in youth hundreds of miles from home with great ambition for his life. After decades of rough rain and storm, when the grooves on his forehead have deepened and the grey strands in his hair grow daily more numerous, one moonlit night he finds it hard to fall asleep because of the longing in his heart for home, and tosses and turns in bed. We might be tempted to judge that the thing called nostalgia is like a messenger of grief that eats up our hearts, but we might also say that nostalgia is like the

31

gentle caress of our mothers, soothing our desperation into vast tranquillity when we have at last realised, after failing to attain the goals of our youth (or perhaps even after having attained them), that what we imagine to be the great ambition of youth consists only of a temporary false dream of the days when we look at life through pink-tinted veils, and is not something profound, lofty and solid that could give lasting repose to mind and body. Alike to those who have achieved the goals of their youth and to those who have failed, nostalgia may be the nest to which we finally return.

The ancient poet of the "Homecoming Verses" chanted that "birds seek their nests when tired by flight"; and Goethe, who is said to have enjoyed a "permanent youth", sang when no older than thirty-one, "On every peak there is repose. ' We could say that they have absorbed the sad and profound meaning of nostalgia with uncommon intuition and sensitivity.

In this respect, happy are people who have spent their childhoods in a beautiful countryside, because they have a warm maternal bosom to nestle against whenever the mind is wearied. But those who were born and have grown up in the city, and who change their abode every few years, or even several times a year, are unhappy people indeed because they have no home to long for even when they long to have a home to miss. One might contend that such a person can live always for the future, but a person's mind cannot stretch rigidly upward like steel all the time; so that after every strain there follows of necessity a slackening of nerves, and every relaxation may be a prelude to greater exertion.

Anyway all of us, whoever we may be, harbour nostalgia. This goes without saying for those of us who have a home in the country to long for, but those of us who do not have a country home also become sad or happy because of our constant longing for something. The object of nostalgia for those of us without a country home may be scenery of mountains and streams that we saw one night in boyhood in a dream, or a girl in our imagination whom we have never met even in dreams. Well, a theologian might maintain that the nostalgia we speak of is nothing but our longing for the bosom of our heavenly father; that men have been fated to suffer nostalgia from the moment they were expelled from the Garden of Eden after tasting the forbidden fruit. Whatever objection there may be to this religious theory, it is an irrefutable fact that men are so made that they can discover the meaning of life only when they feel longing for something.

For myself, born and raised in Seoul, unfortunately there is no beautiful countryside which I could yearn for with aching heart. The house in which I am said to have been born and where I lived until the age of three has been demolished without a trace, and now cold-faced modern houses occupy the whole district. But I, too, have a kind of a memory of home where I can transport my mind when it is wearied. A part of the memory is that of my house in Kyedong, where I lived from six to fourteen, and the other is the memory of Changrangjong Pavilion, which I am going to record here.

2

Changrangjong is the name of the pavilion on the brink of Sogang, the Western Han River, that once served as the residence of a prime minister. His Excellency Kim Jong-ho, a relative of mine—a third cousin of my great-grandfather, and consequently a tenth-degree kinsman to me—had served the government during the Taewongun regency era in a post as high as minister of internal administration. Changrangjong is the pavilion he purchased to spend his gloomy remaining years after Taewongun lost power and he resigned his post because the affairs of the country went contrary to his wish for maintaining national isolation. The name Changrangjong was given to it by His Excellency himself.

My memory is not quite clear on this point, but I think it was in the spring of my seventh year. Therefore, it was about twenty-eight years ago. The season must have been early spring, because it was about the time when the shepherd's purse sent up its shoots into the air from underground. I went there with my father and spent a few days. Strangely, what I saw and heard then became deeply engraved in my young mind, so that even after a lapse of nearly thirty years the events traverse the land of my memory and pierce my heart from time to time in the shape of an almost painfully sweet nostalgia.

Changrangjong Pavilion stood on a huge estate of more than 3,500 pyong,[1] located on a small mountain thickly covered with pine trees overlooking the river, where the land abruptly fell off in a precipitous cliff after sloping slowly toward the river. When you looked at the house from a distance, from the bank of the river, a row of servants' houses stretched in a line on the hill beyond the usually dried-up brook. In the midst of them stood the gate of the great house, tall and imposing.

"Now we're almost there. The house over there—that's your Sogang grandfather's[2] mansion."

My father, holding my tired right hand with his left hand, pointed to the big house beyond the brook, raising his cane in his right hand. The impression of that big mansion standing with the evening sun obliquely on it was so extraordinary that the picture of the house at the moment my father told me that was the house of my Sogang grandfather is still vivid before my eyes, as if it were only yesterday. Seen close by, it revealed itself as a very rundown ancient house perhaps hundreds of years old, with the pillars all leaning or fallen. The surrounding wall of stone and clay was also caved in here and there, and in some places the holes were big enough for cows to pass through. As we entered the gate after climbing the mountain, a huge, dark old gingko tree obstructed our path like a monster in a nightmare. I heard later that the gingko tree was rumoured to be inhabited by an evil spirit, so that when any of the houses in the neighbourhood offered sacrifices to shaman spirits, they always began by offering food and prayers to this gingko tree to appease the spirit dwelling in it, and that whenever unfortunate things happened

1. One pyong is 3.24 square metres or 36 square feet.
2. Terms like 'grandfather', 'grandmother', 'uncle.', 'aunt', 'brother', and 'sister' are very loosely applied to relatives and acquaintances and even to strangers to show respect and affection due to the person's age and station in life. Here, 'grandfather' is used because the person is a relative of the boy's grandfather's generation or older.

in the neighbourhood people trembled in fear, thinking that the wrath of the gingko tree spirit was roused.

Beyond the gingko tree there was another steep slope, and high on the slope stood the middle gate yielding to the men's quarters. Inside the middle gate was a level garden with study and guest rooms on either side, and on the high stone embankment directly facing the river stood the main study occupied by His Excellency himself. Separating the garden from the outside was a wall only a few feet high, and if one stepped on a stone and looked over the wall, there was a cliff falling from right below the wall, so that the dark blue waters of the river were seen rolling a dizzying distance below at the base of the cliff.

His Excellency was ill in bed. On the wooden-floored verandah facing southwest, the gay evening sunlight was shining brightly, but when we first stepped into His Excellency's main study it was so dark that nothing could be discerned by the eyes. My father, after walking towards the warmer part of the floor and making a full bow,[3] bade me bow, too. After I bowed as I was bidden and crouched down on my knees, father introduced me, saying, "This is my son, Your Excellency."

"Oh, that's a good-looking boy." His Excellency raised himself on purpose to stroke my head, and accosted me with "How old are you?"

"Seven, sir."

"Hm. . . Bright sons are our greatest hope at a time like this."

At long last my eyes began to discern things in the room. Though His Excellency was very lean because he was already eighty years of age and had been long ill in bed, even to my young eyes his narrow face, fair skin, silver beard, all bespoke nobility that had grown loftier with the harshness of worldly storms and waves.

While Father and His Excellency were talking about some-

---

3. For a full Korean bow, men kneel down and bend the body forward until the forehead almost touches the floor. Women sit instead of kneel on the floor and bend forward as deeply as is appropriate to their relationship with the recipient of the bow.

thing between themselves, I looked around the room carefully. I had known only the small men's study in my house in Kyedong, so everything seemed to me novel and interesting. Both the double sliding paper doors were firmly closed against the wooden-floored verandah, and over them a dark purple curtain was drawn; on the opposite side I glimpsed a big folding screen, a painting of mountain spirits amusing themselves among clouds above the waves, covering the whole of the long, high wall. On the square table in a corner and atop the pair of stationery chests engraved in floral patterns standing near the pillow of His Excellency lay scattered big ancient books in great piles. The brush holder carved with a dragon placed on the ink slab box, the marble seal engraved with a tiger pattern, the calligraphy pieces of renowned ancient scholars hanging on the walls, the long duster made of white horsehair. . . Oh, I feel as if I am beholding distinctly even now all these mysterious and elaborate decorations in that room.

3

In a little while the door opened and a topknotted[4] young man about twenty years of age came in.

"Stand up and make a bow to your elder cousin," Father told me.

I got up again and made a bow as bidden. That was Kim Jong-gun, the young master of that house, great-grandson to His Excellency and twelfth degree kinsman to me. His Excellency had lost his son and grandson early, so that he cherished this young great-grandson as his heir who would

---

4. In the Yi Dynasty, for a man to wear his hair in a topknot was the symbol of married status and adulthood, and therefore a matter of pride. In this story, however, which is set in the early years of modernisation, Jong-gun's wearing a topknot indicates that he is under the rule of conservative family elders, and he might not have been too happy to wear the topknot, because the more advanced youths of the day wore their hair cut short, in the Western style. We see at the end of the story that Jong-gun promptly got rid of his topknot upon becoming the head of the house.

carry on the family line.

My father and His Excellency began to talk at length again, with Jong-gun seated beside them. I could not make out what they were talking about, but on looking back, as school was often mentioned in their conversation, it was probably a discussion over whether to send Jong-gun to school—His Excellency was consulting my father's opinion on that. His Excellency had of course a great many people to seek advice from on any other matter, but as far as modernisation was concerned, my father was the only one in the whole clan who knew anything about it. My father had been a Korean government scholarship student in Japan, and was employed before the annexation in such offices as the finance ministry and the cabinet organisation bureau. He continued to work in the government after the annexation of Korea by Japan.

I infer that the talk between my father and His Excellency that day concerned whether or not to let Jong-gun have a modern education, from my father's repeated regretful remarks afterwards that His Excellency was too stubborn to send Jong-gun to school. In my opinion, His Excellency, since he had been one of those most violently insistent upon keeping away the barbarians from the West, must have finally decided to keep Jong-gun away from school, adhering to his convictions to the last, though he felt the need to have his precious only descendant receive a modern education because he saw the world changing contrary to his wishes. But he went so far as to consult my father.

Because the grown-ups' talk lasted too long and made me feel impatient, I got up noiselessly and, opening the double sliding doors, came out on the elevated wooden-floored enclosed terrace. The doors of the terrace were shut on all sides, too, but it was intensely bright with the rays of the evening sun filtered through the paper panels of the doors. There was not much decoration there, but the high piles of books and the signboard with the characters "Chang Rang Jong" excited my curiosity. I remember that after studying the signboard for a considerable while, I could make out the characters as meaning Clear Water Pavilion, and that it made me feel very proud. The signboard was written by His

Excellency himself, so that in a corner there was his sobriquet "Do-am" signed with brush.

After looking long at the signboard, I went to the edge of the floor and gave a push at the door that looked down on the river. To my surprise, the door slid open without a squeak and the unexpected sublime view from Changrangjong Pavilion spread out before my eyes. Oh, the magnificent view which rushed into my eyes soundlessly in that one instant! That, too, is vivid before my mind's eye! The dark blue waves rolling right beneath my eyes, the wide, wide sands spreading beyond the waters that filled my view; mountain after mountain stretching from the edge of the sand far, far away to where the sky ended, undulating in peaks and valleys, just like the waves of the ocean—I stood there entranced at the grand scene, unconscious of the passing of time.

After a long while I recollected myself, perceiving gay, translucent colours thrown over the solemn view. The sunset glow had begun to spread. That was the first time I realised that although the evening glow is something that must start spreading slowly, it looks to the beholder as if it has suddenly begun. Even though this was March, thick folds of clouds of all sizes and shapes screened the sky. Some had trailing horizontal tails like smoke, some looked like blossoms of cotton wool whose edges shone silver; some rose up mountain-high and fell back like waterfalls while I was watching, giving the illusion of great beasts at war; some were immobile, shielding the sky high up at the zenith like diaphanous floral-pattern veils. All the various clouds were dyed in yellow, red, pink, purple or orange tints, so that together with the blue of the sky peeping through intermittently, they formed a wondrous sight, like a translucent, rainbow-coloured magic glass. The resplendent sky was in turn reflected upside down in the water, and thus sky and earth together made an entrancing vision, as if the whole universe were a huge, radiant flowerbed. Not only was it an unforgettable sight to a seven-year-old boy, but a sight that would have been indelible to anybody.

But soon, a more impressive and unforgettable event to my young mind than even the beautiful sunset took place.

With my mind wholly absorbed in the ecstacy of the

evening glow, I was unconscious of anyone coming or going in the garden under my feet below the elevated floor, but when I happened to glance down at the ground in front of me, I saw a girl of about twelve looking up and smiling at me. I did not know how long she had been there. Wearing a bright yellow blouse and a red, red skirt, and standing with the gem-like glow of the evening behind her, she was looking up at me, smiling.

I instantly experienced such a strong liking towards that girl that it made me feel as if my body was being gently squeezed. So I smiled at her before I knew, and the girl beckoned me to come to her.

4

I nodded several times and went into the main study to go past it out into the yard. Then Father scolded me for having been away so long, and told me to stay beside him because we were going to the inner quarters to pay our respects to the lady of the mansion. I yearned to go out to the girl, but had no choice except to squat down on my knees beside my father.

The inner quarters stood on an even more elevated plane than the men's quarters, and were of sturdier construction. With a large, grand living-room in the centre, there was the innermost room on the west, the daughters' room to the east, a wooden-floored room adjoining the innermost room, another room adjoining the daughters' room, with a back room next to that, and across the inner garden were two rooms for female relatives or guests. This may sound like an imposing mansion, but since it was very gloomy from age and lack of care, and the rafters were rotten, making the curved edges of the roof droop, it looked like a deserted temple, the kind that appears in ancient tales. The roof line was ragged with dried grass from the year before which grew from the mud plaster that kept the tiles in place.

As soon as we stepped inside the inner gate, a smell of food invaded our nostrils and we could see people bustling all over the living room and the kitchen. Some were scurrying back and forth with cake steamers, some were frying sea food and vegetables, some cutting loop cakes, splitting platycodon, sorting mung bean sprouts, or marinating meat in sauce. The huge, gloomy house was all in a bustle. I was thinking to myself that this must be the scale of daily living at lords' mansions when Father said to me,

"Tomorrow's the birthday of the grandmother of this house. I have to go back home after dinner, so you sleep here with Jong-gun and stay for a few days. Tomorrow your mother will come."

My father, uttering false coughs to announce himself, went into the innermost room in which Her Ladyship was lying in bed. Some of the young ladies in the living-room hid themselves at the sight of a man, but in the innermost room a lot of aged ladies were sitting, and they greeted my father as they might a child. Her Ladyship was lying on the warmest part of the floor and did not move at all except to turn her yellowed face a little, even when my father and I made deep bows. After bowing to Her Ladyship, my father and I had a hard time making bows in turn to all the ladies in that room, who were either some kind of cousins or great aunts to me.

After a round of bowing I was collecting my breath, looking at the intricate geometrical pattern of the ceiling— that was called *sorabanja*—when a murmur rose again in the room, the door slid open, and a young lady as beautiful as a full moon—to my eyes at that time she was really fair as the moon—came in with lowered eyes. The lady made a respectful bow to my father. My father diffidently half-raised himself and received her bow. Looking at the beautiful lady in shapely indigo blue skirt and bright yellow blouse, I suddenly remembered the girl I had seen a little while ago. She must be this lady's sister or niece, I thought.

"Bow to your sister."

Somebody told me to bow again. The lady was Jong-gun's bride.

When dinner was over my father left me there alone and went back home as he had told me. As I had never slept anywhere other than in my own house before, I wanted very much to go back home with Father, but it occurred even to my young mind that if I stayed there I would be able next day to meet the girl I saw that afternoon. So I consented without much protest and went to sleep, my heart throbbing with expectations like one about to set out on a great adventure.

From very early the next day guests began to gather. Most of the guests were women, and most of them were of the family clan, so that there were many aunts and great aunts I knew.

In the meanwhile, my waited-for mother came and greeted me with a glad expression, and asked me whether I had slept well, whether I had washed my face, whether I didn't miss home too much, and what I had eaten. At that moment I forgot all about the girl and resolved never to leave my mother's side, so glad was I to see her.

When I went into the inner quarters with my mother, I found that in a short space of time a great many young women in yellow blouses and trailing indigo skirts had gathered, enough to fill the huge living room. They were making a hundred times more bustle than the day before. The young girls had forgotten their modesty, and were shouting to each other to hand over something or to put something in a corner out of the way. Like a flock of sparrows freed for the first time after long confinement in wooden chests, they whispered, giggled, and poked each other in the ribs, while some of them swiftly put into their mouths some of the food they were making to chew and swallow surreptitiously.

The whole space of the innermost room was filled with party guests as well, so that there was nowhere I could take a seat in any comfort. Besides, none among them kept her mouth closed even for a moment. It is the same any time, now or in the old days—when women gather, they chatter and make noise. I felt I could hardly keep my senses in place, so as soon as I managed to eat a late breakfast, I escaped directly from the crowd to go to the back yard of the inner quarters.

5

To the rear of the inner quarters was another courtyard, and joined to the yard was the hillside park or garden belonging to the house. This rustic hillside garden was enclosed with a baked tile wall, and planted densely with peach, apricot, plum, cherry and other fruit trees, and also with willows, spindle, forsythia and other flowering shrubs. On the slope stood a shrine, the arabesque paintings on its eaves all discoloured. I observed the shrine for a long time and started up the small pathway through the fruit trees, thinking to get to the top of the hill. It was then that someone called me with a "Hey, you," from behind. On looking back, I saw the girl in the yellow blouse and red, red skirt of the day before hurrying towards me.

I was indeed very glad, but did not move from where I was, saying only, "What is it?"

The girl, after climbing up to where I stood, said, "Shall we go up and play over there?" pointing to the top of the hill, and looked into my face.

"Yes."

When I consented, she held my hand and started up the hill.

"What's your name?" she asked, looking into my face again.

"Kim Shi-kun."

"Where do you live?"

"In Kyedong."

"Where's Kyedong?"

"It's very far from here."

While talking, I felt something like soft happiness, for some undefinable reason. I felt like walking to the end of the earth holding hands like that with the girl. Then I thought I would like to know the girl's name, too.

"What's *your* name?"

"My name?" She smiled, perhaps thinking that my question was unlike a child's, and answered, "I'm called Ulsoon."

I felt I wanted to know more about the girl.

"Are you the younger sister of the new bride in this house?"

"No. The bride is my little lady."

I could not understand what she meant, so I asked again, "Your little lady?"

"Yes, she is a bride now, but. . ."

I still couldn't see what she meant but didn't ask further. Later on I found out that Ulsoon was a maid Jong-gun's bride had brought from her own home when she married.

In the meantime we reached the top of the hill, at the base of the baked tile wall. Beneath the wall was a level lawn.

"Let's play here." So saying, Ulsoon seated me on the lawn and sat down herself beside me. Looking down, I saw the inner and outer quarters of the house lying prostrate, the tiled roofs like the backs of huge whales, and beyond them the sweeping view of the river—the water, the white sand, the vast landscape that I had looked upon the day before with such great ecstasy. I felt shy at Ulsoon's fumbling with my hand, so I said: "Why is the river so blue?" pointing to the river.

"It's blue because it's a river," she said, and moving still closer to me, looked directly into my face.

"How old are you?" she asked.

"Seven."

"Do you have an elder sister?"

"Yes."

"How old is she?"

"Fifteen."

"She must be pretty. Is she?"

I had till then never thought my elder sister pretty, but I didn't like to tell other people my sister was homely, so I just said "Yes."

"Do you have older brothers?"

"Yes, I have one."

"How old is he?"

"Twelve."

"Is he also good-looking, like you?"

I was about to say yes but Ulsoon suddenly squeezed my face with one hand on either cheek and trembled. That act of Ulsoon made me somehow deliciously happy, till I felt my whole body in a tremor, but it also suddenly made me afraid. I was afraid, for some reason, that she might get at me to beat me up and pinch me.

"No. No. I don't like it."

I shook my head and tried to take Ulsoon's hands from my cheeks, but Ulsoon just smiled gaily and did not take her hands off me.

"No. No. I really don't like it."

I shook my head more forcibly than before, and my face became tearful. Only then did Ulsoon take away her hands and said, "Oh, poor boy. I didn't mean anything. I just think you're pretty."

Then after a little while she said, "Don't tell anybody we played here together," and looked into my face once more. I nodded my promise.

A little later Ulsoon said, "Oh, my lady must be looking for me," as if suddenly remembering something. Then, springing to her feet and saying, "Let's play again later," she ran down the hill.

Looking at her descending figure from the back, I felt sorry. I felt regretful, too, thinking that she might have gone away because I shook my head. I also thought that if she did that again, next time I would be still. But presently I forgot all about such things and started to trot around on the hill.

6

After that, during my several days' sojourn in Changrangjong, I became fast friends with Ulsoon and we played together as often as we could get together in the hillside garden of the house. Sometimes we gathered shepherd's purse in baskets, and sometimes dug in the earth for bindweed root to eat. Such pleasures were novel and exciting to me, since till then I had never been away from the heart of the city. During that time a most impressive event took place one day which is an indispensable part of my memory of Changrangjong.

One evening we went up the hill to collect bindweed roots again, as Ulsoon suggested. With a wooden stick in hand, we dug up the soft earth here and there and fumbled about in the dirt with our fingers. Then the crisp bindweed root could be sorted out. If you brush away the earth from it and put it into your mouth and chew it, soft juice flows into your mouth together with the smell of the earth. The half-cent Japanese cakes or candies were nothing compared with the taste of bindweed roots. At first, from time to time I chewed on some other tough grass roots, mistaking them for bindweed roots, and spat them out in disgust, but by and by I learned to discern easily between bindweed root and other grass roots. Ulsoon could gather a heap of bindweed roots in no time at all, and after brushing the earth off the roots, she gave them to me to eat. She even stuffed them into my vest pockets for me to take home and eat, till the pockets were in danger of bursting.

It was almost sundown. Ulsoon was collecting bindweed roots a few feet away, and I was digging in the earth also, when the tip of my wooden stick touched something hard. At first I didn't pay much attention to it and poked the ground around. A hard object there blocked the stick again. Wondering what it might be, I dug to find that something like rotted wood came out of the earth. On digging further, a whitish gleam like that of iron appeared.

"Look, what do you think this is?" I presently called to Ulsoon.

"What?" Ulsoon ran to me at once. Leaning down, she dug away the dirt around it some more and looked into the hole, and then suddenly straightened up, shouting, "It's a sword, a sword!" It was indeed a sword. We had exposed the middle of a long sword buried horizontally in the earth. Ulsoon said, "You wait a little. I'll fetch a hoe," and ran down the hill.

After a good while of strenuous digging, we bared a great sword longer than my height and so heavy I could hardly lift it. The rotted scabbard was attached to it in only a few places, and fell away while we were digging it up; but the sword itself, after we brushed the earth away from it, was whole, as if it had been made just the day before, and its blade sharp. The hilt and the grip were covered with strange engravings and the splendid pure gold decoration shone, dazzling the eyes.

"Oh!" I shouted with emotion and, mustering all the

strength in my body, lifted the sword up and wielded it under the darkening sky. The tip of the sword glittered in the evening sun.

"Don't! You'll hurt yourself."

I pushed away Ulsoon, who tried to stop me, and raising the sword again, wielded it with all my might. I cannot forget till this day the magnificent sensation of that day, when I felt as if I had become a mighty general in ancient stories with a great sword.

I don't know how precious a treasure the sword was, or what became of it after that. But that it must surely have been a renowned sword could be guessed from the fact that although it had been buried perhaps scores of years in the earth, so that the scabbard had all rotted away, the blade itself was not rusted to any serious degree.

I can still vividly recall the deeply touched expression on His Excellency's face that night when he repeatedly opened and closed his eyes with the sword before him. His Excellency said, as if to himself, "Not such a great wonder, since this house once belonged to General Chung," and sat buried deep in thought. Of course there is no way of knowing who General Chung was, nor why he had buried such a valuable sword in the ground. But I could tell that there must be a deep secret and a hidden story to the sword from the expression on His Excellency's face that night.

The major part of my memory of Changrangjong is recorded above. But if this had been all, Changrangjong would not have occupied my mind so much, nor would I have written of it in the form of a story. People are apt to feel more attachment to something gone by, something that has disappeared, than to things of the present, things before our eyes. Changrangjong has disappeared without a trace. It evokes my nostalgia the more powerfully because it now is no more.

The chronicle of Changrangjong after that date would in itself make a long novel, so I will not touch on it here, but only tell the main parts of it: Her Ladyship died within a year of my first visit there, and a few years after that His Excellency also passed away at almost ninety years of age. Within one year of his death his daughter-in-law, the grand-

mother of Jong-gun, also died. Not only have people passed
away, but the line of His Excellency which enjoyed glory
and wealth for decades also went down amid the rough
climate of the changing world, like a giant tree that had
withstood the wind and rain of hundreds of years silently
failing to sprout new leaves one spring after a harsh winter.

7

What precipitated the downfall of the house was Jong-gun's
dissipation. When the older people died one after another,
Jong-gun, who had till then studied Chinese classics at
home under tutors, suddenly cut his hair short, put on
Western-style clothes and started frequenting pleasure houses.
By the time of the second anniversary of His Excellency's
death, even the title of the house itself had gone over to
others and Changrangjong looked just like a skull. Thus I,
who had gone to that house with Father as if visiting some
longed-for country home, could not but be astonished and
grieved at such a drastic change in it. Not a shadow remained
of the many people bustling in the house, and it was caved in
in several places, and the garden overgrown with weeds. Only
about a dozen people gathered in all that great house to
commemorate the death of His Excellency. On the hill where
Ulsoon and I used to play, not even a single healthy-looking
fruit tree remained. In the living-room which once teemed
with young ladies in indigo blue skirts, Jong-gun's bride,
looking sallow and shabby as a mouse, was preparing the
offering table with an old cook. I could not believe that this
was my sister-in-law who had looked as fair as the full moon.
    That night, in the main study which used to be occupied
by His Excellency, seven or eight people gathered around my
father to reminisce about the old days in sorrowful, low
voices. I was sixteen then, so I could understand most of
what the older people were talking about. My father was
relating, deep into the night, how the site of Changrangjong
had been a battleground during the Japanese invasion of the
sixteenth century and how, when Admiral Rose of France
sailed up the Han River from Kangwha Island leading three

warships in a reprisal for the execution of missionary priests, and made the whole court tremble in fear back in the Taewongun days, it was right in front of the Changrangjong garden that the admiral and his crew had anchored for many days. It was none other than His Excellency himself among all the courtiers who most urgently insisted on repulsing the Western barbarians.

I listened with emotion to my father's words, looking at the great-grandson of His Excellency, Jong-gun, who squirmed now and then, as if the ceremonial mourning robe of rough hemp bothered him, and who was sitting with bowed head like a coward. My father's voice flowed on like a quiet stream, and the night was deep and all around was silence. When I raised my eyes towards the offering table in the corner, I saw the yellow flame of the tallow candle shiver and stretch upward towards the ceiling without a breeze, and then shrink back again.

In the course of twenty years after that, Changrangjong disappeared without a trace, during which time my father passed away and I have been going my own way. Long since, Jong-gun's family gave up living in Seoul and went down to the country town of our clan. During all this while I had not forgotten Changrangjong, but had not too painfully missed it either, but for some reason I dreamed of Changrangjong no less than three nights in a row this spring. In my dreams I was always the seven-year-old boy, and the evening glow spread in the sky over Changrangjong, and in the main study there was the silver beard of His Excellency and the yellow candlelight, and my father raised his stick to point out Changrangjong to me, and on the garden hill I was playing with Ulsoon in the evening sunlight.

After I woke up in the morning from my third dream, I could not calm my longing, so vivid was the dream of the night before. Looking back, I realised that though I had been living not far away from it I had not been to Changrangjong even once in all the nearly twenty years since the night of the commemoration service for His Excellency. It was a Sunday, and the season was March, too, so after lunch I set out from home as if to go on a walk, with a camera strapped to my shoulder.

Taking a trolley for the first time in my life and getting off at Sogang, I tried to find my way to Changrangjong, reviving my memory. But strangely, I could not find my way to the house; which hill the house had stood on and which was the house itself I could not make out, even though they had been so vivid in my dreams. With difficulty I found a place which looked like the grounds where the mansion used to stand, but the hill on which the house had been standing was one bald mass of red earth, and on the site which seemed to be the old site of Changrangjong a large, unfamiliar factory was standing, shooting up black smoke out of its sky-high chimney.

Disappointed at such a drastic change, I walked about for a good while on the heap of coal ash in front of the factory and tried to recapture memories of the past. The blue water was rolling below as in the old times, beneath the precipice in front of the yard. But from the gloomy scowling heaven only a chilly wind blew, although it was spring. The endless clicking of the machines in the factory mercilessly jolted my mind that was trying to revive old memories.

Was Changrangjong a thing that could exist only in the fairyland of memory, in a dreamland enveloped in cloud and fog? My mind, which had been bemused in languid revery, slowly woke up to the hard reality before me.

A loud noise of some engine streaked the sand beyond the river. Looking up, I saw an ultra-modern twin-engine passenger aeroplane gliding down the runway in the far distance at Yoido Airport. While I was watching, the aeroplane took off and, with an atrocious explosive sound, ascended into the air slowly, then swiftly. It was an ultra-modern all-metal passenger plane that glides over rivers and mountains, over national boundaries, threatening to encompass the whole sky over many continents in one dash.

Chae Man-shik

Born in 1902, Chae Man-shik was, like the uncle of 'My Idiot Uncle' (1937), an intellectual in colonial Korea, in which Korean intellectuals had few openings for decent white-collar jobs, and few opportunities for constructive work. Like many such intellectuals of the day, Chae Man-shik became a writer and a sympathiser with the leftist movement. He was a charter member of the Korean Artists' Proletarian Federation (KAPF), but resigned his membership when the federation turned extremist. He worked on and off as a reporter on Korean newspapers and wrote short stories depicting the plight of intellectuals in a society where they felt themselves to be superfluous, or humourous sketches of unenlightened rural people trying to adjust shrewdly to the changing world.

From 1938 he began writing novels, distinguished by his keen satirical wit, power of description, fluent narrative and penetration into the complicated maladies of the rapidly changing world and the subsequent collapse of values. Although today Chae Man-shik is celebrated mainly as a writer of satire, his contribution is more substantial and far-ranging. He was burdened with tuberculosis and poverty for many years of his life, and therefore his promise was not quite fulfilled when he died of the disease at the age of 48 in 1950.

My Idiot Uncle

Chae Man-shik

My uncle? Oh, you mean that husband of the lady who's my father's first cousin? The one who went around preaching. . . what do they call it?. . . socialism in his youth and went to jail because of that, and is now sick in bed with tuberculosis?

Oh, don't speak of him to me. All that foolishness of his! There's simply no word fit to describe it.

Was there ever another man who ruined himself like that! His ten years of studying, his college education, all gone to waste; his youth spent with no useful outcome to it, his name besmirched as a jailbird; his body eaten away by that evil disease; and he just keeps lying there doing nothing in a cave-like room in that hovel, with eyes closed, day in and day out.

Needless to say, he has no property nor estate. How could he? Swing your arms right and left as freely as you like in that room, there's not a piece of furniture to hinder you. Not a thing in that dingy room but cold poverty.

It's my aunt, my nice, kind, gentle aunt who keeps him from starving, what with sewing and washing for others, peddling cosmetics, or doing whatever work she can come by.

It'd be better for everybody, for himself too, if he were to die, but he doesn't even have the decency to drop dead.

My aunt, what a pitiful woman she is! Why didn't she try to improve her lot when she still had her youth? Why go on toiling away like that? What kind of future comfort can she hope for out of that kind of life?

53

It's nearly twenty years since she was abandoned by her husband.

It's a pitiful sight, her going around like that trying to get work and making a living, tending his illness, after sighing and weeping away the whole twenty years of her youth, having taken back for a husband a half-dead corpse that he was.

What sins does she have to expiate that she must shoulder a burden like that? She says it's her fate, but why shouldn't one change one's fate? That's what the old-fashioned Chosun[1] women are like, ignorant and backward.

It would be a kindness to my aunt if he'd die soon.

Kind-hearted and skilled in all kinds of household work, she could surely find a comfortable home anywhere.

Let's see. She was sixteen when she married that fool, and that was when I was three, so it's been eighteen years. That's nearly two decades, isn't it?

Well, that uncle of mine was a mere schoolboy at the time, true, but for almost ten years he roamed around Seoul and Tokyo on the pretext of studying, and then when he got old enough to know women, he just drove my aunt back to her home, asking her to give him a divorce, as if anybody would think him advanced for that.

Why, after he came back from his studies, he just jumped into that God-damned thing, socialism, like crazy, and got himself a so-called educated woman. I saw that mistress of his three or four times, but believe me, she was no beauty, that woman. How could a woman presume to be a man's mistress with that kind of face? Well, there's an old saying that beauties get cast aside but the uglies don't. Anyway, my deserted aunt was at least five times as pretty as that mistress of his.

And then he got arrested and served a jail term of no less than five years. Meanwhile both my aunt's and my uncle's families had gone broke, so my aunt had no support. So she came to Seoul to try and make a living, and also to prepare to meet my uncle when he got out of prison. She looked to me for help in getting on. That was the year before that uncle

1. Chosun is the old name for Korea.

of mine came out of jail.

I was hardly more than a kid at the time, but I tried all I could do, and luckily I soon found her a place as a house-maid at Mr Kurada's.

At that time I counselled my aunt over and over again that she should get married again, instead of living like that. Young as I was then, I felt sorry for her, she looked so pitiful.

And there was a good eligible man, too. That was a Mr Minne, who sold bananas in front of the Mitsukoshi Department Store. A nice man, too, I'd say.

My master knows him well, too, and Mr Minne asked me time and again to make a match for him with a Chosun woman, saying that he'd like to live with a Chosun girl.

He hasn't got any great wealth to speak of, but he makes a comfortable living, so wouldn't my aunt have an easy life if she lived with a man like that? But my aunt, she just rebuked me for saying shameful things, and wouldn't listen to me. There simply was no helping her.

Well, apart from that, I really did give her a lot of help. I'm not saying this to boast about my goodness. And to be frank, it isn't that I don't owe her something, too.

I lost my parents at seven. I was left destitute with no one to look after me. So my aunt, who was living at her own house after being cast aside by that husband of hers, took me in herself and brought me up. Until that time, her family was not badly off. My aunt was very fond of me, and her grand-parents—my great-grandmother and great-grandfather—loved me dearly, having no small children in the house.

I grew up in that house until I was twelve. And I was given four years of schooling, too, even though only a primary education. If that family hadn't been ruined like that, I'd have been living with them till now, and maybe I'd be going to college.

Well, you can't say I didn't repay her for what I owe her as well as I could. Nobody can say I'm ungrateful.

Oh, well, my aunt comes to me to beg for help from time to time, saying she has run out of grain. And in truth, it's pretty bothersome. If I were to give her help every time she asks for it, I wouldn't be able to manage my own affairs. So most of the time I give a definite no.

But of course I don't neglect to send them a couple of pounds of meat at New Year, and drop in on them from time to time to make conversation. So you can't say I neglect them.

However that may be, my aunt saved her five won monthly salary for a whole year while she worked as Mr Kurada's housemaid, and she also made some small extra income by sewing, and the Kuradas, they gave her a bonus of seven won for having been a good servant when she left them. All in all, she really did manage to save a good hundred won.

With that money she rented a room, bought some pots and pans, and took that precious husband of hers there after he had finished his prison term.

The day he was released, I went with my aunt to meet him. Though he had cast her aside like that, I saw tears gather in his eyes when he saw my aunt waiting there at the prison gate.

The mistress he doted on so much, not even a shadow was there of that woman. Well, that's what mistresses are like, the whole lot of them. But this uncle of mine, he looked around to see if that woman had come to meet him. That's the kind of idiot he is. Except for my aunt and me, there wasn't a soul in sight, not even a puppy, to say nothing of a woman.

We were just putting him into a taxi when he vomited blood. I heard later that he began vomiting blood in prison about a month before his release. So we carried the half-dead body to aunt's room and laid him down there. And from that day my aunt went everywhere, did everything anyone could possibly do, to get a cure for his illness. So by and by he got better, and he's almost all right by now. He's a dragon now compared to when he came out of prison. A dragon, I say.

It's an amazing thing, a woman's devotion.

It's been three whole years. For three whole years she's been working like that for him. Honest, I couldn't have done that even to bring my dead father and mother back to life.

So if that uncle of mine has any kind of conscience or anything like that, he would have to make up his mind to get well as soon as possible, to earn as much money as possible to secure his wife some comfort, and repay her for what she's done for him and expiate the sins of his past. Now, isn't that what he should be doing?

If he were to repay her for what she's done for him, it wouldn't be enough even if he were to carry her on his back all the time, so as not to let her step on dirt again.

Anyway, he should have some resolution by now. Well, since he is a jailbird, he wouldn't be able to get a place in the government or in a business, however determined he might be, but that's nobody's fault but his own, so he has no one to blame. He ought to be making a living anyway, even by rough labour.

Say, it would be a spectacle, wouldn't it, for a university graduate to work as a day labourer, but what help for it can there be?

When I compare his case and mine—considering that if my great-grandfather's family hadn't gone bankrupt like that, perhaps I'd have finished college or a university by now, and would perhaps have been like that uncle—then I think it's fortunate that I didn't get to be a college graduate but was placed early in the way I'm going now.

This pitiful uncle, he's gone to college and finished it too, but now he has nothing ahead of him but to become a day labourer. But look at me, I've got no more than four years of schooling, but I have a bright, shining future ahead of me. My uncle's lot isn't one whit better than a page boy's, compared to mine.

But now look at what he's doing, the fool, now that he's out of death's grip, instead of trying to make a living by hard labour or something like that. I can only laugh!

What devil has got into him, that he should dive into it again like a madman? Why can't he just leave it alone? What is there to be got out of that? Food? Fame? What except persecution and imprisonment? Maybe that thing's just like opium. One can't leave it alone, I guess, once one's had a taste of it.

But if you get to know something about it, there's nothing exciting or sweet or anything like that in it. It's nothing but gangsterism. That's it, gangsterism, nothing more, nothing less.

Let me tell you what it is. My master told me all about it. In a faraway country, somewhere in the West, some lazy bums got together in a sunny place one day and tried to think of a way they could eat without working. So these bums, they said to each other: in this world there are rich men and poor men. And that's not fair at all. All men have the same features and limbs. It's utterly unfair that some are rich and some are poor, all being born alike. So it's only justice for us to take from the rich what they have and divide it equally among us poor people.

Oh, that's right! Well said! Let's all eat what the rich have.

So, that s how it became a move. . . a movement at first, started by those bums.

What is it if not a robber's game, pure and simple?

In this world, each man has his own share of luck, so that if one is born at a fortunate hour or if one is diligent he will become rich, and if one is born at an unlucky hour or is lazy, he will live poor. That's the way it is, and that's the fair providence of heaven. How dare anybody say it's unfair? What are they but gangsters, those who would take away and eat up what other people have earned?

Not only is it gangsterism, but if the world goes on the way they want it to, the idle ones will go on idling and keep on pillaging the rich, so wouldn't the world come to be filled with robbers, the whole world? And won't the world be ruined when the rich people don't have anything left to be stolen?

If everybody stopped tilling the land, waiting for other people to grow grain so they could eat for nothing, and if everybody stopped weaving, waiting for other people to weave so they could be clothed for nothing, where in the world would grain and clothes come from? That would be the end of the world for sure!

Ignorant poor creatures, especially the lazy ones among them, not knowing that it's such an accursed thing, jump into that move. . . movement headlong, decoyed by the notion of taking away and eating up the possessions of the rich.

That's what s happened in Russia. As sure as anything, the farmers there, they wouldn't till the land to grow grain, so people are dying of hunger by tens of thousands. Didn't I tell you it's clear and simple like that? Serves them right, too.

But this pestilent fad, it spread like mad everywhere in the East and West, and for a while it spread pretty vigorously in Japan, and all the bums in Chosun, they imitated that, sure enough, because it was the fashion in Japan, not knowing what it was all about. But now the movement's pretty weak, and not many bums are active in it, thanks to the strong government repression.

And that's how it should be, too. If it's a good thing, why on earth would the government forbid it, and arrest those byms and put them in jail?

If that were a good and profitable thing, the government would spur it on and would give prizes to those who do it well, too. The moving pictures, the comedy shows, the wrestling matches, the colourful ceremonies for sending dead souls to the other world, the carnivals and the exercises to radio music, they are all good and profitable things, so the government encourages them. Right?

What is a government, anyway? A government is supposed to know what's good and profitable for the people, and tell people how to do this and that and what to do and what not to do, so the people could live in peace, as well as they are able.

Take that. . . socialism, for example. What would have become of the world by now if the government had let them do as they liked? Lots and lots of people would have been ruined, and *I* would have been ruined most of all! All my plans would have been upset and me ruined, ruined!

Here's my hope and my plan. My master, he's especially fond of me and trusts me, so in ten years or so he's going to set me up in an independent trade, that's almost for sure. Then, with that as springboard, I'll work hard at commerce for thirty years, and I plan to make a hundred thousand won by the time I'm sixty. With a hundred thousand won, that's as good as owning land yielding two thousand bags of rice a year. So I can be as proud as I choose to be.

And what with what my master told me, I've set my mind on marrying a Japanese woman. My master said he will make a match for me with a good Japanese girl. Oh, Japanese girls are swell!

I wouldn't have a Chosun woman, even if anybody offered me one for nothing. The old-fashioned women, they are modest but ignorant, so they can't help me make friends with Japanese people. And the new girls, they wouldn't do either, because they may not be ignorant, but they are conceited. So, old-fashioned or new, I wouldn't have anything to do with Chosun women.

Japanese women are the best. Every one of them is pretty, proper, tender, and even the ones that aren't ignorant are modest. How lovely they are!

Not only will I marry a Japanese woman, but I will change my name to a Japanese name, too, and live in a Japanese house, wear Japanese clothes, eat like the Japanese do, give Japanese names to my children, and send them to Japanese schools. . .

It must be to Japanese schools that my children will go. The Chosun schools, they're so dirty, my children would be ruined. . .

And I wouldn't speak this language any more either, but speak only the national language. You have to live like the Japanese do first. That's the way to earn money like the Japanese.

So I have my plan all set up for making a hundred thousand won, and I have my road clear before me, and I'm going that way with sure, giant steps. So how can I help but have the shudders to hear of these mad, murderous ruffians pushing socialism to ruin the world? Oh, it gives me the creeps to hear that name!

What would become of me if the world is turned upside down by them? All my plans and my hard work, they would all have been to no avail. Nothing could be more unfair than that.

Oh, my master, his words are all true, every one of them. Crimes like theft, robbery, swindling, those kinds of crimes take only the amount stolen or swindled one time, so they are not such dreadful crimes, compared to this damned. . . socialism. This socialism just turns the whole world upside down and upsets the whole country, so they can never be forgiven, that's what my master said.

Forgive them! If it had been left to me, I'd have ground to powder every single one of. . .

To be frank with you, when I think of such things, my uncle also looks almost like a ruffian. If it hadn't been for my aunt, why on earth would I bother to drop in on him now and then, when he has that dreadful disease? I couldn't care a straw even if he was to drop dead.

Well, I wouldn't be so harsh on him if he had repented of his past crimes and mended his ways, but he wouldn't. Like the saying has it, like, you know, "Dye the white dog's tail a hundred times, it will turn white again," and stuff like that. . .

That's why he's so hateful to me, and that's why, even when I do get to chatting with him when I drop in on them, I just throw in sarcastic words to hurt him or drive him in the corner by picking on what he says.

Just the other day, I gave it to him good. And look what he did. He told my aunt that I've been completely spoiled, that I was a good-for-nothing.

Boy, did that make me laugh! What kind of gall does he have anyway that he could call *me* spoiled, a worthless good-for-nothing? He, of all people?

If I was him, I wouldn't have had a word to say, even if all the dummies in Chosun could suddenly speak, but he seems to think that anything coming out of his mouth will be considered a revelation.

So I suppose that was an admonition? And he admonished me through my aunt, indirectly, because if he said a thing like that to my face I'd certainly teach him a thing or two, I suppose.

Oh, what presumption! That's why God gave us two nostrils instead of one, so that people could breathe, even when they hear stupefying things like that.

So he thinks I am spoiled, a good-for-nothing, a washed-up man! Me, a promising youth with a bright future ahead for sure, and who's praised all around for being a bright, able, proper boy; one who got awarded for model service no less than twice, even though I didn't have as much schooling as he had, and am still a mere clerk?

Oh, yeah, that's it, of course! He thinks anything he does is right, so naturally everything I do is wrong. He'd have thought me a good, sound young man if I'd followed that accursed thing socialism and became a jailbird and a consumptive like him, instead of a spoiled, ruined man! Good heavens!

I guess the proverb about the log in one's own eye or something like that was made for people like my uncle. This is how it went that day. I just gave him a good lesson, and that made him say things like that about me to my aunt.

That day was a holiday for me, so I called on them in the morning because I had a few words to say to my aunt. Aunt was away at work sewing for a bride-to-be, and only my uncle was there, lying on the warm part of the floor as usual.

Well, he had a heap of old magazines in the Chosun alphabet by his pillow (wherever did he collect all those dusty things?) and was looking through them. So to while away the time I picked one up and thumbed through it. But that was no amusing magazine, nothing interesting for reading.

Chosun people, they can't even make a magazine right. No pictures, no comic strips. And then they are full of all those difficult Chinese characters. How do they imagine anybody can read them?

For the likes of us, we can manage to read the Chosun alphabet, but it's not very easy. We can't understand things written in difficult Chosun alphabet mixed with Chinese characters. Those written only in the Chosun alphabet are novels, and believe me, they *are* hard to read. Besides, the novels Chosun people write are not the least bit interesting. Oh, it's been a long time that I've kept away from those Chosun newspapers and magazines.

Speaking of magazines, there's no magazine to top "King" or "Shonen Kurabu". Gee, are they swell! All the Chinese characters are annotated in Kana, so no matter where you open it, you can just start reading right on at top speed, and there's not a thing you don't know the meaning of. And every passage in them has either a profitable moral lesson or an exciting adventure.

Oh, the novels are good, too. Those by Kang Kikuchi,

especially. Are they tender, romantic, and exciting! And the glittering, jingling historicals of Eichi Yoshikawa, they make my shoulders dance, just to read them.

The novels are exciting, all of them, there are plenty of comics, lots of pictures, and are they cheap, too! For just fifteen cents you can buy a Japanese magazine no more than a month old, and after reading everything in it, you can return it too and get five cents back.

Now that's how a magazine ought to be made. But these Chosun people, they always boast about everything, but they can't even make a magazine right.

So that day too, I wasn't going to read any of it, but was just leafing through one of them, hoping to find a picture or a funny paper, when my eyes happened to light on my uncle's name! That was a surprise, so I lifted it closer to my eyes and glanced through it. In the title there were words like economic and social and others, which were explained in the footnotes in small letters.

That was enough for me. Economics, that's what my uncle learned in college, so he ought to know all about it. And social, he ought to know a great deal about that, too, because he followed socialism. So that's what he must have written, what's economy and what's socialism and which of them is right and things of that sort.

Oh, there was no need to read it all. Since he's a man who went all the way through college to learn economics, but got caught up in socialism instead of making money, he must have insisted that economy is wrong and socialism is right.

But I glanced through it all the same because that was the first relative of mine that got his name in a magazine, but there was simply no way to read it. I could make out most of the letters all right, except the most difficult ones, but any way I put them together, I couldn't make head or tail of what it meant.

It didn't make me feel too good, so I gave up reading and placed the article before him, to have a word or two with him.

"Uncle?"

"Yes?"

"You write here economic something and then social something. Then, which do you mean one should follow— economy, or socialism?"

"What?"

He rolled his eyes, not understanding my question. Maybe it was so long ago he wrote it that he had forgotten it, or maybe he couldn't answer it right away because I put my question in too difficult words. So I began questioning him further.

"Uncle! Economy means that one should make a lot of money, save it and become rich, doesn't it? But socialism means that one should take away the money that rich people have saved, doesn't it?"

"What on earth are you. . ."

"No, listen to me."

"Who on earth told you those definitions of economics and socialism?"

"No need to be told. Doesn't economy mean to earn as much money as possible, to spend as little of it as possible, and save the rest of it?"

"Oh, no. That's just what we mean when we say economising. Economics and economy have far different meanings."

"How different? Economy means accumulating money. So economics must mean the science of how to become rich."

"No. Not at all. That may be management of finance, but economics isn't anything like that at all."

"Then you have gone to college in vain. What use was it for you to study economics for five years if you haven't leanred how to become rich? I often wondered why, uncle, though you went to college to study economy, you still haven't made any money. Now I see that it's because you didn't learn your studies right."

"Didn't learn my studies right? Well, that may very well be. I guess you're right! You *are*."

Look at that! I had him nailed down at once. That's the kind of fool he is, even though he went to college and everything.

"Uncle?"

"Yes?"

"Then, since in college you didn't study economics to save

money and become rich, but studied socialism to take money
away from rich people. . ."

"Now, what are you thinking socialism is?"

"I know perfectly well what it is."

And I explained to him everything about socialism. He just
lay there, looking up at my face, and then he smiled, like a
fool. Then listen to what he says:

"Is that socialism? That's gangsterism."

"So you know that socialism is gangsterism, uncle?"

"When did I say socialism is gangsterism?"

"You said it just now."

"Well, I said what you described was not socialism but
gangsterism."

"There! So that's what socialism is—sheer gangsterism.
You say so yourself, and then you insist it isn't."

"Now, is this boy trying to pick a quarrel?"

Look at that! He just didn't know how to answer me.
That's how he is with me most of the time.

"Uncle?"

"What?"

"*Do* change your mind, uncle."

"How do you mean?"

"Aren't you worried?"

"What kind of worry would a man like me have? I'm
worried about *you*."

"Oh, I have my plans all set, well and good."

"How?"

"Here's how." And I explained all about my future plans.

Then listen to what he says after listening to all I told
him: "My, what a pitiful boy you are!"

"Why?"

He couldn't say why.

"Now tell me. Why do you say I'm pitiful?"

He still couldn't say.

"Why? Uncle?"

Still no response.

"Uncle?"

"What?"

"Did you say I'm pitiful?"

"No. I was just talking to myself."

"But you did say. . ."

"Listen to me, boy."

"Yes?"

"For a man, whoever he may be, there is nothing so shameful as to be a flunkey."

"Flunkey?"

"Yes. Be he king or beggar, everyone must live within his means, in this world under this system. Nothing's more shameful than to flatter for a living, debasing one's own character, and no one's more to be pitied than those flunkeys. Two bowls of rice cannot make a man's stomach fuller than one bowl of rice."

"What does that mean?"

"I mean about your wanting to marry a Japanese girl and changing your way of living completely to Japanese style, even going the length of changing your name."

"Why, isn't that good?"

"That's what I'm talking about. If you have decided to do that out of deep conviction, it would be different; it might even be good. But it seems to me like you have other intentions."

"What other intentions?"

"That you mean to flatter and please your master and your neighbours by doing so."

"Why, of course! I must earn the trust of my master and get along nicely with the Japanese neighbours. Isn't that what I should do?"

He had no words to contradict me with.

"How little you know about the world, uncle! Though you are older than me and had university learning, you don't know the world as well as I do, me who has struggled in it from early years. What kind of a world do you think this is we are living in now?"

"Look."

"Yes?"

"You're talking about the world?"

"Yes."

"And you say you have a guaranteed bright future ahead of you?"

"Sure."

"And you say you'll have saved a hundred thousand won by the time you're sixty?"

"Sure."

"Well, I suppose you and I mean different things when we speak of knowing the world, but keep in mind that the world is not as easy to live in as you think."

"Why?"

"A man, however hard he may strive, cannot escape the power of the force that sweeps the world, that flows invisibly but strongly—this is what we may call the current of history— one has to be governed by it, and there's no helping it at all."

"What?"

"In simple words, however good plans one may set up, and however many opportunities one may make, things don't always go the way one wishes."

"Gosh, uncle! The other day in the magazine *King* I read about the hero of the West, Napoleon. He said that one must create opportunities oneself, and that 'impossible' is a word to be found only in the dictionary of fools. What is there in the world that wouldn't go the way it should, if one keeps on thinking, planning, making opportunities and struggling hard? If one fails once, one must stand up again with redoubled courage. Don't you know about rising up for the eighth time after the seventh fall?"

"Well,
Napoleon had success when he went along with the tide of the times, but failed when he tried to go against it. Have you seen only those who rose up and succeeded after the seventh fall, but never heard that there are many who fall for good after collapsing at the ninth try?"

"But just wait and see! I will succeed, whatever happens with the world. That's what's wrong with you, uncle. You just despair even before you try and fight for something."

"Do you always have to try climbing up to the sky to know that it's high?"

Look at that. Making a preposterous comparison because he doesn't know how to contradict me. What kind of reasoning is that? Would there be such idiots on earth as not to know the sky's high without trying to climb up to it?

I was going to let him get away with that, but it was kind of boring, sitting there in that dingy room, so I talked some more.

"Uncle?"

"Yes?"

"What are you going to do after you get completely cured?"

"What do you mean?"

"About your future?"

"My future?"

"What are you going to do?"

"What have I to do, at this stage?"

"So you're going to live like that, without any plans?"

"Why do you say without plans?"

"Do you have any plan, then?"

"I may have."

"What is it?"

"Living like I have been living."

"You mean doing that thing, the. . . what you call it, again?"

"I suppose so."

"Uncle?"

No response.

"Uncle?"

"What?"

"Leave off now."

"Leave off?"

"Yes."

"Do you think I do it for pastime?"

"Don't you?"

No response.

"Uncle?"

No response.

"Uncle?"

"What?"

"How old are you?"

"Thirty-three."

"So why don't you just leave that thing alone now and try to look after your home?"

"Look after home for what?"

"What are you doing that thing for?"

"It's not because it's of any practical use that I follow it."

"Then you do it without any hope or goal?"

"Goal? Hope?"

"Yes."

"Well, personal goals and hopes, they're on a different level. . . They do not matter. . ."

"My, what kind of law is that?"

"Law?"

"Law!"

"Hm. . . Law. . ."

"Uncle!"

No answer.

"Uncle?"

"What?"

"Aren't you grateful to my aunt?"

"I am."

"Aren't you sorry?"

"Sorry? Yes. I am sorry."

"So you know she is to be pitied?"

"Yes. I know."

"You know she is pitiful, but you insist on living like that?"

"Well, there are people in this world who incur pain willingly, who savour sweetness out of the bitterness of pain. I don't mean there are unusual people of that sort. I mean that when a person concentrates his heart and mind upon one thing, then one tastes sweetness in the bitterness of pain. Then pain becomes a pleasure. It is like that in the case of your aunt. She is suffering much, but she does not take it as pain. She is taking pleasure out of her hardships."

"Then you're happy about it?"

"No, I'm not."

"Then why don't you try to repay her for what she's done for you?"

"It's not that I don't know what I owe her, but. . ."

"Then when you get all right again, you must. . ."

"Oh, I've got such a big task!"

Now, just listen to that! Saying he's got a big task, a guy who fritters away his time lying on his back! Oh, he's just impossible. He'll never be any use to anybody, any more than a clipped-off fingernail. As long as he lives he will live on other people, troubling them, doing harm to the world.

A person like that ought to die as soon as possible. He ought to die, and deserves to die over and over. But he just won't do it, but keeps on squirming like that. Ah, it's just so annoying. . .

Chung Bi-suk

Born in 1911, Chung Bi-suk, at the beginning of his career, produced works marked by a strong romanticism, expressed in his loving contemplation of nature and in his yearning for an undefiled life surrounded by clean and healthy nature. His early stories are also marked by a longing for pure, romantic love and reverence for lofty, unworldly character. His romanticism may have been a reflection of his dissatisfaction with, and yearning to escape the humiliating reality of, a country under the colonial yoke, and the powerlessness of intellectuals to change the situation. As did many other writers of the day, he made his living by taking reporting jobs, and made writing his avocation.

His literary career made a sharp turn in 1953 when he surprised the world with his serialised novel, The Liberated Wife, *which depicted an ennui-ridden professor's wife drifting into adultery. The novel caused a moral shock in conservative Korea and called forth angry protests, but it was a huge commercial success, and the author from then on wrote many commercially successful newspaper serials with heavy erotic contents. It is generally conceded that his career as a literary artist was over by 1953. He stopped writing from the late sixties and is residing quietly in the suburbs of Seoul.*

The Ceremony of Apostasy

Chung Bi-suk

T he steam train pushed up the steep slope pantingly. From the top of the mountain the plateau spread out, eight hundred metres above sea level.

A plateau. Even the air itself felt thin. The frosty fog peculiar to mountain areas clung to the windows of the train, so that however hard you kept wiping them, you could not even look out of the window at the scenery.

Inside, the train was hollow as a cave. Although this train bustles with rich holiday-makers in the summer, on a late autumn day like this passengers are few, and shabby. The scanty number of passengers were mostly old men wearing rustic horsehair hats, or railway construction workers in baggy trousers and canvas shoes. Everyone was quiet, as if silenced by decree, so that only the rhythmic cacophony of the engine reverberated in the car.

Holding the railway timetable open in my hands, I sat for a long time turning over in my mind only the memory of Aira, like a man out of his wits. Then, realising that Y station, which was my destination, was the next stop, I sprang up and opened the window.

Autumn came much earlier in that area than in Seoul, so that the evening wind blowing in through the window felt cold as ice. I buttoned up my sports jacket and looked up at the mountain that blocked my view.

Mount Sorak—wasn't it just last summer that we, my betrothed Aira and I, looked at Sorak Mountain together from this window and shared our joyful expectations of

73

summer at the villa?

I have to seek in this chilly season the mountaintop villa where Aira and I spent a full summer of happiness, because I cannot meet Aira again except by invoking memories of the days we spent together.

Although she had never been strong, and though the mountain air must have been too harsh for acute pneumonia, not having seen her death with my own eyes I could not believe that Aira could have died less than a fortnight after I left her in the villa. Time and again I tried to reconcile myself to her death by telling myself that death cannot be revoked, or by remembering the Bible phrase that had been drummed into my ears throughout my three years in the seminary, "Except a corn of wheat fall into the ground and die, it abideth alone: but if it die, it bringeth forth much fruit." But even the sacred Bible verse failed to have any effect on me in this case.

In my trunk I had the crisp new diploma I received from the seminary. It was to take the final examination for this diploma that I had left for Seoul alone, leaving Aira at the villa. And then, as soon as the exam was over, I joined the roving evangelistic team of graduating students and set out on a preaching tour to Cheju Island and other places.

Wherever I went, I delivered fervent sermons from the strength of my happiness at the prospect of meeting Aira as soon as the tour was over. And every night I confirmed my vow that we would be faithful disciples of God by dreaming dreams of her.

At the end of the two-and-a-half-mouth tour I stepped down at the Seoul terminal, my heart bursting with joyful expectation. But all my hopes and dreams vanished like vapour. The first moment I heard of Aira's death from Aikyung's lips, I really could not feel anything. Perhaps because, during the two-and-a-half-month tour, I had used the word "death" almost every day. Did I not preach from the pulpit day and night, "Death is not something to be dreaded. There is nothing like death that can purify our lives"?

But when I came back to reality from the spiritual world of God, Aira's death caused me rending sorrow. It was a

sorrow that chilled me like icy water poured over my naked
body. I had wailed to numerous congregations that "Death
is never to be feared". Ah, was it not a fraud? What a horrible
hypocrite I was! Believing in an illusion as truth, how many
seeds of unhappiness had I sown in how many people, and
what a great price I am paying for that!

Time and again I tried to comfort myself with words
from the Bible. But all the sacred words that used to give me
so much inspiration and strength sounded now like a meaningless murmur uttered in sleep. I wanted to be buried deep in
sorrow as a human being rather than to behave like a model
Christian. Now I miss human beings—not men who are sons
of God, but earthy, numerous, sinful men.

The story I am going to record is a mere rambling discourse concerning how I became a descendant of Judas.
The good citizens of the spiritual world will call me an
apostate for writing such a record, but I will dare to write.

The train stopped at Y station.

I took down my suitcase and stepped down to the platform. It was a deserted little station, and I was the only one
who got off. I had been standing absently for a while, like
one who did not know his way, when the station master
approached me and asked for my ticket.

I handed him the ticket silently. After glancing at it carefully, he asked in a friendly tone, "Are you here for the
first time?"

"Yes. Er. . . no."

I could hardly speak. Hot tears welled up in my eyes. The
cordial and courtly manner of the elderly station master
aroused in me undefinable feelings of trust and sorrow. I felt
a longing to embrace this elderly station master and tearfully
explain why I had to visit the mountain villa at such an
unseasonable time. I felt as though if I asked him why Aira
had to die, this old man could give me the answer.

But just then the train gave off its stentorian starting
whistle, so that the old station master had to raise his hand
and signal to the conductor. The train that had brought me
here left the station without hesitation. After gazing at the
station master's back for a long time, I stepped into the

square in front of the station dejectedly.

I walked up the mountain along the narrow pathway stretching through forests of huge trees along a running brook. In full summer water ran high in the brook and you could bathe in its rapids but, as it was late autumn, stones jutted out above the shallow water in the bed of the stream.

When you go up some distance, you come to a big rock called the Buddha Rock. I can never forget the time last summer when I bathed in the rapids while Aira waited sitting on this rock. Aira, bored with waiting, was humming "Milky Way", and exclaimed on seeing me in only my briefs, "Oh, you look like a deer! A long-legged deer!" and beamed, as if she had really found a deer.

"Deer? Oh, I do envy the deer who takes his fill of all this sylvan freshness, until he could burst for joy."

"Well, I guess you aren't as handsome as the deer of the forest," she said, and threw the stone in her hand into the rapids, splashing water on me.

But upon this rock where once Aira was seated now only fallen leaves lay scattered, adding to the feeling of desolation. Halting my steps, I stood for a while buried in the memory of Aira, and without thinking picked up a stone and threw it into the water as Aira had done. But only a hollow splash spread in the air, and the next moment the silence was even heavier.

I resumed my heavy steps. I did not want to be freed of the searing longing that would not let me alone but made me recall Aira in every tree and every stone. Isn't it a blessing that though death can take away a person forever, it cannot deprive the living of memories?

When I reached the topmost point of the peak at the end of a mile's walk, the villa of my memory—which had been covered all over with ivy and roses but now looked deserted, with the ivy leaves dyed red and more than half fallen—came into view.

The cosmos plants that thickly hedged the yard now looked ugly, withered by the frost of late autumn. Cosmos had been Aira's favourite flower, so that she watered them with great care throughout spring and summer, in happy anticipation of the autumn cosmos season. But Aira had

passed away before the flowers bloomed. It must be lucky
for those destined to die that they do not know when death
will come, but what dire misfortune is that good luck to
those who must go on living!

The flowers in the garden were all withered and drooping,
as if they too were in mourning for Aira. After looking at the
flowers for a long time, I pushed at the gate of the villa. All
the doors were firmly locked and the place maintained a
solemn silence.

"Aira! Aira!"

I called out the name of my beloved and knocked on the
gate, because I felt as if in one corner of this firmly locked
villa Aira was waiting for me. But however many times I
wailed her name, no response came from Aira.

Swallowing a heavy sigh, I circled the villa once and went
up the hill behind with emptiness in my heart. To visit Aira's
grave. Aikyung had said that because Aira liked to look at
the sea even more than she liked music, they buried her on
this hill.

I was going up the hill peering here and there, when someone from the distance called out, "Oh, it's you, young
master!" It was Soonshil, the wife of Kim, the villa keeper.
Soonshil, as she walked up to me, almost smiled, but at once
lowered her head modestly.

On seeing this country woman whom Aira and I used to
call "Madonna" between ourselves, thoughts of Aira pierced
me once again and tears welled up in me. I was at once sad
and glad to meet Soonshil, who had liked Aira so much and
whom Aira also had liked. Soonshil, though she was the wife
of the villa keeper Kim, was an unusually intelligent woman.
I felt as if there were only Soonshil and me in all the world
who could mourn the death of Aira sincerely from the
heart's bottom.

Soonshil and I stood facing each other for a good while
without speaking. At long last I said, "Thank you so much
for nursing Aira in her last hours." I recalled having heard
that Soonshil had nursed Aira day and night, and I felt I
had to express my thanks. But Soonshil did not say anything
in reply. I realised belatedly that it must be painful for
Soonshil to be thanked for what she had done out of love.

When at last I began to move, Soonshil at once guessed what I wanted and led me to the grave. Aira's grave was built on a sunny spot on the hill that overlooked the vast expanse of the East Sea. And right below the grave was the orchard, the everlasting orchard of our memory, in which Aira and I shared our first embrace last summer.

Soonshil, when she reached the freshly built grave, just lowered her head, not having the heart to tell me that it was Aira's.

In this new grave whose earth looked red in the twilight sun—could it be true that Aira was lying in this grave? The Bible had taught me that when a man dies the flesh will rot in the grave and the soul will ascend to Heaven. And I had firmly believed it; but oh, how much greater was the pain of sorrow this grave was giving me than the consolation that Aira's soul must have ascended to Heaven. With what sad reality did the tombstone, the chisel marks of whose inscription "Here lies Lee Aira" were still vivid, pound on my heart.

I fed incense into the incense burner and made three deep bows before the grave. After I bowed three times and smelt the incense, for the first time I felt with my flesh the reality of Aira's death. Not being able to suppress the torrent of grief flooding my heart, I threw myself down on the grass and wept aloud.

I realised that I had been crying only when, after a long time, Soonshil shook my shoulder and called me. And only then did I realise that I had made bows before the grave. That was my first act of apostasy before my God.

"Thou shalt have no other gods before me."

That is the first of the Ten Commandments. But how powerless were the words over me now! How could I endure the sorrow without bowing before the grave, when my heart was pierced and torn apart with longing? It may be that that bowing was a totally meaningless act. But how could I help it when the ceremony had for me a meaning of reality?

"Aira, Aira, wake up now! I've come, your Hisoon has come, so wake up!" I wailed silently.

Aira's soul, why don't you answer me if you are there? Instead of feeling the reality of the soul, I felt with my whole body the reality of death before that unresponsive grave.

After Soonshil had gone back to the villa to prepare supper, I kept calling and calling Aira's name in front of the grave in the spreading dusk.

When Soonshil came to the grave again in search of me I was already soaked through with evening dew. On coming back to the villa, I found that Soonshil had cleverly prepared for my use the room Aira had been using. Entering this room, which had been preserved as on the day of Aira's death, I could not but mourn Aira's death again.

I lay down on the very bed where Aira had breathed her last, and waited in vain for Aira to return, and also thought about how I could follow Aira to where she was. In the vase on the piano beside the window facing west still stood the white roses, withered and dirty. With longing for whom in her heart did Aira gaze at those flowers?

Looking absently at the opposite hill which showed its distinct outline amid the spreading dusk, I lay soaked with infinite longing for Aira.

At last the cold beams of the tenth-day moon struck my window. Like one startled by something, I sprang up and ran outside. When I recovered my senses, I found myself circling Aira's grave like a wild animal.

The next moment I realised my foolishness and walked down to the orchard. When we came here last summer the leaves were thick, and on every bough hung ripe, dark-red apples, so that the whole orchard seemed to be vibrating with passion. But now the fruit had been picked and the leaves had fallen, and only the moon fell coldly on it, making it look as desolate as the ruins of a battleground. The moon shone brightly like this on the day when Aira and I first shared our lips under the apple trees. With what rapt feeling of mystery did we look at the globes of apples shining red in the moonlight! Though we were too happy in the present even to think about the future, hadn't we been able, in that moment of happiness, intuitively to gaze at eternity?

Although we were excited with the temptation of earthly passion, we did not pluck the forbidden fruit that night, because we felt that bliss would be ours forever very soon. But before the summer changed to autumn, our radiant hope was mercilessly shattered.

I wandered in the orchard where not even a cricket chirped. I felt as if it were the memory of Aira that I was treading under my feet at every step, so I leaned on a tree for a while and called out "Aira!" I felt as if Aira were peeping at me from behind the moon.

But surprisingly, the woman who appeared before my eyes at my urgent call for Aira was Soonshil. "Sir, you must go in and sleep now." Soonshil was beside me presently and urged me with gentle words. At that instant, Soonshil's eyes, reflecting the cold beams of the moon, shone translucent as two drops of mercury on a silver tray.

"Is Kim back from the market?"

"No. He may be planning to come back tomorrow."

After a few more brief words I came down to the villa, preceding Soonshil. In the room the lamp was already lit, and on the piano stood a small pot of autumn chrysanthemums instead of the white rose vase. The half-blown white chrysanthemums seemed to be welcoming me silently. I gazed at the chrysanthemums absently for a while, and realised with some surprise that Soonshil had the rather elegant hobby of growing chrysanthemums.

Past midnight I lay on my bed, but the thought that until only a couple of months ago Aira had lived in this room made it hard for me to fall asleep. After tossing and turning for a long time, I fell asleep, but woke up, startled, dreaming of Aira opening the door and stepping in. I did not feel I could fall asleep again, so in ten minutes I sat up and decided to write to Aikyung, Aira's younger sister in Seoul.

"Aikyung.

"It seems my heart is too small to contain all the memory of Aira. Aira's grave says nothing to me. When I fed incense into the burner before the grave, it was only fragrant smoke that rose. I inhaled the smoke deeply, as if it were Aira's soul.

"Aikyung, why didn't you tell me of your sister's death earlier? If I could have seen her dead even for a moment it might have been some consolation. Just now I met your sister in my dream. When I opened my eyes with joy, holding out my arms to welcome her, she had already disappeared. It was too real to be a dream, and too fleeting to be real.

"Aikyung, I think this is the sixty-fourth day after your sister's passing away. In four days it will be the fifteenth of September by the lunar calendar, so I will commemorate her birthday with a sacrificial rite for her here. 'How awful of a Christian to offer sacrificial rites to the dead!' you might say.

"But that which to you must be shocking and ridiculous is to me a solemn wish. As the high priests of the Levites made offerings of doves and lambs to God in token of their piety, the only way I can express my love for Aira is to make offerings before her grave. I have decided to stay the whole winter in this villa, just to make offerings before her grave. You might laugh at me and think me sentimental. But I have realised for the first time that every human truth has a tinge of sentimentality in it."

The next morning I stepped down to the yard before the day had fully broken. It was a rather cold morning. After walking around the deserted garden, I was starting up the hill to the rear when I met Soonshil coming from the hut. When she saw me she made a friendly bow and said, "Good morning. Did you get very cold last night?"

I answered her greeting, and said, "The frost is thick," looking around the yard. The night before must have been extremely cold, for the garden was coated with a thick layer of frost, and the cosmos stalks looked sparser. "The flowers have all withered."

"Oh, I think I'd better cut down those cosmos plants."

Soonshil must have guessed my feelings, for she walked away to the hut. In a little while she appeared with a sickle, tying her apron, and began to cut the withered cosmos stalks.

Watching the stalks being cut down one after another, I recalled once again that all of them had been planted by Aira's own hands. Therefore, seeing them cut down pained me, as if the memory of Aira in my heart were being sheared off.

When the garden at last looked clean and spacious, I became enveloped by a nameless feeling of emptiness.

"Now it's clean, isn't it?" Soonshil straightened up, putting down the sickle.

"It's too empty."

"I think the place had better be planted with chrysanthemums next year," Soonshil said. Those casually uttered words seemed to me to presage something fateful, and I could only stand there in silence for a while, my heart heavy. Soonshil, looking at me with her deep eyes, also stood there in silence.

The dull silence had lasted for quite a while when Soonshil and I were both startled by the sound of a sudden false cough. When we looked around, coming back to our senses, we found to our surprise that Kim, the villa keeper, was standing like a wooden image within the hedge, and staring at us with eyes sharp as daggers. They were keen, poisonous eyes that cut through flesh. I intuitively felt that Kim suspected Soonshil and me, and after a brief, confused silence I said, "Ah, are you back from the market?" and moved a few steps towards him.

"Oh, the young master's come? Why, this is a surprise! I heard you were in Chejudo. When did you arrive? I went to the market yesterday and, er, a few bowls of makkoli did me up and, er, I guess I'm getting old. So, I'm sure the master and the mistress are both well in Seoul?" Kim, at once softening his expression, guffawed and bowed time and again, rubbing the back of his head with his palm, and chattered on busily.

After exchanging a few words with Kim, I went up the hill. But I could not help feeling uncomfortable, and kept recalling Kim's poisonous eyes. It was an ordinary enough scene, but perhaps it could not have failed to breed suspicions in Kim, who had stayed out all night, leaving his young wife alone in the villa.

I felt regret more on account of Soonshil than of Kim. Even though Kim chatted and laughed immediately, I could not believe that the suspicion once conceived could be erased that easily. I recalled reading somewhere that foolish imaginings always breed mischief, and my mind was heavy with the fear that some dreadful misfortune might overwhelm Soonshil in the future.

Three days passed. Perhaps nothing had happened in the Kim household, because Soonshil was as composed as usual.

On the evening before the birthday commemoration offering to Aira, I was sauntering in the orchard. The sun had just set, and the moon had not had time to spread its beams, so that I was stepping on fallen leaves and walking among the trees in semi-darkness for a long time. Now and then a desultory wind swept past, making the boughs weep, and the earth fell to sleep by degrees.

At last the moonbeans filled the space and conjured up a myriad shadows like those of scarecrows in the orchard. After a gust of wind, the whole orchard was about to sink into fathomless quiet again. A voice called from somewhere, "Young master!" The woman who was calling me from among the apple trees was Soonshil.

I was glad. I had never been so pleased to see Soonshil before. I did not know exactly why I was so glad, but I was. I knew it was unwise to meet Soonshil alone in a moonlit orchard like this, but still I was very glad.

Soonshil approached me and without a word handed me a telegram.

"Will arrive at nine. Hope to be met at the station. Aikyung."

Aikyung was coming, probably to participate in the sacrificial offering to her sister, after reading my letter to her.

"The little miss is coming, isn't she?" Soonshil asked. Soonshil could read, as she had attended elementary school up to the third form.

"Yes. Because tomorrow is Aira's birthday."

"Going to stay long?"

I was silent for some time, because I did not know who she was talking about, but I answered, "Well, I think Aikyung will go back soon. I will stay the winter in this villa."

Soonshil did not make any further remarks.

"It must be very cold here in the winter, isn't it?"

"Not so very. But there's nothing but snow in the winter."

"Snow?"

"Yes. Everything gets covered with snow in winter— mountains, fields, houses. All you can see is snow, so that in winter you long for people."

Hearing Soonshil's words, I strengthened my resolve to stay the winter in this snow-covered villa, feeding myself on

memories of Aira. I felt that it would be a good thing for
Soonshil, too, who said she missed people in winter.

"I guess you can see hunters in the winter?"

"Yes. We see hunting parties from Seoul shooting now
and then."

"What animals are they after?"

"Mostly roe deer."

At the word roe deer, I remembered Aira's having called
me a deer, and I recited the word several times. And then,
picturing the tragic and beautiful sight of the wounded deer
falling in the snow bleeding red, I felt an aching in my limbs,
as if I had been the stricken deer myself.

Ten minutes later we went down to the villa in haste.
When it was time for me to go to the station and I started
out, putting on a heavy coat, Soonshil came up to me and
said, "Let me come along to meet her too."

"Oh, no. I can go alone."

I did not feel like dissuading her, but I recalled once again
the furious eyes of Kim. Soonshil did not insist, but raised
her head and looked at me. The moment my eyes met her
pearly eyes glistening in the moonlight, I was startled, as
one who has seen something that must not be seen and,
running down the hill like a frightened deer, I wailed, without knowing what I was doing, "Soonshil! Soonshil!"

At that moment I realised, almost with pain, that in this
world there was only Soonshil to comfort me now that Aira
had gone forever.

When I reached Y station it was already time for the arrival
of the train. I walked back and forth alone on the platform
dimly lit by street-lamps. There was no one there except me.

The train came in shortly. I ran to the door of the third-
class carriage. A man in old-fashioned garb and an old woman
who looked nearly sixty—only these two people got out of
the train; Aikyung could not be seen.

"She must have missed the train," I murmured, and was
turning away when from behind me Aikyung called out
"Hisoon!" in her resolute voice, and ran towards me
spiritedly, like a mare.

"Oh, Aikyung! Where did you get off?" I asked, running

to her.

"I came in the second-class car."

'In the second-class car? Why, you had a luxury trip!"

"Yes. As if I was on a honeymoon."

"A honeymoon?"

Feeling dazed for a moment by the word "honeymoon", I looked at Aikyung. She was wearing a western suit over her supple, elastic body, and her permanent-waved hair blew in the wind. In fact, Aikyung looked as seductive as dancing Salome.

When we were past the street and had entered the mountain pathway, Aikyung said, "Oh, I forgot to thank you for the letter," and smiled.

I ignored the smile and asked, "Do your parents know I'm staying in the villa?"

"Of course they do! When they heard you were going to stay the winter in the villa, they were frightened. They were worried about what the mountain winter would do to your sensitive health, and told me to persuade you to leave the villa. I came as their emissary, so to speak."

Tears filled my eyes to learn that Aira's family's love for me had not changed even after Aira's death.

"But what good could the air of Seoul do for me?"

"They don't want you to come to Seoul, but to go to a hot spring or somewhere like that. And they want me to go with you and console you."

"To a hot spring? And with Aikyung?" I retorted and looked at Aikyung hard, till she shrank back from embarrassment.

I was a little displeased, and I wondered whether going to a spa with Aikyung was her parents' idea or her own. To me, the idea of trying to allay my grief from the loss of Aira with anything other than the memory of her was profanation.

There had been an incident of sorts last summer when all three of us—Aira, Aikyung and I—were staying in the villa together. One bright moonlit night we were chatting on the verandah when suddenly Aikyung, without heeding her sister's presence, took hold of my arm, pressed it to her bosom, and said jokingly, "I like Hisoon more than anybody else in the whole world!"

That was all, but from that day Aira lost her appetite for three days, and was buried in anxiety. At that time I thought Aikyung was simply joking so I told Aira not to be over-sensitive but, on looking back, it might not have been all a joke.

All during the walk from the station to the villa, Aikyung did not pronounce her sister's name even once. I regretted having written to her. Upon arriving at the villa Aikyung, without bothering to look once into Aira's room, rushed up directly to her own room. When I suggested that she look into Aira's room, she said, "No. I like my room better. Come to my room at once. I will tell you exciting things."

I was more than a little disappointed, because I thought it was Aikyung more than anybody else who should be grieved by Aira's death. Again and again I confirmed my plan to stay the winter in the villa so that I would not betray the memory of Aira.

I had a hard time falling asleep that night, with the sad fact in my mind that Aikyung was betraying her sister less than three months after her death. That Judas betrayed Jesus could be deemed human; it can happen that I, as a human being, might forsake Jesus. But how could Aikyung forget her own sister in less than three months' time? The worlds of life and death seem separated by only the thickness of a thread; but are the two worlds even so far apart from each other? I could not help feeling resentful of Aikyung. As the night deepened, my nerves became tenser and tenser, and at last I kicked out of bed and went outside.

I breathed deeply to steady myself and walked towards Aira's grave. Does Aira know that I have come to her? Thinking that if her soul were there it would come before me and comfort me, I threw myself down on the grass beside the grave. It was midnight, and all around was silent as death; the moon was clear and cool. The rhythmical puffs of the breeze sounded sad, or sometimes happy, or forlorn. I was thinking that it was in moments like this that sound, colour and sentiments blend into one, when I seemed to hear a quarrel from afar.

Pricking up my ears, I could perceive it was a man's voice, and upon listening more carefully I recognised Kim's hoarse roar. I felt my heart sink, and at once I recalled his fiercely suspicious glance. I got up. I felt my way towards the direction of the voice, picturing in my head the sorry state of Soonshil.

As I approached the hut of the Kims, I could hear wild curses.

"You, Goddamned bitch! Why did he come, if not for you? Now, tell the truth. Confess everything, if you want to live. You bitch, you deserve to be torn to bits!"

With these savage curses I could see a shadow like that of a demon on the paper-panelled door. And the atrocious sound of palms hitting flesh also came. It was obvious that Kim was beating Soonshil.

But not a sound came from Soonshil.

The blows were cutting my heart like an axe. I could picture only too vividly the terrible sight of Kim beating his wife and Soonshil biting her lips, trying not to groan.

"You bitch who ought to be torn to pieces! If that dog's meat is more to your taste, get yourself out of my sight! You dirty whore." With this, another bout of curses and blows began.

"Bitch! Have you become dumb all of a sudden? Why don't you answer me? Oh, yes, what *could* you have to say? Defend yourself if you can!"

But Soonshil was still silent.

"Well, you as good as admit your guilt with that silence! Do you have to go all the way to the orchard to do that dirty thing?" There was murder in Kim's voice.

I shuddered, realising that Kim's eyes had been following Soonshil and me all the time. We had done nothing sinful, but it was terrible nevertheless to have aroused such suspicions in other people.

I felt like jumping into that room right then and telling him that nothing like what he suspected had ever happened. But such a declaration would not convince Kim, and to have eavesdropped on a domestic quarrel would further increase suspicion, so I suppressed my urge with an effort.

It was painful to listen any further to the quarrel which I could do nothing to put an end to, so I ran to my room, but could not fall asleep. I felt I had to give up my plan of spending the winter in the villa. I realised it was best for Soonshil that I leave this villa as quickly as possible.

The night was almost spent. In Aikyung's room right next to mine I heard something hitting the wall. I listened, thinking that perhaps Aikyung had turned in her sleep, when a little later came a deep sigh. What was she sighing about? After a few moments' silence, Aikyung called me. I kept silent, and a little later Aikyung called me again, this time in a clearer voice, "Hisoon! Hisoon!"

I suddenly remembered Aikyung's seductive body, and realised that Aikyung was not a girl any more.

'Hisoon! Hisoon!" She called again, this time knocking on the wall.

"Aikyung! Why don't you go to sleep?" I said reprovingly, but that was an admonition to myself as well.

"Hisoon! I'm scared to death! Please come to my room."

"What's there to be scared about when you have me in the very next room? Go ahead and get some more sleep. It'll be a long time before day breaks."

"Oh, I'm scared to death. Please come quickly." Aikyung sent off an agnoised plea.

I raised myself reluctantly. I walked out to the hall and grasped the knob of Aikyung's door. But at that moment I instinctively felt that if I went into that room something horrible would surely happen and, telling myself that I must overcome this temptation by all means, I shuddered. I took my hand off the doorknob.

"Come in quickly!" Aikyung pleaded. I grasped the knob again. At that moment, the phrase in the Lord's Prayer, "lead us not into temptation", flashed through my mind like lightning, and I released the knob quickly. And I rushed outside as fast as I could.

When I came back to the villa about two hours later, the sun was already shining above the hill. I met Aikyung in the hall, but she was sullen, and did not even say good morning.

I came out to the well in the backyard to wash my face. Soonshil, who had been washing rice beside the well, calmly greeted me with a bow just as on any other day. She did not at all look like one who had gone through hell during the night. Only, there were some bruises on her neck. I was touched to think that there could be such beautiful patience.

At that moment Kim appeared from nowhere.

"Good morning, young master. Don't you think the weather's a bit warmer today? Oh, today is the fifteenth, so this is the day for the birthday offerings. Time flies like an arrow. Why, it's almost three months since the elder miss passed away. Oh, isn't it unbelievable?"

Kim babbled on, without waiting for any response. How could a man who had acted that way the night before talk so glibly in the morning? I was stupefied. The phrase "with honey in the mouth and a sword in the belly" must have been coined from examples of his kind.

At about ten o'clock we prepared our offering table and carried it to the grave. On the table were simply a bowl of white rice, fried fish and cooked vegetables. After burning incense, I poured out wine and bowed three times before her grave. Sorrow spread in my heart like fog. Soonshil wept quietly, and Aikyung kept looking up at the sky. Nobody spoke. After Soonshil had made her bows, Kim prepared to bow, too, but I cut him off decisively.

It was a simple ceremony, but for the first time I felt as if I had paid part of my debt to Aira. Aikyung, after we came back to the villa, said, "Hisoon! Now that the commemoration ceremony is over, let's leave, shall we?"

Where does she want me to go from here? Not comprehending, I answered vaguely. Had I been ignorant of the tragic scene that took place in the hut last night I would have insisted on spending the winter in the villa, but since I knew about it I could not do that either.

"What's there to make you hesitate? Now you've made the commemorative offering; let's go down by the first train tomorrow."

"I don't know."

"Why are you so indecisive, you, a man? You can't live here forever, so why not leave at once?"

"There's no difference."

"But you'll have to leave sometime."

I kept silent. By that time I had given up trusting human emotions.

All that day I roamed the hills, fields and the orchard like a mindless man. Life and death and all seemed meaningless to me. I envied the mental state of those who could trust in God as the highest reality.

All day I did not see anyone.

Night came again. And I feared the night. I kept thinking of what had taken place in the hut the night before, and towards midnight I got up, without knowing what I was doing. Fearing that the same thing might be happening again, I noiselessly approached the hut with trembling heart. Oh, what nightmare was this? The same tempest between the husband and wife was heard again tonight. Moreover, Kim was drunk this time.

He kicked and hit his wife, threw things, fell down in the frenzy of his own fury, cried aloud like a child, and then sprang up and tortured his wife again. There was only the papered door between the dreadful scene and me.

I could not stand it. And I could not step between them and bring peace, so I had to run back to the villa again with clenched fists. Well, I would have to leave the villa as Aikyung had told me to as soon as it was daylight.

How could I shield Soonshil from the misfortune that engulfed her? The only thing I could do for her was to leave the villa as soon as possible. It was a very painful thing for me, but I had no choice. I must hesitate no longer but leave this villa with Aikyung today. Whatever the rough waves that might await me in the world, I had to go away with Aikyung in order to save Soonshil from greater misfortune.

When day broke, I met Soonshil beside the well as I was going into the villa to wake up Aikyung. Soonshil was as calm as always. I was about to inquire about the night before, but I bit my tongue and swallowed the words. Then I said, "We're going to leave today."

"Yes? Why? You said you were going to spend the winter here."

Reading disappointment on her surprised face, my heart beat wildly.

"Because I think it is fate."

Soonshil just dropped her head at my answer.

It was one of those moments when mind and mind meet

in silence. I put my hand on Soonshil's shoulder unawares and called, "Soonshil!"

Soonshil just trembled. And she gazed at my chest silently, with blame in her eyes.

"Soonshil!" I cried out again, and grasped her hand. "You said you miss people in winter. Wherever I go, I will never forget that. But I think meeting and parting are beyond our will."

Soonshil was still silent, her head lowered.

"Soonshil, I have realised for the first time what great happiness it is to cherish a mute love for someone. Now, goodbye."

Soonshil and I held hands for the last time. Then she raised her eyes and poured her moist glance directly into my eyes. Our eyes met. Beholding Soonshil's eyes ecstatically for a moment, I raised my arm and gently patted her on the shoulder. I did not feel any guilt in my act. On the contrary, I felt as sanctified as at the moment I was baptised before God.

So at last I left the villa, accepting as destiny my eternal hovering over the boundary between the flesh and the spirit, but no longer with sorrow in my heart.

Kang Kyung-ae

Born in 1907, Kang Kyung-ae seems to have lived the lonely existence common to the women intellectuals of the day. Not much is known of her life, especially as she spent the major part of her adult years in Manchuria. There, in Kando, she worked as a reporter and head of the branch office of a Korean daily before her return to Korea in 1943 and subsequent death.

In common with many of her contemporaries, her subject was the life of poor, struggling, underprivileged people. The trend of naturalism is softened and rendered more poignant in her stories by her tenderness toward her characters and her sensitivity to their emotions, as is shown in 'The Underground Village' (1935). The mother of this story is emblematic of the enduring Korean woman, who submits unprotestingly to her lot as a beast of burden, and whose sighs may sometimes be exhausted but whose affection never is.

The Underground Village

Kang Kyung-ae

The sun was burning above the western hill. Chilsung, as usual, staggered past this village with his beggar's sack slung over his shoulder. He kept pulling down his crownless straw hat, but the sun continued to scorch his forehead, and drops of sweat rolled down. Dust rose up from the parched road like smoke and made it difficult for him to breathe.

"There he comes again!"

"Come on!"

The little urchins at play by the roadside shouted and ran towards him. Chilsung swore to himself and hurried his steps, but the children soon overtook him and pulled at his clothes.

"Cry, lad, cry!" One of the urchins blocked Chilsung's way and laughed. The children surrounded him in a circle.

"Hey, boy, how old are you?"

"Show us what you earned today."

One of the urchins snatched at his beggar's sack, and all the others clapped their hands. Chilsung stood immobile and glared at the biggest of the group. He knew that if he tried to push ahead or swore at them they would pester him still more.

"Oh, he looks like a gentleman today." One bristly-haired urchin brandished before his face a stick with a bit of cow-dung at the tip. The children all giggled and made as if to smear cowdung on Chilsung with their sticks. Chilsung could not stand it, so he ran as fast as he could.

He raised both his shaky arms high and twisted his neck convulsively as he placed one foot ahead of the other. The children mimicked his gait and followed him. They blocked him in front and behind, and jumped up to smear cowdung on his face. He scowled fiercely, and could only mutter "Goddamn!" after twitching his mouth for a long time.

The children imitated the mouth and the "Goddamn!" and roared with laughter. When cowdung touched his lips Chilsung spat vehemently and scowled fiercely.

"Why, that's a terrible gentleman there," the children mocked, but perhaps they thought he really looked terrible, for they began to retreat. Chilsung wiped his mouth with his sleeve and looked at the noisily retreating children. He felt furious and forlorn, like one cast aside by the world.

After the urchins had gone away, there was utter silence. Chilsung walked on along the new highway. He tried to brush away the cowdung, but the effort only spread the bluish stain on his clothes. He stared into space, and flopped down on the slope at the foot of the mountain.

A breeze stirred the tall grasses, and insects chirped now and then. A running brook sang from somewhere, too. He scratched his head and looked ahead absently. The sun showered its oblique rays upon the forest, and the songs of the birds sounded plaintive. "Why am I a cripple like this, so that I have to be ridiculed and persecuted even by little children?" he thought, and plucked a blade of grass beside him, which hurt his palm.

"Well, at least I'm not as miserable as Kunnyun," he thought. "Kunnyun is blind yet she lives," he mused, looking at the down-covered berries of a nearby plant. He pictured Kunnyun in his head. Her softly closed eyes! He trembled as he pictured them. He looked at his beggar's sack beside him and thought he would give Kunnyun the most delicious unbroken biscuits that he had garnered that day. "How shall I give them to her? Shall I hand them to her over the brushwood hedge tonight? To do so, Kunnyun will have to be made to come out and stand beside the brushwood hedge. Someone will have to tell her to come out. Who? No, that won't do. Then I will send Chilwoon over with them. Oh, no, that way Kunnyun's mother and my mother will know. I will hand them over the hedge tomorrow at midday after people have gone out for weeding." His heart throbbed, and he got up.

The sun that had been pouring down heat as if to fry his skin disappeared among the mountains, and a cool breeze from somewhere stirred the grasses and cooled his body. Chilsung fumbled with his beggar's sack and then, slinging it over his shoulder, resumed his tottering walk.

The sky spread before his eyes like a vast sea, and far off towards the horizon a red evening glow spread in waves. He pushed up his straw hat and came out of the shadows of the valley. As he moved, the smell of cowdung stung his nostrils.

When he had passed the mountain and approached the entrance to the village, his younger brother Chilwoon ran up to him with the baby on his back.

"Oh, you're late. I've been waiting for you all day." His big eyes beaming happily, Chilwoon went up close to his brother and, taking hold of the beggar's sack, tried to find out what he had obtained that day.

"Did you get biscuits today, too?"

"No." Chilsung quickly shifted his sack and retreated a step. Chilwoon moved with him.

"Give me one, will you? Just one." Chilwoon swallowed and stretched out his soiled hand. The baby on his back also spread both her hands and looked at Chilsung.

"Goddamn!" Chilsung turned away quickly. Chilwoon followed him hastily.

"Will you, please? Give me one."

"I haven't got any." Chilsung scowled. Chilwoon became tearful at once and looked up at his brother.

"I'll tell Mother you won't give me a biscuit. She said when she went out to the field that if I looked after the baby you'd give me sweets. I'll tell on you, I will." Chilwoon twisted his mouth and wiped his tears with his fist.

The baby, without knowing what it was all about, also began to cry. Darkness was setting in, but Chilwoon sobbed and ran towards the mountain where their mother was supposed to be.

"Mother! Mother!" When Chilwoon shouted sobbingly, the baby also cried "Mama! Mama!" The echo from the

mountain sounded somewhat like their mother's reply of
"Coming!" Chilsung, deeming it fortunate to be rid of
Chilwoon and Yong-ae, turned and began to walk.

The village was sunk in darkness and nothing could be
discerned, but the old locust tree loomed tall and erect, as if
it were trying to reach the stars. He walked on, resolving that
he would meet Kunnyun by whatever means, and give her the
biscuits without fail.

"Is it you, Chilsung?" It was his mother's voice. He looked
back. Her face could not be seen under the big bundle of
brushwood, which made her neck tilt until it seemed about
to break.

"Why are you so late today?" She had looked down the
road again and again to see if her son was coming until her
eyes ached, before she went up to the mountain from the
field. She had worried that he might have fallen down somewhere or been stoned by urchins, and had thought of going
to town in search of him. At his mother's question Chilsung
recalled the mortification he received from the urchins and
at once became tearful.

His mother walked close up to him. She smelt of leaves.
She was carrying the big sheaf of twigs on her head and also
the baby on her back.

"Mother, he won't give me any sweets." Chilwoon hung
on to his mother's skirt. His mother staggered, about to fall
down, but recovered her balance and stroked Chilwoon with
one hand.

"I'll kill that damned boy." Chilsung raised his foot to
kick his brother. His mother lurched in between them.

"Don't! He's had a hard time all day, looking after the
baby. He's got heat rash all around his waist." Then his
mother sighed deeply. Chilsung suddenly fancied he smelt
cowdung and his anger rose.

"Do you think I've been sitting in the shade all day?"

"Oh, that isn't what I meant, Chilsung!" His mother's
voice choked and she could not go no speaking. They walked
in silence.

When they got home they sat down on the sheaf of twigs.
His mother talked about this and that to divert Chilsung.

"Oh, there are so many stinging insects this year. My

hands are all numb from their stings." She would have liked to take a look at her hands, but restrained herself and caressed the baby. She bared one of her breasts. Chilwoon kicked at the bundle and went on whimpering. Chilsung could not stand to look at his mother and sister, so he got up and looked around in the dark to see if Kunnyun was somewhere around.

Entering the room, Chilsung sat down crosslegged, pressing under his thigh the toe he had bruised on the stepping stone, and noiselessly latched the door. Then he poured out the contents of the beggar's sack. Matchsticks and rice grains scattered with a rustling sound. He winced and rapidly felt the things one by one. He thought of the money that was in the sack, so he took it out and looked down at it absently. Nothing could be discerned clearly because the room was dark, but he imagined he could see everything distinctly.

He piled up the matchboxes and the rice and the biscuits separately in a corner and thought of Kunnyun. What should he give her? He picked up the biscuits quickly and, thinking that he would give her those, put one in his mouth. It crushed with a crisp sound between his teeth, and sweetness spread in his mouth. He smacked his lips and listened again to make sure Chilwoon was not eavesdropping.

He counted the money held tightly in his hand and, when he thought how happy Kunnyun would be if he used it to buy her material for clothes, his heart beat wildly. "Why doesn't she come to visit us at home? If she does, I'll give her money and biscuits and everything she wants." When he imagined her visiting them, he felt somehow reverential. So he wrapped the matchboxes and biscuits together and put them under the straw mat, pushing the money in under the mat too, and moved the rice near to the kitchen. Then, sitting near the back door, he looked over at the hedge of Kunnyun's house.

Squash vines were winding round the hedge and stars were floating above it. "How can I meet her?" His hand touched his toe and it hurt. A cool breeze caressed his cheeks. His heart ached. It ached more than his bruised toe.

"Eat your supper."

Chilsung looked back, startled. When he realised it was his

mother who was standing outside the door, he felt an emptiness in a corner of his bosom.

"Did you lock the door?" His mother pulled at the door.
He felt as if she were pulling at the door to ask for biscuits or
for money. He thought he hated his family and all.

"I won't eat," he shouted. His whole body shook.

"Did you eat something in the market?" His mother's
voice became thin. Every time Chilsung got angry, his
mother's voice became weak like that. After a long interval,
his mother pleaded again, "Why don't you have some more?"

"I don't want to," he shouted again. His mother murmured something to herself and fell silent. Chilsung, left
alone, yearned to eat the biscuits under the straw mat. He
lifted it. A sweet scent floated up and also the disgusting
smell of bedbugs. He replaced the straw mat and turned
around, thinking that the biscuits must go to Kunnyun tomorrow, but his hand was again fingering the mat. "I will give
them to Kunnyun." He took his hand away quickly and
grabbed the doorsill.

A breeze squeezed in through the gap between the door
panels and chilled his sweaty brow. He quickly took off his
jacket and hugged the wind. He felt itchy all over, so he
rubbed his body against the wall. It made him feel good, so
he kept on doing it harder. That made him breathless, and
the skin on his back tore and ached. So he got up, clinging
to the wall, and went outside.

As he moved, every part of his body ached. His fingertip
hurt as if pierced by a thorn, and his wrist ached and his arm
felt sore and his toe stung. He ignored them all and walked
on.

Among the onions planted in orderly rows beside the bush
clover hedge a few white flowers shone like stars, and the
smell of scallions that drifted with the wind made him feel
as if a girl were sitting beside him. He stepped nearer to
the hedge.

From Kunnyun's house floated the poignant smell of
mugwort burning to keep away mosquitoes, and the fire
itself flickered now and then. As he pricked his ears towards
the conversation in Kunnyun's yard, the hedge rustled and
the furry spines of squash leaves stung his cheeks. His face

burned when he suddenly thought Kunnyun might be peeping at him from beyond the hedge.

After a long while he looked around. His clothes were all damp with dew, and scallion blossoms shone like pebbles under water. The mosquito fire could not be seen any more, and all around was darkness. From somewhere insects chirped. When he stepped into his room he felt stuffiness fill his chest up to his throat.

When he awoke the next morning, the backyard was full of sunshine already. As soon as he got up, Chilsung looked around to see whether his mother and Chilwoon were in the house still. Making sure that they were not, he sat on the doorsill and looked at the hedge of Kunnyun's house. Kunnyun's father and mother must have gone out to the field to weed, and Kunnyun must be home alone.

"Could there be some visitor? I must see her today." Thinking thus, he looked down at his arms, which hung limp inside the tattered sleeves and looked as if they were made of no bones and no flesh, but only shrivelled greenish-yellow skin. Suddenly he felt sad and, raising his head, sighed deeply. How fortunate it was that Kunnyun was blind! If she could see, she would have taken to her heels at the sight of these arms. But what if Kunnyun felt these arms and asked why they were so thin and limp? And what could one do with such weak arms? His heart tore at the thought. He kept heaving sighs and suddenly thought, "Couldn't there be a medicine for them? There must be some medicine." On the spider's web spread over the hedge of Kunnyun's house hung innumerable dewdrops. "Maybe those are medicine." He sprang up and went outside.

Praying that the dewdrops shining on the spider's web would be medicine for him, he pulled the web down carefully. His arms were weak and trembled, so that the dewdrops fell on the ground in a shower. He tried to catch them in his palms, but not a drop fell on them.

"Goddamn!"

He had a habit of swearing "Goddamn" and glaring at the sky whenever he failed at something. As he was standing thus fuming to himself he turned his head at the soft sound of rubber shoes. The furry squash leaves touched his eyelids and

he became tearful. Kunnyun seen through tears! He suppressed his urge to rub his eyes and opened them wider.

Kunnyun, walking with a heavy wooden laundry basin on
her head, came towards the hedge and, after putting the basin
on the ground, straightened up. Her eyes were closed as if in
sleep; or they seemed just slightly open. Perhaps from exertion, several red spots shone on her cheeks, and her chin
seemed sharper than usual, making her look like someone
who had been ill for days. Kunnyun shook the laundry
piece by piece and spread it on the hedge.

Chilsung could not breathe. As he tried to inhale noiselessly, his heart felt about to burst and the skin of his belly
contracted. He bowed down once to brush away his tears
and kept looking. Nothing was in his head now except every
movement of Kunnyun. Kunnyun came near him with her
last piece of laundry. Chilsung wanted to stretch out his hand
and take hold of Kunnyun's, but he flinched back instead,
and his whole body shook.

As the hedge rustled under the spreading laundry, a
thousand birds' wings flapped in his chest, sirens sang in his
ears, and darkness descended on his eyes. He could move and
part the squash leaves to look beyond the hedge only when
Kunnyun's footsteps had retreated to a distance. Kunnyun
was walking towards the kitchen door with the empty
wooden basin on her head. He felt an urgent desire to call
out to her and make her stop, but his voice would not
function. Kunnyun's bare legs showed once or twice through
the torn skirt and disappeared. He stared at the kitchen door,
hoping that she would come out again, but she did not
reappear. He heaved a deep sigh and came away from the
hedge. The sun shone hot. He wished he had given her the
biscuits. He wished he had given her the money. "No, I will
save the money and buy her material for a skirt," he thought,
and peeped in again. Only the hedge rustled; otherwise all
was silence. The laundry washed by Kunnyun shone so bright
that he averted his eyes and turned away. If he didn't buy
her clothes, Kunnyun would go around showing her legs
through the torn skirt forever.

"Give me sweets, will you, please?"

He looked back to see Chilwoon coming out of the kitchen

door with the baby on his back. He moved away from the
hedge like one discovered in theft. Chilwoon, thinking that
his brother was coming to beat him, ran into the kitchen,
but looking back approached him again.

"Will you? Just one." He held out his hand.

The baby also tilted her head to look at her elder brother,
and spread out her hand. The baby's head was covered with
sores and the sores oozed all the time. The baby's thin, light-
brown hair was pasted to the sores, and flies always swarmed
around her head. The baby kept pulling at her hair with her
tiny fingers and ate the scabs that she tore from her head.

The baby held out that hand before her brother. She
thrust her hand before her brother with fingers spread like a
fan. Chilsung scowled at them once and went into the room.
Chilwoon blocked the doorway and importunately begged
again. "Will you? Give me just one and I'll go away." He
snuffled up his snot.

"I don't want to see you!"

Chilwoon had no shirt so he was clad only in a pair of
pants. The skin of his back, parched and grilled by the sun,
was peeling in flakes. The baby did not have even pants, so
she was naked all the time. His eyes burned as he looked at
the bare bodies of his younger brother and sister. As he
turned his eyes to look at the wall, he pictured the pile upon
pile of cloth stacked along the walls of the town store. His
hand that had been raised to strike Chilwoon fell limp.

"If you don't give me any, I won't look after the baby."
Chilwoon put down the baby and ran away. The baby
began to cry, screaming. Chilsung did not cast a glance at
the baby, but turned away. Flies were swarming around the
rice bowl. His mother always went out to the field after
setting his rice and soup in the room under a cloth, because
Chilsung got up late. He went up to it and took away the
cloth. A drowned fly floated in the soup, and the countless
flies that had been sitting on the rice flew up startled. He
picked out the fly from the soup and put a spoonful of rice
into his mouth. The food consisted of a little rice and many
acorns. The scanty rice, when crushed between his teeth,
was so soft and glutinous and sweet that it almost made
him choke. But immediately the crunched acorns filled his

mouth with bitter juice. He tried to swallow the acorns without chewing, but they did not go down his throat, lingering
in his mouth and spreading bitterness.

When he looked a while later, the baby had already
stopped crying and was crawling towards her brother. She
looked at her brother and looked at the rice bowl and then
looked at her brother again. Chilsung, as a reward for having
stopped crying, sorted rice grains in the bowl and gave the
baby a spoonful. The baby swallowed the rice in no time and
then looked up at her brother again. This time Chilsung gave
her an acorn. The baby did not put it into her mouth but
kept fingering it.

He cursed loudly at the baby who could tell rice and
acorn apart. The baby twisted her mouth and began to cry.

"Stop it!" Chilsung kicked the baby. The baby closed her
eyes tightly and lay prostrate on the floor. The flies on her
head flew up once but settled down again immediately.
When Chilsung raised his foot again to kick, the baby just
sniffled and stopped crying. But tears kept flowing out of
her eyes. Chilsung went on eating but turned his head at
an urgent cough.

The baby, who had eaten the acorn, in the meantime had
sicked it up. The acorn sicked up with the baby's reddish
saliva was not chewed at all. The reddish tint was of blood.
The baby's face was flushed and muscles stood out on her
neck.

Chilsung instantly felt the acorn in his mouth taste like
sand, and a bitter smell rose up. He flung away his spoon,
picked up the child, and put her down on the dirt floor.
When he spanked the baby's fleshless buttocks, her face
turned dark but she kept sobbing silently. He kicked the
rice bowl and walked across the room. He could not bear
to hear the vomiting sound. He remembered the biscuits
underneath the mat and, taking them all out and throwing
them down in front of the baby, went out into the backyard. He circled the yard for some time and spat.

When he came into the room again, it was hot like the
inside of a stove. He kept standing up and sitting down,
and when he turned his head to look he found the baby
asleep on the dirt floor, head pillowed on hand. On her

vomit flies were crawling, and on the baby's head and inside the baby's open mouth were swarms of flies. Biscuits! Startled, he looked. Not a morsel of the biscuits remained. The baby could not have eaten them all so fast. Chilwoon must have been home. He regretted that he had given them all to the baby, and thought he would beat up Chilwoon when he saw him. He ran outside, kicking the baby on his way. He hated to look at the baby lying on her side with one hand under her head like a grown-up, and he hated to look at her thin limbs.

Hearing the baby's cry, he searched for Chilwoon. Chilwoon was playing with other children under the willow tree. He walked towards them, breathing hard. Although he walked as stealthily as he could, Chilwoon caught sight of him and ran away. The children, chewing on Indian millet stalks, eyed Chilsung and giggled. Some of them imitated Chilsung's gait.

Chilwoon could not be seen anywhere. When Chilsung fell down because his foot caught in a vine, the children who had been following him laughed and chattered noisily. He stood up with difficulty and scowled at the children because he was afraid that they, too, might attack him in a body. The children, perhaps frightened by his scowl, took to their heels. To Chilsung they did not look like children, but a horde of hungry monkeys after prey. He stared at their backs, thinking that all the children of this village were hateful. His forehead burned in the sun and his toe stung. The husks of Indian millet stalks that the children had peeled off hurt the soles of his feet. The children were running towards the brook. He thought Chilwoon must be among them, and went towards the willow tree.

There were more Indian millet husks around the willow tree, and cowdung was scattered here and there, because people tied their cows to the willow tree. He leaned against the tree and looked. His eyes moved unconsciously to Kunnyun's house. He yearned to see Kunnyun again. She'd be alone at home now. But what if somebody were there? Something stung him. Several huge ants were climbing up his legs. He brushed them off and looked again.

Far away on the hedge of Kunnyun's house were spread

white garments, looking as if they would fly up like birds at the faintest sound. "No," he said to himself, "Nobody's there. Everybody's gone weeding." At the sound of footsteps he looked back. Kaedong's mother was walking towards him heavily, carrying a woman on her back.

Normally when they met she would accost him jokingly, with banter such as "Have you earned many boxes of matches? How about making a present of one to me?" But today she passed him without a word, her face tearful. Sweat poured in torrents from her forehead, her legs tottered, and she was panting like mad. Chilsung saw that the woman being carried on her back looked like a corpse. The dishevelled hair, the foamy mouth, the torn clothes. When he looked at the face inside the chaos of hair, he recognised Kunnyun's mother. He wanted to ask questions, but Kaedong's mother had already gone past the willow tree. What happened? Did she faint? Did she have a fight with somebody? He got up and followed them. He wanted to overtake Kaedong's mother and find out what was the matter, but his legs did not carry him as fast as he wished. He staggered even more than usual and did not advance much. He got angry, swerved wildly, and fell down. After writhing for a long time he got up and began walking slowly.

Smoke rose up from Kunnyun's chimney. Oh, what had happened to Kunnyun's mother? As he went near Kunnyun's house, his feet moved towards it of their own accord, but he checked himself and walked round it, hoping to overhear something.

When he stepped into the dirt yard the baby was defecating in the midst of a swarm of flies. As she strained hard, her anus jutted out like a finger and red blood dropped from it. The baby's eyes were dilated to the full and muscles stood out on her face like the blade of a sword. The small forehead streamed with sweat. Chilsung averted his face and went into the room. He wished he could step on the baby and kill it or cast it away on a distant mountain.

Putting into his mouth the acorn that was kicked by his feet, and scowling fiercely at the baby's groans, he came out into the backyard. He remembered about Kunnyun's mother again and stepped up to the hedge.

He raised his head at the sound of a baby crying. He recognised at once that it was not his sister but a new-born infant. He realised Kunnyun's mother must have delivered a baby. Then his anxiety subsided a little, but he felt a bitter taste in his mouth at the thought of a baby. He thought that babies had better be killed as soon as they were born rather than survive like his baby sister.

Had she given birth to a girl like Kunnyun again? A blind girl? He giggled for no reason at the thought. Before his giggle died down he wondered to himself why it was that the women of this village produced such deformed children. Well, Kunnyun wasn't blind from birth. And as for himself, he also became a cripple at four after suffering paralysis following the measles. Then he recalled what his mother always said about his illness.

At that time his mother went to the town hospital, walking miles in knee-deep snow, carrying him on her back. After waiting in vain for an eternity in the unheated hall in the hospital, she pushed open the door of the consultation room, but the doctor raised his eyebrows and motioned her out, so she went into the hall again and waited another eternity, till at last an errand boy came out with a finger-thin vial.

Whenever she recalled that day she cursed the doctor vehemently, and cursed the world, too. Whenever his mother talked about it Chilsung always cut her short and told her not to say any more. He couldn't bear to listen to it.

"Would I get better if I took medicine? Would Kunnuyn be all right if she took medicine? Oh, no. After you are crippled no medicine can cure you. But who knows? Maybe if I could take some good medicine I might be able to move my limbs freely like other people and go up the mountains to gather wood, and not be mocked by little urchins." He felt a heaviness in his chest. He opened his eyes. Shall I go to a hospital and inquire? "The doctors, they don't care about anything but money," he repeated his mother's words and flopped down on the ground.

Silence came from Kunnyun's house and the baby's crying had ceased. Chilsung felt hungry. He looked at the sun and thought that when his mother came back presently she would look at him through her unkempt hair with anxiety and ask him why he didn't go begging today, and what then would they eat tomorrow? He looked at the bush clover trees.

"Could this bush clover tree be medicine for my disease?" he suddenly thought as he smelt the cool scent of the bush, and bit off a stalk. When he chewed on it, the smell of grass nauseated him and he felt like vomiting. But he closed his eyes tightly and chewed and swallowed without breathing. His throat felt torn, and saliva flowed and flowed. He thought the medicine would work only if he swallowed the saliva too, so he blinked his eyes and swallowed the saliva. For some reason tears flowed from both his eyes.

He looked up at the sky and prayed that he would be able to gather wood instead of his mother. He had never had such a thought before; he used not to feel too sorry even when he saw his mother walking with difficulty under a big bundle of wood, but somehow he prayed such a prayer at that moment.

He stood perfectly still for a long while and then raised his arm before his eyes with a pounding heart. But the arm was still withered. He vomited suddenly and, hitting his head against the ground, began to weep.

It was after deep darkness had fallen that his mother came back, again with a load of wood.

"Are you sick?" The dim figure of his mother looked as if it would fall down any moment from the weight of fatigue. And the thick smell of grass, soaked through and through in her skirt, smelt like garlic.

"Dear, why don't you answer me?" His mother's hand as she touched him felt like a piece of log, but it had some warmth in it.

Chilsung pushed away his mother's hand and turned away. His mother, sitting a few feet from him, studied her son and said, as if to herself, "Why doesn't he tell me if he's sick?" and got up and left the room. After some time his mother came in with boiled rice in vegetable soup and helped her son sit up. Chilsung sat up and held the spoon with a trembling hand.

"Darling, are you sick?" Now his mother's clothes smelt of smoke, and with her breath came the smell of boiled rice. Chilsung felt better.

"No."

His mother set her mind at ease and looked at her son eating soup.

"Kunnyun's mother had a baby today in the field. Oh, why do babies get born in poor homes?"

Chilsung recalled the sight of Kunnyun's mother as he saw her under the willow tree, and the cry of the new-born infant rang in his ears. The miserable sight of Yong-ae as she tried to defecate revived before his eyes. He scowled.

"Oh, why should the likes of us conceive? Heaven's too inconsiderate." His mother sighed and went out with the empty bowl. Chilsung, partly because it was too hot in the room and also because he wanted to know what was happening in Kunnyun's house, went outside.

From the pile of wood in a corner of the yard a strong smell of grass rose up, and the stars in the dark-blue sky shone like babies' eyes. He chased away the annoying mosquitoes and sat down on the heap of dry wood. Leaves rustled, and the warm mist rising from the wood warmed his bottom. His mother walked up to him.

"Is that you, Chilsung? Why did you come out?" She sat down beside him and the wood rustled. Chilsung turned his head away because of the smell of sweat and baby's dung. His mother suckled the baby and sighed. It seemed as if she wanted to say something to Chilsung, but kept fretfully caressing the baby, who looked like a sick cat.

She had weeded all day and at night had gone up to the mountain and gathered wood. Although she was dead tired, she had to look after the baby at night. Every night she felt she wouldn't be able to wake up again once she fell alseep. Chilsung hated his mother for not looking after herself.

"Go to sleep, you chicken!" Chilsung shouted. Yong-ae began to cry.

"How can she go to sleep? She's sick and she's starved all day and my milk's dried up," his mother wanted to say, but swallowed the words. Tears gathered in her eyes.

"Oh, it's all right. He didn't say it to you. Suck your milk." She finished the words with difficulty. Tears streamed down her cheeks. She wished she could quench Yong-ae's thirst with her tears.

At long last his mother said, "Why would a baby get born and almost mill its mother if it didn't mean to live? When I looked in next door just now the baby was dead. That's better for everybody, but. . . Oh, poor things. She had writhed so in the furrow that the baby's head was all matted with earth, I heard. If it had lived it would have become nothing but a cripple. I heard that earth went into its eyes and ears, too. Oh, it did well to die," his mother murmured fretfully. Chilsung breathed hard because of the oppression in his chest. Then he thought he would not have to be like this if he had died as a baby.

"Oh, what's so good about living that we have to keep alive? Kunnyun's mother said she'll go weeding again tomorrow. She needs to rest at least one day, but this is no time for resting. Oh, why do babies get born to poor folks like us?"

She recalled the time she had threshed barley the very next day after she gave birth to Yong-ae. The sky had swirled and looked yellow, and the ears of barley became in turn big balls and tiny dots. Whenever she lifted or brought down the flail something kept sinking down from her body. Later on she felt something heavy hanging between her legs, but she could not take a look at it or do anything about it, afraid that others might notice. When at last she looked at it in the privy, a lump of flesh as big as her fist was hanging down from her insides and blood was all over her thighs. She was frightened but too ashamed to consult anybody about it, so she left it as it was. The flesh still hung between her thighs and oozed.

Because of that she was hotter in summer, and she stank. In the winter it was worse; she ached all over and felt chilly as with an ague. If she walked far, the lump burned as if on fire and it also got so inflamed and swollen that she couldn't walk. Swellings erupted all over it, and as they festered and burst they pained her beyond description. But it was a pain she could not even talk about to anybody.

The mother sighed, thinking of the flesh hanging down damply even now. The dried leaves rustled. Yong-ae bit her mother's nipple.

"Ouch!" she cried but, fearing that Chilsung would curse

the baby if he knew, swallowed her next words and pressed Yong-ae's head to let her know it hurt. But at once, fearing again that she had pressed it too hard, she caressed the baby's head.

"Oh, in the midst of that bustle they had guests at their house, but they had to leave without going in."

Chilsung raised his head. The fragrant smell of mugwort burnt for the mosquito fire brushed past them.

"The people who'd been thinking of taking Kunnyun had come to take a look at her. Maybe you don't know about them. The man runs some sort of business in the town. I heard that he has some money. But he hasn't got a son yet. So he has taken in about a dozen women up till now, but still hasn't got a child. Oh, babies have to get born in houses like that."

His mother looked down at Yong-ae. Chilsung didn't like to see his mother minding the baby even while talking. But he sat still waiting for her next words.

"So somebody talked to him about Kunnyun and the man said never. I heard it's because he felt sorry for his wife, but he came to take a look at her today. Why today, of all days? Maybe that's a sign Kunnyun will have luck. And she deserves it too. She's gentle and she can do any kind of work better than people who can see. Well, she'll get married into an heirless family and she'll bear a big healthy son. She has to live a better life."

"What would anybody want to take a blind girl like that for!" Chilsung yelled abruptly. He was now all aflame with jealousy, and he resolved that if anybody tried to take Kunnyun away he would fight till the death. That made him hot in the head and shaky in all four limbs.

"So, is she going to be married?"

His mother looked at her son and found it difficult to answer. When she reflected that Chilsung was already old enough to yearn for girls, she felt sad and anxious about his future.

"It's not quite settled yet."

Chilsung calmed down a little at that, but he felt sad and got up.

"Go in and sleep. And go to town tomorrow. We can't

manage otherwise."

Chilsung got angry and left his mother, to walk around aimlessly. As he walked he left behind the odour of mugwort, but the smell of grass floated on the crisp, cool air. Along the wind came the sound of grain stalks rubbing against each other; the cool, light breeze wrapped his body softly. His pants became wet with dew and the sound of insects undulated this way and that as if he were kicking at them with his toes.

He stood still. Before him, all was hidden under cover of the impenetrable darkness, and only the outline of the burnt mountain stood like a heap of clouds under the sky. Over the mountain stars shone competitively. When starlight lingered on his eyes, tears gushed down and he felt like crying his heart out. The mountain and the sky all looked too unsympathetic to him.

"Let's go in, dear." His mother's weak voice reached him.

"Why do you follow me around all the time?" All the resentments that had been suppressed in his heart threatened to burst out at once.

"Please, let's go in. Don't walk around like this." His mother held his hand. Chilsung tried to shake her hand off, but he lacked strength. His mother begged, half-crying. Walking back with his mother, Chilsung decided to see Kunnyun the next day and ask her if she was going to get married, and also if she would marry him. When he had resolved thus, his heart beat fast and he seemed to behold before him a ray of hope.

"Please have pity on me and your younger brother and sister." His mother tried to soothe him by any means. Chilsung walked home in silence.

Chilsung got up late the next day and decided again that he would have an answer from Kunnyun that day. "What if she is already pledged in marriage?" The thought made him feel faint. He came out into the backyard and stood beside the hedge. All was silence inside Kunnyun's house; only the buzzing of flies around the dirty water basin could be heard. "I can't!" He stepped away from the hedge at once. The white stones in front of him looked yellow for some reason.

He went into the room panting. He looked at himself and

thought, "I can't go to meet her like this!" There were traces of cowdung on his clothes and they were also torn here and there. But he quickly reminded himself that Kunnyun couldn't see, and tried to figure out what to say to her, looking up at the ceiling. He swallowed many times, but he could not think of a word to say. He felt as if he had never known how to speak in all his life.

Suddenly he felt weak when it crossed his mind that she might already know he was a cripple. He looked outside spiritlessly when he imagined Kunnyun saying, "Who would marry someone like you?"

The leaves of the squash and the gourd vines that wound around the hedge, of the corn stalks and apricot trees and the bush clover that stretched upward towards the sky, all shook freely and blithely in the breeze. He felt somehow less free than those plants and trees, and he sighed till his whole body shook.

At last Chilsung emerged from his yard with firm resolution and, after pacing in front of Kunnyun's house several times, pushed open the bush clover gate and strode in.

The door to the dirt-floored room was shut, and only a bush clover broom lay in the yard. When he opened the door a cat jumped out, mewing. He was so frightened that his heart throbbed wildly. He stepped on to the dirt floor and after much hesitation opened the door of the inner room. Only heavy air moved out towards him; Kunnyun was not there. He suspected at once that she had been married already, and searched the kitchen and the backyard. As he was about to give up and turn back, he heard the bush clover gate open. Frightened, he ran to a post and stepped close to the straw mat stored behind it. The door of the kitchen opened noisily and Kunnyun came in with the wooden laundry basin. He felt faint and weak. He felt as if Kunnyun could see and would come up to him; that she was not blind, but could always open her eyelids and see with her starry eyes. Feeling he was about to suffocate any moment, he suppressed his breath and went behind the straw mat. But his breath came in wilder pants, and he felt as if the straw mat would block his nostrils and make him swoon.

Kunnyun went out into the backyard. Hearing the dragging of her shoes, he stuck out his head, peered about, and tried to move his feet; but his whole body twitched convulsively and he could not move a step. He thought of giving up and going home. He felt as if his body had been made of stone. But then the hedge rustled as Kunnyun spread laundry on it and he remembered "Kunnyun is going to marry a man in town!" His feet began to move in wild staggering.

Kunnyun, in the middle of spreading a piece of laundry on the hedge, sharply turned her face and halted. Chilsung dared not look at Kunnyun but stood there like one out of his wits.

"Who is it?"

Silence.

"Who is it?" Kunnyun's voice was trembling. Chilsung thought he had to say something, anything, but his lips refused to move. At long last he moved forward one step.

"Oh, it's you." Kunnyun moved close to the hedge and bowed her head. Her softly closed eyelids were tremulous. Chilsung became a little bolder as Kunnyun recognised him. He began to worry about the outside now, and he kept looking out.

"Go away! My mother will be back soon." Kunnyun spoke decisively. Her voice was the same as when she was a child.

"I heard you're going to get married. You must be happy."

"What foolish talk. Go away!" Kunnyun, fingering her laundry, sighed softly. White flesh peeped from between the rents in her thin blouse. Chilsung stepped close to her unawares.

"Oh, Mother!" Kunnyun shouted, grasping the hedge. Chilsung became fearful and thought of retreating. He felt faint and the ground swirled before him.

"My mother's coming."

Chilsung opened his eyes at the sound of Kunnyun's trembling voice. The thick braid of glossy black hair on her back smelt intensely of Kunnyun. Chilsung pressed Kunnyun's foot with his foot. Kunnyun blushed and, withdrawing her foot, moved away. The laundry in her hand fell limply to the ground.

Chilsung feared that she might pick up a stone and hit him, but Kunnyun stepped close to the hedge and just fingered the bush clover twigs. Her hair ribbon blew in the breeze. She did not speak any more words, but just fingered the twigs of the hedge.

"I'll give you sweets and. . . and clothes, too. You won't get married, will you, if I do?"

Kunnyun kept silent for a long time and then, raising her head a little, said, "Who cares for sweets?" and laughed softly.

Chilsung also laughed and asked again, "You won't, will you?"

"How do I know? My father knows."

Chilsung was at a loss for words at that. So he just stood there like a fool.

"Get out at once." Kunnyun turned her face towards him. She had thick eyelashes over softly closed eyes, and hanging at the tips of her eyelashes were drops of anxiety.

"Well, are you going to marry, then?"

Kunnyun dropped her head and rolled a stone with the tip of her shoe. Chilsung felt like crying.

"You won't? Promise?"

Kunnyun, instead of answering, sighed and turned away. The baby cried just then. Chilsung, startled, ran out.

When he got home, he saw Chilwoon tying the baby with a strip of cloth. She was rolling on the floor of the kitchen. The baby moved her thin limbs wildly and struggled. Chilwoon hit her as if she had been a dead fish.

"Are you going to sleep or not? If you won't sleep, then I'll kill you." He waved a fist at the baby, his nose dripping from both nostrils. The baby shook like a leaf and was shedding constant tears from her closed eyes.

"Yes! Close your eyes like that and sleep!" Chilwoon lay down beside the baby and squeezed his side with one hand.

"Mother, it hurts here so much, I can't carry the baby any more. I can't," Chilwoon murmured, snuffling. Presently, drowsiness filled his eyes and he fell asleep. Chilsung looked down at his brother absently and stepped onto the dirt floor.

"Mama!" The baby he thought was sleeping opened her

round eyes and looked up at her brother. Chilsung got
frightened. Unconsciously he lifted a foot and raised an
eyebrow, as if to kick her. The baby twisted her thin lips
and closed her eyes.

"Mama! Mama!" the baby's mouth was calling and tears
were running down her cheeks. Chilsung went into the room,
paced it in a circle a few times and came out into the backyard. Hoping Kunnyun was still standing in her yard, he
carefully parted the brushwood of the hedge and peeped in.
Kunnyun was not there; only the laundered clothes lay
spread over the hedge.

He came into the room and, looking up at the beggar's
sack hanging on the wall, thought about how he would buy
material for Kunnyun's clothes. He thought to himself, who
knows but that that might show his feelings to Kunnyun and
her parents, too? He slung his sack over his shoulder sideways
and, putting the straw hat on his head, went outside. In
passing he saw the baby lapping up something. When he
looked around he saw that the baby was drinking her own
urine beside the stove.

"You! Dirty thing!" Chilsung growled and went out to
the street. It was hot, as if he had stepped into hot water.
Taking the new highway, he arranged his clothes and hat and
tried to walk with dignity. He thought he would have to look
more like a gentleman from now on. He coughed a solemn,
false cough and tried to walk slowly. Well, if he walked like
that the children wouldn't pester him or the grown-ups make
fun of him. He recalled Kunnyun's face as he thought so. He
looked back stealthily, but his village was already out of sight
and only the Indian millet field met his view. As he walked
near the field the smell of young Indian millet leaves floated
past and sweat ran down his back. He jerked his body once or
twice and looked in no particular direction.

The burnt mountain that shone green beyond the Indian
millet field looked so close that it seemed he could reach its
top if he moved only a few steps. It was the same mountain
that he could see at leisure from the window of his house,
and it was also the mountain that he could look at while
trying to walk inconspicuously past an Indian millet field
like this.

He exhaled a deep sigh. Whenever he looked at the mountain he felt his torn mind compose itself, and recalled things from childhood he had quite forgotten.

One spring day when mist was rising up from the distant mountain, he woke up in the morning and from his window he saw his friends going up the mountain in single file with panniers on their backs and long staffs stuck sideways across the panniers. He envied them so much that he sighed and looked at them like a mindless boy, thinking, when will I be all right again and able to go up the mountain to gather wood like those boys, with a staff stuck in the pannier slung over my back? And he thought that when he grew up he would climb the mountain and split thick boughs and bring down more wood than the pannier could hold.

He sneered at himself when he recalled that thought. All the joints in his bones ached, and his heart contracted. He shook his head a couple of times and trudged on. Before his eyes was only Kunnyun now.

Two days later.

Chilsung was standing at the entrance of the town of Songwha, six miles from his village. He could not earn much by begging in the town near his village, so he had roamed on to Songwha. After two days and nights of begging he at last managed to buy some cotton material for Kunnyun's dress and was going back home.

He thought of spending that night somewhere, but decided to start homeward at once because he wanted to give the gift to Kunnyun quickly, and also because he was worried about Kunnyun's rumoured marriage.

The starless sky and the furry-soft darkness dazed his eyes, but for some reason his mind was at rest, and a certain degree of hope brightened his eyes. He could distinctly discern the mountains and the waters, as if they lived in his mind's eye, and even the pebbles on the highway seemed to be amicably inviting him to play with them.

He thought he liked the road at night much more than in the daytime, when cars ran past raising dust and pedestrians walked on it without end. So he walked on, without feeling any pain in his legs. When he halted his steps, the smell of the mountain welcomed him and the running brook whispered to him. The smell of rice paddy mud also wafted up to him, and when mountain birds resumed singing the distant glow of lamps seemed to float up and fly away.

Every time he breathed, the material for Kunnyun's clothes touched his chest like the skin of a girl and made his flesh thrill down to the toes. "How shall I give it to her?" He opened his mouth unconsciously and made as if to mouth something. He pictured himself standing face to face with Kunnyun. "When I give her this cloth, Kunnyun will blossom with smiles to the tips of her thick eyelashes!" His heart pumped noisily.

Raindrops began to fall as dawn broke in the eastern sky. He became frightened and started to run, but the rain came thicker and the wind scattered it with a sound like the fluttering of a flock of sparrows. He hesitated over what to do for a while, and turned his steps towards a village that showed its dim outline through the thick screen of rain. If it hadn't been for Kunnyun's cloth he would have marched on, rain or no rain, but he feared that the precious material would get wet from the rain, so he decided to seek shelter in the nearby village.

When he looked back after walking a good while the highway could be seen distinctly, and for some reason he felt unwilling to move, but he forced himself on.

When he reached the village, a smell of wet straw invaded his nostrils and as he walked past a privy the stink stung them. He stepped under the eaves of a house. He felt chilly all over and his eyes were tired, so he moved next to the wall and crouched down beside it. An image of the spindly tree at the entrance of his village flitted before his eyes. Kunnyun appeared before him. He opened his eyes wide.

· Day had dawned amid the rain. The distant mountain could be seen, the cluster of roofs revealed itself, and water dripped from the eaves noisily. He mustered his courage, stood up and looked around.

He saw that the house he was standing by looked like a rich man's. The walls were of cement, and the roof was of dark, baked tiles; the wooden gate was large and studded with nails with heads as big as his fists. He felt his frozen heart thaw.

The marble nameplate looked dignified. Surrounded by the sound of raindrops, Chilsung looked at the nameplate hard, and kept on thinking.

"Maybe this is a lucky day for me. Maybe I can get a good breakfast at this house, and some rice or money too." He squeezed his eyes shut and thought, "Shall I pretend to be blind, too? Maybe that would make me look more pitiful and they might give me more rice and money." He tried to keep his eyes shut but his eyelids itched and his eyelashes trembled, and the marble nameplate criss-crossed his view, so that at last he opened his eyes.

"What shall I do? Maybe my clothes are too clean." he ran at once towards the muddy spot where he had been squatting. He felt even more chilly, and his lips trembled. As he was about to peep in through the crack between the two panels of the gate he heard a sound of steps and quickly moved aside. The gate opened with a loud squeak. As always when people looked at him, Chilsung dropped his head and stood uneasily.

"Who is it?" It was a thick voice. Chilsung looked up. The man had long, narrow horizontal eyes and looked like a servant, clad in black clothes.

"I. . . want some food."

"So early in the morning?" the man muttered to himself and turned back toward the main building.

"This is a charitable house. Other people would have tried to chase me away first." Chilsung congratulated himself and looked in.

The elevated building with the wooden porch attached looked like the master's study; to one side of it was a small gate, and beyond the gate the living-room floor of the inner quarters could be glimpsed. Stretching from the left of the study up to the front gate was a room that looked like a storehouse, and in front of it lay stacks of straw. Yellowish water dripped from the straw stacks. In the spacious front yard water flowed forcefully in a stream, creating a furrow.

"I'll have to go in there to get some food," he thought, and began walking awkwardly towards the inner gate. When he stepped over the threshold of the middle gate, a dog shot out from the inner kitchen like an arrow. When it growled at him, Chilsung stepped back one step and clucked his tongue to appease it. The dog bared its sharp teeth and, jumping up, pulled on the beggar's sack with its teeth. He shouted and ran out past the middle gate. He hoped someone was in the study to call back the dog, but no sound came from there. The dog rolled its eyes and, raising its forefeet, tried to jump up to his face. Chilsung held his begging sack with his teeth and kept bending and stretching his body. But the dog did not abate its attack, and Chilsung had to make a further retreat. The dog followed him to the main gate and, when Chilsung hesitated to make an exit, ran up to him and pulled at his trouser leg with its teeth. Chilsung screamed and ran. The man came out from inside.

"C'mon, c'mon."

The dog ignored the call and kept barking with its sharp muzzle. Chilsung looked back at the dog with murder in his eyes. The man beckoned to the dog with his hand. The dog slowly retreated with backward steps, still keeping its eyes on Chilsung.

Chilsung suddenly felt nauseated and a chill ran down his spine. He felt feverish all at once. He looked for the dog but it was not there. Instead, the big, ugly gate blocked his view impudently. He thought of going back inside, but he shuddered to think of encountering the dog again. He gave up and staggered on.

The rain whipped him mercilessly, while the wind and the sounds of the trees shaking and the water flowing in the ditch almost split his eardrums. On the surface of the muddy water that flowed in swirls floated whitish straw, and leaves whirled swiftly like green birds.

The wet clothes clung to his body mercilessly and the tempestuous wind made him pant for breath. He looked around, hoping to find something, but all the gates of the houses were tightly shut and breakfast smoke rose from the chimneys. He hoped to find an empty house or a water mill, but before his heavy eyes the dog kept jumping up and down, and he felt as if it were following him. The trouser leg torn by the dog flapped as he walked and disclosed his yellow, withered leg. The rain dripping from his tattered straw hat, worn low over his eyes, felt as salty on his lips as tears. He suddenly felt like crying when he thought of the material getting wet.

He stood still. The rain was so thick that he could not discern where was the mountain and where the brook, while through the madly flapping grain stalks a loud, heavy sound like a huge animal roaring shook the earth.

He ardently wished to advance, but his feet refused to move. He looked back, to note that he had almost passed the village. He moved towards the two or three houses at the end of the village, but kept gazing at the field, as if he had some unfinished business.

It was not the first time that he had been chased away by a dog; and countless times he had been abused and persecuted by men, too. But somehow he felt an uncontrollable fury today.

"Why are you standing there like that?"

He looked back in surprise to find that he was standing before a small building which apparently was a water-mill. The man who was looking at him with outstretched neck looked between forty and fifty, and Chilsung could instantly tell that he was a cripple and a beggar like himself. The man grinned. He did not feel like going in, but entered after some hesitation. With a strong smell of rice husks came also the stink of horse droppings.

"Come over here. Oh, your clothes are all wet."

The man raised himself, leaning on his crutches, spread the straw mat he had been sitting on, and sat down on one corner of it. Chilsung quickly noted the man's grey hair and beard. He feared that the man might try to take away his earnings.

"You must be cold because of those wet clothes. Just put on my old jacket and take them off and dry them." The man searched his bundle and said, "Here it is. Come on."

Chilsung looked back. It was a dark, western jacket patched in several places. He envied the man such a good garment and looked directly into his smiling eyes. The man did not look like one who would try to snatch away other beggars' earnings. Chilsung dropped his glance and looked at the water dripping from his sleeves. The man walked towards him, leaning on his crutch.

"Why are you standing there like that? Put this on."

"Oh, no." Chilsung retreated one step and looked at the western jacket. His heart throbbed before a garment the like of which he had never worn in his life.

"Oh, aren't you a stubborn fellow! Then come here and sit on this mat." The man led him by the hand and made him sit on the straw mat. The man pretended not to notice Chilsung's twisted legs.

"Have you eaten anything for breakfast?"

Chilsung was fearful lest the man wanted a share in any food he might have in his sack, and cast a glance at the sack. It was dripping also.

"No."

After a silence, the man murmured, "Then you've got to eat something."

He searched his bundle for a while. "Here. Eat this, though it's only a trifle." He took out and spread before Chilsung something wrapped in a piece of newspaper. Inside the newspaper was some half dried-up boiled millet.

His appetite suddenly whetted by the sight of food, Chilsung stretched out his hand to take it, but his hand did not work, it just shook. The man noticed it and placed the paper on Chilsung's raised knees close to his mouth, saying, "I'm sorry there's so little."

Shyness weighed heavily on his eyelids, so he looked down, sniffed to hide his embarrassment, and sucked in the millet on the paper placed on his raised knees. The smell of printer's ink spread in his mouth and the slightly spoiled millet tasted sweeter the more he chewed it. As he smacked his lips over the last grain, his tongue yearned for more. His ear felt itchy and hot.

The man regretted there was no more. Chilsung took his mouth away from the newspaper and smiled at him. The man smiled, too, and turning his eyes caught sight of Chilsung's leg.

"Oh, you're bleeding! You must have hurt yourself!" He stooped down to look at it. Chilsung felt the pain reviving and looked at it, too. His trouser leg was soaked red with blood and his leg had begun to bleed once more. He felt a pain in his bowels suddenly, and bent his leg and raised his head. He felt as if he were smelling the fishy smell of wet dogs in the wind.

"I got bitten by a dog."

"Oh, have you been to that tile-roofed house? The house that raises those bloody dogs? And there's more than one, too. Let me look at it. You mustn't leave a dog bite unattended."

The man grasped his leg. Chilsung quickly pulled away but felt a smarting sensation across the bridge of his nose. He twitched his nose a couple of times. Tears ran down his cheeks. The man noticed that, and laughed and patted him on the back.

"Are you crying? If one were to cry at every. . . Well, you mustn't cry."

Chilsung raised his head quickly to look at the man. The man's eyes were full of fury. When his eyes travelled to his leg again, Chilsung felt heavy in the chest and dry in his throat. He dropped his head and, scooping up soft dust that lay piled on the floor, rubbed it on the wound.

"Oh, no! Don't ever do that again. Leave it alone if you don't have any ointment. Don't run dirt on wounds again. That makes them fester."

Chilsung bent his leg from embarrassment and looked out. The man was sunk in thought again.

Wind whipped in the rain, and the countless spiders' webs hanging from the ceiling swayed like smoke. The leaves of the willow tree shook like a frightened child and muddy water ran along the earth in a torrent. He looked up, startled to see a big bat covered with white chaff flapping its wings threateningly.

"Are you a born cripple?" the man asked suddenly. Chilsung bowed his head and, after much hesitation, answered, "No."

"Then it was because of an illness. Did you get any treatment?"

Chilsung looked long at his legs again, hesitating. At last he muttered, "No. None at all."

"Ugh, in this world sound legs get broken. It's nothing unusual not to get treatment for illness." The man laughed into the void. The laughter made Chilsung shudder. He glanced at the man. As the man looked out at the road with fiercely dilated eyes, blue veins bulged on his forehead and his lips were clenched shut. "Oh, I curse myself to think what a fool I was! I should have fought to death! What a damned stupid fool I was!"

Chilsung pricked up his ears and tried to understand the meaning of the man's words, but could not make it out. The man looked back at Chilsung. The two or three thin wrinkles under his eyes reminded Chilsung of his own father.

"Listen, my boy. I was the head of a family once. I was a model worker in a factory, too. A first-rate engineer. After my leg was broken I was fired from the factory, and my woman ran away and the children cried from hunger. My parents died of sorrow. Oh, there's no use talking about it."

The man stared at Chilsung. Chilsung's heart pounded for some reason and he could not meet the man's eyes, so he looked at his broken leg, and at the mute earth under that leg.

Outside it was misty with drizzling rain, and the distant mountain looked tearful. The croaking of frogs gave him the illusion of being in his own village, and he fancied himself looking at Kunnyun's back under the locust tree. Chilsung got up.

"I've got to go home."

The man got up, too.

"Oh, do you have a home? Then go."

When Chilsung raised his head the man came near him and arranged his straw hat for him, smiling. Chilsung felt like leaning on him as if he were his mother.

"Goodbye. Hope to see you again, too."

Instead of answering, Chilsung smiled at him and left. When he looked back after a long time the man was standing there before the mill, absently. Chilsung wiped away his tears with his fist and looked back again.

The patches of millet and the Indian millet fields were flooded with rain, and the stalks were half sunk under water. A frog croaked, and he thought to himself this was going to be a lean year again. The frog sounded like the heavy groan of a man.

It began to drizzle again. His clothes that got wet once

more and the rain weighing down his eyelashes made his heart heavy with swirling indefinable doubts.

When he reached his village the rain thickened again and wind also began to blow. Even the locust tree that always looked cool seemed gloomy under the scowling sky, and the low mountains screening the back of the village looked dim through the rain. His steps faltered when the hedges of the houses and the vegetable gardens came into view, and when he thought that Kunnyun might be going to the well below the mountain with the water jar on her head.

When he arrived home his mother came out to meet him with eyes full of tears.

"Oh, you bad boy! Where have you been all this while? Didn't you ever think your mother'd be waiting?" Taking the sack from him, his mother wept. Chilsung didn't answer, but came into the room where the floor was more than half covered with bowls and basins for catching the rain leaking from the ceiling. The water hit the bowls and basins rhythmically. Chilsung stood there and didn't know what to do. He shivered and shook more severely from cold than when he was walking.

Chilwoon and the baby were lying on the floor, and the baby's head was wound round with some whitish cloth. On their small bodies too the water fell.

"Sit down somewhere. Oh, I roamed the town all night searching for you last night. I even looked into taverns and bars. You bad boy, why didn't you tell me you'd be away if you weren't coming back at night?"

His mother wept aloud now. Since she had lost her husband she leaned on her crippled son as the pillar of the family. Chilwoon woke up from the noise.

"Oh, it's Brother! Brother's back!" He jumped up, rubbing his eyes. Swarms of flies flew up, and the baby fretted. Chilwoon rubbed his eyes with both hands and tried to look at his brother but couldn't, so he rubbed harder.

"Oh, son, don't. That will hurt you more. Oh, the children have been sick while you were away and made me so worried. And Chilwoon's got those sore eyes, too. I wonder what's come over this village. Everybody, young and old, has sore eyes."

None of these words came to Chilsung's ears. He dearly wished to lie down somewhere where water did not fall and go to sleep. Chilwoon broke out crying from irritation and then, going out of the back door, urinated and washed his eyes with the urine.

"Wet your eyes well. Not just the lids but the eyeballs, too. Look how he wants to take a look at you. He asked for his brother all day yesterday." His mother wept again. Chilsung moved aside to avoid the water dripping on his back. This time water dropped on his nose and ran down to his lips. He struck his nose angrily and swore.

"Oh, why should it rain now? And the wind! What fierce wind! It will break all the millet stalks. Oh, God, what can be done?" She raised her clasped hands as if in prayer. Her hair was all matted with the rain, and her eyes were bloodshot, the eyelids blue-black and sunken. Her soiled clothes were stained with rain.

Chilsung sat down on the sill and closed his eyes. His eyes felt unbearably sore and his eyelashes stung his eyeballs. As he rolled his eyes a couple of times, he suddenly recalled the water-mill.

"Yesterday the dike of Kaedong's rice paddy burst and everything was swept away. Oh, what a dreadful curse is that wind! What's going to happen to our field?"

His mother ran outside. Chilwoon, crying, tried to follow her but tripped on the doorsill, fell down on the ground and screamed. Chilsung raised his eyebrows. "I'll kill that thing!"

His mother quickly picked up Chilwoon to take him out of her elder son's sight and walked around in and out, casting anxious eyes towards their field.

Chilsung did not want to see his worried mother, so he turned aside and closed his eyes. Startled, he opened his eyes. The baby, who had been lying in a corner of the room drawing quick breaths, tried to get up and fell down repeatedly, weeping. She kept rubbing her head on the straw mat and fretfully scratched the cloth wound round her head, making a sound that made him feel creepy.

Chilsung tried not to open his eyes but he could not help opening them and catching sight of the baby's yellow fingers tearing at her head. He wished the baby dead, and closed his eyes.

Wind blew more fiercely. One could hear the branches of the apricot tree breaking, and also a sound like a pillar toppling that shook the back door. Chilwoon came into the room and lay down.

"Brother, get me some eye medicine tomorrow. Kaedong's father bought him eye medicine from the town and his eyes are all right now."

Chilsung listened to his brother in silence and thought of the material inside his shirt. The thought that he should have bought eye medicine instead crossed his mind but quickly disappeared, and he tried to think of a way to give the cloth to Kunnyun.

A match struck in the kitchen and soon his mother came in.

"Water got into the stove, up to the top. What can I do? The little ones haven't had anything yet, either. How hungry you all must be!" She went out and came running back presently.

"The dyke broke in Kunnyun's rice paddy, too. The strongest dyke in the neighbourhood. Oh, what's going to happen to ours?"

Chilsung dilated his eyes.

"Oh, why doesn't this little girl go to sleep? Don't tear at your head like that! That little girl hasn't slept a wink for days. Kaedong's mother told me rat skin's good for sores so I killed one and plastered its skin on her head, but she keeps tearing at it like that. I guess it itches because it's healing. Don't you think so?" His mother seemed to want some reassuring concurrence. But Chilsung didn't want to hear anything except about Kunnyun. He asked patiently, "Then everything's swept away in their rice fields?"

"Yes! Oh my milk's dried up." Looking at the fretting baby, his mother massaged her breasts. They were limp.

The baby panted more urgently and her hands tried to reach her head but dropped down tiredly. His mother listened again to the sound of the wind.

"Oh, our millet will all be swept away now! Our field can't escape a flood if Kunnyun's field got swept away. Oh, Kunnyun's lucky she doesn't have to live through this.

She got married yesterday."

"What?" Chilsung screamed. The precious material kept inside his shirt struck his skin like a rock. His mother looked at her son, startled.

"Mum, look at that!" Chilwoon jumped up and groaned. They all looked.

The cloth wrapped round the baby's head was about half torn off, and maggots as big as rice grains were crawling out of it.

"Oh, God! What happened? What *happened?*!" His mother went over to the baby and snatched away the cloth. The rat skin came away and from it dropped masses of maggots bathed in blood.

"Baby! My baby! Wake up! Oh, wake up!" Hearing his mother's scream, Chilsung ran outside frenziedly.

The rain poured down fiercely and the wind stormed madly, and the sky, torn mercilessly by the lightning, roared with thunder.

Chilsung glared up at the sky.

Hwang Soon-won

Born in 1915, Hwang Soon-won is one of the most respected masters of fiction in the literary world of Korea today. And he fully merits this respect, too. Through the decades when being a writer meant writing trivial popular novels or starving, Hwang Soon-won steadily refused to compromise, and adhered stubbornly to his artistic vision.

Hwang Soon-won's stories deal with the timeless elements of life in Korea. He pursues, through a series of illuminating and suggestive images, the meaning of being a Korean and living in Korea. The tired old troupe leader in 'Pierrot' (1951) is one such image, although here the particular circumstance of the Korean War makes him somewhat more timely than his other images. As in 'Pierrot', in most of his stories the harsh circumstances of life, rather than being indicted or attacked, are mournfully gazed upon with lyrical tenderness and quiet resignation. The focus of attention, in other words, is not the circumstances themselves but the characters' emotional reactions to them. This is why Hwang Soon-won is a genuinely Korean author, and why he represents so strongly the main tradition of Korean literature.

In his longer works he exhibits a more ambitious historical perspective, examining the meaning of Korea's past history and the problem of what attitude to take towards the heritage of the nation's past, which is a mixed blessing.

The author is still active as a writer, and also teaches creative writing at a university.

Pierrot

Hwang Soon-won

As had happened in Taegu, in Pusan also we came to
be beholden for our shelter to a lawyer's family.
I sent my family on ahead of me for refuge, and
when I followed them to Pusan later, I found that my family
had not come down to Pusan but had stopped in Taegu. The
reason was that it cost less to live in Taegu than in Pusan.
So I went up to Taegu on Christmas day. My wife and
children were living in a rented room in the great mansion of
a lawyer next to the burned-out courthouse, which stood like
a skeleton. The nest of my beloved wife and darling children
was a shed in a corner of the spacious garden of this majestic
mansion.

It was much colder in Taegu than in Pusan. As the room
was built for storage, with the only door facing north, not
a ray of sunshine strayed into it all day. It was chilly and
sinister, so much so that the children all went out as soon as
day broke, although it was freezing cold outside. But we
deemed ourselves lucky. It was fortunate that we had among
our acquaintance a friend of this family, so that we could
obtain some kind of shelter, which was needless to say a
great good fortune for refugees like us.

There were some rules we had to observe at this house. By
decree of the mother-in-law of the lawyer, we were forbidden
to draw water from the well in the inner yard after dusk, or
in the morning before they did, or to do laundry of whatever
kind in the inner yard, where there was a well and also city
water. The prohibition against drawing water in the morning

was no inconvenience for us. As we ate only twice a day, we needed to draw water only late in the morning for late breakfast, after the lawyer's family had all finished breakfast. It was the same with laundry. We had only to carry water to the outer yard and wash our things there. But on days when we had used up our water, if somebody got thirsty at night, especially if any of the children got thirsty, it was painful not to have any water. Well, people don't die or get ill because of one night's thirst.

There was another prohibition decreed by this august old lady, and that concerned the use of the lavatory. We were forbidden to use the one in the inner yard, so my wife had to build makeshift facilities in a corner of the garden behind the bushes. It was hidden from view by straw matting hung like a curtain. It was very embarrassing for grown-ups to use this crude latrine in the daytime, but about such small inconveniences we were not in a position to complain.

It did not take too long for us to perceive that the household was managed entirely by the mother-in-law of the lawyer. My wife was informed by the maid of the house that, as the lawyer's wife was the only child of this old lady, she had come to live with her daughter and son-in-law when the daughter married, and from the first governed the whole household. The children had a separate room to themselves, and the old lady occupied a big heated-floor room alone, from whence she reigned. Nobody in that family ate in the morning until after the old lady had finished her breakfast.

The old lady's hobby was playing cards with friends, and for that purpose they met in one of their homes in turn, and they also went to Buddhist temples in a group to offer prayers every now and then. We could often see the old lady going out in a silk dress, and she looked so erect and trim that one could hardly think of her as nearing sixty. Her friends who frequently visited the house were all well-dressed and well-groomed women who did not look as if they had ever known hardship in their lives. Maybe life is something that has to be lived with at least that much decency.

About ten days after I joined my family, we woke up one morning to find that one of the rubber shoes of my eight-year-old daughter Son-a had disappeared. It was in vain that we searched everywhere nearby. The whole family covered every square inch of the spacious garden. It could not have been stolen, because if anybody meant to steal shoes why should he have taken only Son-a's, and only one shoe at that? So we had to conclude that the shepherd dog of the house had carried it away and left it somewhere far off.

Although we were extremely short of money, we couldn't let our daughter go around barefoot in winter, so my wife went out to buy a pair of shoes. When she came back with a new pair, she recounted what she had heard at the shoe shop: sometimes one shoe is stolen by someone who has a sick member in the family, in the belief that the sickness would be transferred to the owner of the shoe, if he or she is of the same age as the sick person and the shoe is disposed of in a certain manner. Then my wife said that a child of the lawyer who was about Son-a's age had been ill in bed for several days. When she said that she looked worried, and angry, and also sad.

I shook my head and said that could not be the case. But I, too, could not help having an anxious and angry feeling in my heart. Granted that it was a foolish superstition, and granted that we were people of no consequence at all; still, if one loves one's own child, one should know that other people's children are dear to their parents, even as his own are to him. Moreover, Son-a was the most fragile of our four children. If she got ill in refugee life like this, there was no way to bring her back to health at all.

A few days of anxiety and uneasiness passed. We heard that the sick child of the lawyer was well again. And our Son-a did not take ill. The disappearance of the shoe must have been the shepherd dog's doing. The old lady, who spent many days praying to Buddha in the temple, could not have done anything so inhuman as that.

It was a few days later.

When I got home my wife was sitting alone in the cold, dark room and told me in a voice laden with anxiety that the old lady of the house told her that we must vacate the room. The reason was that they needed the room (which was in fact a shed) to store coal. But my wife had heard a different story from the housemaid.

At midday, a large group of friends of the old lady came to play cards, as often happened. One of the old women caught sight of the straw mat screen behind the bush in the corner of the garden. Why don't people's eyes grow dim as they should with old age? She went up to it to see what it was. When she found out what was behind, she spat with vehemence and complained ferociously about the monstrosity of the thing. She ran up to the old lady of the house at once and blamed her very loudly for letting people defecate in the garden. So the old lady of the house herself began cursing the uncivilised paupers who only wore the masks of men but were not fit to be treated as human beings. She went on to declare that since her house was not a refugee asylum she would order us out at once. Then she went to my wife and ordered her to vacate the room. But she could not very well tell my wife that we had to leave the house because we had made a latrine in the garden, so she gave a different reason— that they needed our room to store coal. Well, that proved the verity of the old lady's saying that human beings should so behave as to be worthy of being regarded as human beings, because it was the old lady herself who had forbidden us to use the facilities of the house, and thereby forced us to relieve ourselves in the garden behind the straw mat screen. After all, she had not forgotten that, since as human beings we had to defecate, we were forced to resort to such an uncivilised method, however reluctant we might have been to do so. And moreover, she made it clear to us herself that our room was no room for human beings to dwell in, but a shed for storing things like coal.

So this was how the shabby Hwang Soon-won family, evicted from the shed in the lawyer's mansion, drifted into Pusan at last around the end of March, after a few more attempts at securing shelter in Taegu.

We had planned to stay with my sister-in-law's family in her rented room for a while until we could rent a room for ourselves. I had seen that the room the family was living in had space to accommodate a few more people.

This house happened to be a lawyer's house, too. It was located at the rear of the Kyungnam Middle School. It was a pretty big house of mixed Japanese and western style, and my sister-in-law and her children were using a room of about twelve square yards. As there was an old cabinet and a small table to one side of the room, usable space consisted of only about nine square yards, but that was enough for my sister-in-law and her three children and the six members of our family.

But when we came to Pusan we found that another family was already living with my sister-in-law. It consisted of a mother and two children. The husband of this lady was an army judge advocate stationed at the front. Originally the lawyer had promised to give this family a separate room, but later on he said he needed to keep the other room for guests, so this lady and her children came to live in the room my sister-in-law was occupying. That had caused no inconvenience, as both families consisted of women and children (my brother-in-law had gone to the United States for technical training and was now staying in Tokyo because the war made it impossible for him to return home). Moreover, the acquaintance of my sister-in-law who had helped her rent this room from the lawyer and this lady's husband were both in the legal profession, so my sister-in-law and the lady became good friends very soon.

But the convenience did not last long. The landlord suddenly demanded that they vacate the room. The reason was that they needed the room for the maid. The strange thing was that the demand had been made on the very day the transfer of my sister-in-law's acquaintance, in respect for whose position the lawyer had rented the room to my sister-in-law, was unofficially decided. My sister-in-law learned of the transfer a few days later when it was officially made known, but the lawyer could have obtained the information easily enough through private channels in legal circles. It is rather extraordinary that the decision on the transfer and the demand to vacate the room had been made on the same day, but I suppose it is only proper to regard it as a coincidence. A man of such prominent social position would not have behaved so hastily and impolitely from a calculation of immediate advantage. So that was the state the room was in before we got to Pusan.

What could we do? Needless to say, we were not so rich as to be able to stay at an inn. After lengthy deliberation we decided to take lodgings in separate groups. It was decided that I should sleep with my aged parents in their eighteen-square-yard room in Nampodong, inhabited by nineteen people of three families, and our two eldest children were sent away to where their maternal grandfather's family of six lived in a four-square-yard room, while the two younger children and my wife could do nothing but stay with my sister-in-law.

I had to hear every day from my wife or from my older children who had been to see my wife how fierce was the demand of the landlord for evacuation of the room. While in Taegu, we had heard that many of the refugees had left Pusan, so we thought we'd be able to rent a room if we tried hard enough. It was true that Pusan was not so crowded as when I first came last winter, but there were still no rooms. My wife and I searched everywhere and inquired of everybody we knew, but it was all in vain.

The demand for eviction was so persistent that the lady who had been living in that room with my sister-in-law moved away to her husband's uncle's. And early in the morning after that a tempest broke out in the lawyer's residence.

While everybody was still in bed, the door of the room was thrust open with great force, and there stood the lawyer himself with fierce glaring eyes. He thundered in an angry voice, "Do you behave like this and yet call yourselves human beings? Get out of my house at once. Go to an inn if you don't have anywhere to go. Human beings must know how to behave. If you don't leave this house this very day I will settle the matter legally."

My wife and my sister-in-law could not keep silent at that. They declared that they could not go out in the streets to live, or go to an inn. The two grown-up daughters of the house came to support their father, and his wife and eldest son were also mobilised. The eldest son of the house, who was said to be attending a law college in Seoul, threatened to use his fists, but the old lawyer dissuaded him and led him away, perhaps having determined that such violence would work to their disadvantage if the matter were brought to court.

I listened to this report from my wife in a corner of the room in Nampodong inhabited by nineteen people. That we were not worthy of being looked upon as human beings was no surprise, our worthlessness in that regard having been settled quite beyond doubt by the old lady in Taegu; and that the landlord would deal with the matter legally was perhaps natural, since he was a lawyer. But we could not very well go and stay at an inn. If we could afford that, we would have done it long before. As to the reflection that we did not behave properly, I know there may be truth in it, because refugees cannot very well afford to behave well all the time. But we had not really been all that barbarous. What my sister-in-law spent for mending the flooring of the room was as good as paying nearly twenty thousand won rent a month, and only the day before we had told the lawyer's wife that we could give her some key money when we managed to sell all our remaining clothes. The lady of the house then said that it was not because they wanted money that they had demanded the room back, but because they needed the room to give to the maid. My wife then asked the lady to let her provide space in the room for the maid of the house, but they still refused. There was no helping it. My wife had to ask her to give her some time until she could rent a room. As the maid is mentioned, I might as well set down here that the woman who was working as a maid in that house had told my wife and my sister-in-law that she was a not-too-distant relative of the family who had come for a visit and was staying in the house to help with the household work; that in this house no maid ever stayed beyond a couple of months, that the current servant was an old woman who was now away on a visit to the country to see her son, and that this room had never been used by people but as a sort of storage room. Anyway, my sister-in-law knew that an old woman worked as maid in this house. Well, the judgment that we did not know how to behave all derives from our lack of ability to rent a room.

My wife then said solemnly, with a sad and tearful face, as if she had made a grave decision, that all our family should live together in the room from that night. Her reason was that, since our situation was at its worst, it might be better for the family to live together until we could rent a room. I hesitated to agree with her.

I thought of the law student. A young man who had threatened women with his fists would not let me alone. But how could a man with a weak constitution, nearing forty, confront a young man in his twenties? But at the same time how could I, as head of the family, leave wife and children in that kind of plight, however much of a weakling I am acknowledged to be? Of course it was not that my wife wanted me to protect her from the brute force of that young man. On the contrary, if she had thought of that she would never have suggested that we live together in that room. My wife only thought of my poor old parents, who slept almost every night sitting up because of me, so she suggested that the family keep together until a room could be found, as the state of things had reached a point that could not get worse.

I went to school. The school at which I had been teaching in Seoul had moved down to Pusan, and had begun to hold classes every other day in a park. This was one of the school days. I asked several colleagues who had come down to Pusan before me to look for a room for me. Although I knew it was not a very proper thing to do, I even asked some of my senior students to look out for a vacant room for me.

In the afternoon I sat in a tea-room without drinking any tea and asked some friends to help me out of this plight.

Towards evening I went out to drink cheap rice wine in one of the liquor stalls roofed by awnings that stood in a row along the quay. I emptied one bowl. I looked up to notice that a couple of sailing vessels were anchored beyond the bulwark. Oh, the sea was always good to look at. Right in front of my eyes gulls kept darting up and down. Oh, that was nice to look at, too.

But in fact I was not in a mood to appreciate the poetic beauty of the sea and the gulls. I felt as if a fishbone were stuck in my throat. That fishbone was the thought that from now on I had to go to the lawyer's house, and consequently to confront the law student. I had never seen this young man, but I had once seen the lawyer himself when he was pruning trees in the garden. He looked past forty, but his well-combed hair was as glossy and black as a young man's, and he was of a sturdy constitution. I thought that if the son took after his father he must be well-built and strong. I was rather unwilling to meet him.

I gulped down another bowl of wine. I had had many a fist fight myself when in my twenties. My face had a lot of souvenirs of those battles. My nose had bled many a time and I also made other noses bleed not a few times. Once I had broken two front teeth of a man, and received in return a scar like a vaccination mark on the crown of my head. To be frank, at the height of my youth I had never lost in an even battle. But after thirty I had always avoided a confrontation of fists. Today, nearing forty, I begin to have fears at the mere thought of a fight. I emptied another wine bowl. But if challenged, I could not just sit crouched in a corner. There is such a thing as self-defence. Yes. I will rise to the challenge. After this long interval, I will exhibit my finesse as of old times. A fight cannot be won with physical strength alone. With the help of alcohol, I made plans about how to tackle the young man according to his various possible methods of attack. I pictured the scene in which I knocked my adversary down, and got excited. It was not before my pocket was emptied and dusk covered the entire quay that I left the liquor stall.

Nothing happened that night. Nothing happened the next day, or the day after that. In the meanwhile the woman who had been working as maid went back to her home town and the old servant woman of the house returned from the country. She was a really old woman, her hair all grey and her back bent. This old woman cooked, washed and cleaned all day.

Once, I saw my wife and my sister-in-law whispering in a corner. When I asked what it was about, they told me that the old servant woman wanted to sell secretly two bottles of soy sauce belonging to the lawyer's household because she was in need of money to settle an old debt for medicine to a herb doctor, and the lawyer's family would not pay her her salary. I tried to figure out to myself whether this kind of stealing would constitute a crime in the eyes of the law.

On the evening of the fourth day after I moved to this house I talked it over with my wife and, in the hope that the landlord might accept a compromise, decided that my wife would go to the lady of the house to pay her one month's rent and plead for mercy. The problem was the amount of rent to take. We reckoned that twenty or thirty thousand won would never do, so we thought of offering forty thousand won, but at last decided on fifty thousand from desperation. We didn't know how we could pay fifty thousand won a month for the room and manage to live, but we had heard that the current price of rooms was ten thousand won per two square yards, and we knew that some people demanded to have a room vacated with the ulterior purpose of raising the rent. Moreover, we thought anything would be better than to have the matter brought to court as the lawyer had threatened, and to be thrown out into the streets. So we decided to try to reach an agreement about the room by any means, and then go out and work hard with our minds at ease to earn a living. And in fact we were already engaged in trade. My wife was going to the Kukje Market with what remained of our clothes, and the two older children were trading with the American Army troops. The fifty thousand won in question was taken out of my wife's business capital.

My wife went into the living room and returned after a short while. The money was not in her hands, so we thought a compromise had been reached. But my wife said no. They still insisted on our vacating the room. The master of the house and the eldest son slept in a sixteen-square-yard room; and in the main room the master's wife and the younger son slept; so I suppose they could not very well say they wanted the room back because the house was too crowded. The lady of the house said that she had to have the room back because her grown-up daughters could hardly sleep because of the snoring of the old servant woman. Then my wife suggested that we make space in our room for the old servant woman to sleep. The lady still insisted on having the room back. She further said that a friend of her daughter offered to make a present of a gold wrist-watch if her family could rent the room, but they had said no.

I felt a chill in my liver. A gold wrist-watch! That was

certainly not a trifle. So I asked my wife what she had done with the money, and she said she just put it before the lady of the house, suggesting that she buy books for her daughters with it. Our ardent hope was that the money would not be returned. But the next day the money was returned.

The following night, it happened. I always stayed away from the room in the daytime, spending the time mostly in the room where my parents lived, except for teaching at school every other day. Most of the refugees in Pusan went out to the market to sell cigarettes, leaving only children in their places of shelter. My parents also sold cigarettes in the market. So in my parents' room I waited for my older children to return, to go with them to the Kukje Market to pick up my wife so we could come back home in a group. Thus we did that night.

When we got back in the evening, we found two strapping girls standing majestically in our room. They were the daughters of this house. We could not discern which was the elder of the two, but anyway we heard that the elder daughter was in the sixth form and the younger daughter a fifth former. The two said they would sleep in our room that night. I wondered to myself which of the two girls was the one who had a friend who would make a present of a gold wrist-watch for renting the room. I felt I had to escape from the scene.

But before I had time to do so, the two big girls declared to no one in particular that the room would have to be vacated within a couple of days and, after giving me a look, went out. It does not matter whether the look was of contempt, derision, or whatever. Anyway, I had to admit to myself that the tactics of these girls were much more effective on me than a few boxes on my ears from their elder brother would have been.

Well, anyway, every morning when I went out of the house I always wished I wouldn't have to return.

The next day was a school day. When I opened the belled door of the entrance porch and stepped out, the lawyer was there pruning boxwood trees in a stooping posture beside some flaming red camellia blossoms. Even at a fleeting glance one could perceive that he cherished and carefully tended the garden plants. It was an elegant hobby. Maybe life is something that has to be lived with at least that much elegance and leisure. I escaped from the porch as if pursued.

At school I again asked my colleagues to look for a room for me. I also asked some sixth formers to help me with this problem. After school I again sat in a tea-room without drinking any tea and begged my friends for help.

Then in Nampodong I waited for my elder children to return. The children came back after dark. I thought my wife was sure to have gone home by herself because we were so late. We decided to go straight home. The road from Nampo-dong to the Kyungnam Middle School was dark.

We pushed at the iron gate. It was locked from inside. We peeped in and saw that our room was not lighted. I thought my wife must still be in the market waiting for us, and my sister-in-law had turned off the light to put her children to sleep. We decided to wait for my wife so we could all go in together, and I led the children to the footbridge over a ditch where my wife must pass on her way home, and crouched down.

My second son crouched down beside me. My eldest son also sat beside me. But my wife did not come for a long time. Nam-a, my second son, began to nod from sleepiness although it was early in the evening. What he did must be tiring for a boy his age. I turned my eyes to the ditch. I took out a cigarette. The match did not light. Rain began to drip.

Dong-a, my eldest son, stood up and walked to the house. In a little while he came running back and said that my wife was already back home and that the gate was open. He said he heard his mother's voice from our room when he drew near the gate.

When we arrived we learned that the light in our room was out for reasons we had not guessed. The electricity in this house was on a special line so that the house had power all day and all night, and all the other rooms in the house were brightly lit even now. For a while we sat silently in the darkness.

My sister-in-law said, as if to herself, that she would leave the room tomorrow even if she had to sleep under the bridge.

She said that though the landlord's family had always been
harsh to the children, of late it had become wellnigh unbearable. If my sister-in-law's seven-year-old and my six-year-
old began to sing or went out in the hall to go to the toilet,
someone in the landlord's family never failed to shout at
them not to be noisy. If the children in our room joined in
when the seven-year-old son of the lawyer marched in the
hall singing a military march, they were reprimanded for
making noise. What was still more painful to see was the keen
anguish of my girl, Son-a, at the least noise her younger
brother and her cousin made, for fear they would be scolded
by the landlord's family.

My sister-in-law wept in the darkness, suppressing her
voice. I felt fire burning in my chest, too. This was a different
kind of anger from what I felt when one of Son-a's rubber
shoes was stolen. But whatever tactics they adopted, we
could only endure and seek ways of minimising the pain
produced by those tactics.

So the countermeasure we thought up was to leave the
room vacant during the daytime from the next day. My two
younger children were to stay at Nampodong, and my sister-
in-law was to spend the day with her children where her
parents were living and return alone in the evening to prepare
dinner. Only after we had thus set up our plans did we
swallow cold food in the darkness.

I spent the whole day next day in my parents' room in
Nampodong with Son-a and Kyung-a. I was relieved that the
day had brightened up, although it had rained the night
before.

My wife came to us before dark, but the elder children had
not come back although it was already dark. Kyung-a said he
was sleepy and fell asleep in his mother's arms.

The two elder children came back only after it was completely dark. They said it was hard to get a ride on the tram
lately. The two children excitedly took out of the secret
pockets in their clothes cigarette and chewing-gum packets
with deft hands before their parents and grandparents. Their
deft hands gave me sorrow. I averted my eyes.

We came out into the street. I was carrying the sleeping
Kyung-a on my back, and my wife carried her bundle on her

head. We walked up the wide street in front of the Dong-a
Theatre. My elder son Dong-a walked close to me and showed
off his conversational skill in English, telling me that he could
easily make purchases if he walked up to GIs and said "Please
sall to me." I corrected him, saying that it was not "sall to
me" but "sell to me". Dong-a is a third former. I would have
to send him to school so that he could graduate from primary
school and enter middle school. But the boy had already
begun to learn English conversation. And the father corrects
him, too.

Nam-a also walked up to my side and began telling me
about the clever boy he had met that day. When the lad was
in danger of being caught, Nam-a said, he sprawled on his
back in a nearby rice paddy. It was a flooded rice paddy. The
lad, sunk in water up to his ears, kicked all four limbs, rolled
his eyeballs and moved his mouth wildly. The boy had a few
GI bucks hidden in his shirt. The men who were going
to nab him looked at the sight for some time and then poked
his belly a few times with a rather worried expression. The
boy took no notice of it, but kept on rolling his eyes and
moving his mouth wildly. Maybe they thought he was an
epileptic. The men went away. Hearing that, it struck me
that my Nam-a, who was chatting away like this beside me,
would also have to learn how to fake an epileptic fit to guard
a few military bucks.

We turned to the right at the Busongkyo Bridge. The road
along the ditch was dark. Stars twinkled in the sky but the
road was dark.

Nam-a suddenly suggested that we all sing together. I was
going to say no, but Son-a, who was walking beside her
mother, began singing as if she had been waiting for the
opportunity. "Stepping over the dead bodies of our com-
rades. . ." It was the military march the lawyer's son could
sing, but our children could not sing along with him in that
house. I recalled how Son-a always tried to prevent her
younger brother from singing and making noise in the lawyer's
house. I did not have the heart to tell her not to sing. Nam-a
and Dong-a added their voices to Son-a's.

As soon as the march was over, Nam-a began to sing the
cycling song and to run in the dark, pretending to be riding a

bicycle. How come he's so sprightly tonight, when he was so sleepy yesterday? Could it be that he had luck with his trade today? "Look out, you old fellow over there, or you'll get run over!" Nam-a's bicycle now turned towards us and swept past between his father and mother. This old fellow of a father had to dodge to avoid being run over.

That made Kyung-a on my back wake up. He joined his sister in singing "Come, sweet, pretty butterfly". Son-a waved her arms, dancing to her song, like a butterfly fluttering in the dark.

When his sister's song was over, Kyung-a, now wide awake, began to sing "Beautiful wild rabbit". He began the wild rabbit jump, too. Not content with jumping on my back, he climbed on to my shoulders and jumped, sitting on my neck. "Whither are you jumping like that? I'm going over that hill by myself and'll come back with lots and lots of chestnuts." Kyung-a continued jumping until he finished the song.

Trying hard not to totter under Kyung-a's gyrations, I thought, if he is a rabbit, then his mother and father are rabbits, too. But his father rabbit, far from jumping over the hill and coming back with lots and lots of chestnuts, is staggering under his slight weight, as if walking straight were a great and formidable feat.

Then I suddenly thought of the word "pierrot". Oh yes, I am performing a circus act now with Kyung-a on my shoulders. Well then, Kyung-a is also performing a circus act on my shoulders. Son-a was also acting the butterfly in this circus. Nam-a was the trick cyclist. And it would be a sad circus if Nam-a had to put on an epileptic fit in order to guard a few military bucks, like the little lad he saw today. Dong-a's "please sall to me" is also a circus act, and their deft putting away and taking out of cigarette and chewing-gun packets are all polished circus routines. So they are the little pierrots of the Hwang Soon-won Circus Troupe, and I am their master of ceremonies. Our stage today is this Bumindong road beside the ditch.

Pierrot Dong-a began to sing "Sorrento". Yes, show off all your accomplishments. I do not know whether, when you look back on today's circus performance a long time later, you will grieve or laugh over it. And you, also, do not have to know whether your father and mother witnessed your circus acts today with tears or with laughter. I only wish, my dear little pierrots, that when each of you has his own circus troupe, you will not have to repeat this kind of circus on this kind of stage with your young pierrots. Oh, excuse me, ladies and gentlemen, it was just the maundering of an old clown. Well then, shall we listen to Pierrot Dong-a's solo?

My wife, who had been walking a few feet behind me, came up to me and placed an arm around my waist. This wife of the leader must have thought her troupe leader husband's circus act was in danger. I grasped my wife's hand by way of telling her not to worry. At that moment, Pierrot Dong-a's solo abruptly stopped in the middle of the last bar. We were already at the entrance of the alley leading to the lawyer's house.

Well, ladies and gentlemen, that will have to be the end of today's programme. I am ashamed to have shown you such a poor circus, owing to lack of rehearsal. But tomorrow we may be able to present you something better. Thank you so much for your kind attention. I thank you all on behalf of the entire troupe. Well then, a warm good night to you all.

Park Yong-sook

Park Yong-sook, born in 1934, is interested in both literature and the fine arts, and is currently active as a writer, art and music critic, and lecturer in fine arts. He began writing in 1959, and since then has written fiction, literary criticism and art criticism in a variety of media.

As an author his main concern was at first the inner reality of man's unconscious, and he used the stream-of-unconsciousness technique extensively. But from the late 1960s he became more interested in the meaning of history, and has written works retracing the historical process in an attempt to probe into the meaning of historical experience and its relation to the reality of today. 'Eroica Symphony' (1965), an essayistic short story, is delightful for the tentative tone of its philosophical revery and the innocence of its romance. From the viewpoint of strict realism, the story has considerable gaps and improbabilities, but it is true to its internal logic, and we watch the two sweethearts with sympathetic concern, even though the man's actions, if he existed in real life, might well have been regarded as outlandish. As a writer, Park Yong-sook is still developing his style and expanding his interests, so it is rather early to assess his achievements.

Eroica Symphony

Park Yong-sook

Men carry such heavy burdens! Some of the load is
acquired by individuals for their own purposes, but
most of the burdens we shoulder were there even
before we were born into the world, so that in fact a man
struggles through life with the load he has inherited. Some,
of course, add burdens of their own invention. At first
glance, this kind of man may look very stupid because he
makes his already heavy load heavier. But these men, although they seem stupid, may not necessarily be so. It may
really be that they are wiser.

Be that as it may, we are born into the world to find, on
first opening our eyes, many burdens, whose purpose we do
not know, scattered about in mountainous heaps all over the
place. As we grow up, we learn the use of these loads one by
one. Some are heirlooms of our own ancestors, some are
remnants left by Westerners, but at all events these loads
tend to become bulkier as time flows onward and centuries
go by. So much so that the earlier you lived, the lighter the
load you were likely to be burdened with. Of course, you
might say that our wisdom grows and thereby we learn how
to discriminate among the burdens, but anyway it is more
troublesome than having fewer to deal with. In any case, in
all periods people worry a lot over how to dispose of their
ever-increasing burdens. For, however hard you may try, you
are never able to shoulder all of the load you have inherited.
But, of course, the burdens do not go away because you try
to avoid them. No. In fact, no man can keep completely

149

away from these burdensome inheritances. Therein lies
man's fate. The loads are too heavy to shoulder in their
entirety, but one can't simply refuse to shoulder them. What
on earth, really, are these loads for? But with the lapse of
ages, people have even stopped pondering this point. They
just take it for granted that the loads are there because that's
the way things are, and they live among the piled-up loads
they do not understand the meaning of.

While engaged in living, it sometimes happens that they
discover from among these burdens something they need.
But most people go no further than imitating other men, as
do apes captured in the jungles. Let a man wash his face in a
basin, and an ape would do the same. Why does the man
wash his face in a basin and put on an apron? The ape does
not know. Likewise, men ordinarily regard their enormous
inherited burdens as an ape would. Now let me talk about
one of our many burdens, that which is called music.

As I understand it, there has never before been a time
when music has pervaded our everyday life as much as it
does these days. Music flows into our ears any time, anywhere, whether we are walking on the street, entering town,
stepping into rooms or whatever. It is like living all the time
in music except when we lose consciousness. It usen't to be
that way until some five or six years ago. If we wanted to
listen to music, we had to go to a stereo parlour or buy
records. In those cases it was mostly Western classical music
we heard. But the circumstances changed 180 degrees with
the importation of popular music from the United States,
where it was booming. Classical music lost its sway and
instead pop music reigns. Moreover, people don't have to go
to a stereo parlour to listen to music anymore. All they need
is a good pair of ears to be visited by music all the time. As
apes put on skirts in imitation of men, so do men shake
their bodies to pop music rhythm, as other men do.

There was a controversy once over whether pop music is
music or not. The more conservative people, who preferred
classical music, were of the opinion that pop music is not
music, but the young people, who liked it, argued that it is
modern music. Anyway, as in all such cases, conflict does not
lead to any clear-cut conclusion, unlike the case of boxing

matches. So the argument becomes inconclusive, and people go on listening to pop tunes, not knowing whether they are music or mere vulgar worldly noise. In short, pop music has been imposed on men, an added burden.

It is true that in many cities there are still stereo parlours in existence patronised by music lovers, but the atmosphere of such places is not so soothing as in former times. There aren't any commentators to explain the pieces, nor do they always play request records promptly enough for busy people to wait for. It is a recent phenomenon, but city tea-rooms are increasingly taking on the function of stereo parlours. Come to think of it, it is a welcome phenomenon, indicating that tea-rooms are recovering their proper function, which had been abandoned in the destitute days of the Korean War. That may be a proof, also, of the fact that living has become less strenuous to a certain degree in recent times.

The story I want to tell here is about a disc jockey in one of these tea-rooms. Disc jockey is a new kind of job that has been proliferating recently in Korea. The job is taking root in radio and television stations, and also in stereo parlours and tea-rooms. This new occupation is having its day since the advent of pop music. A disc jockey is not exactly a professional, he's just a worker. There is the English word "technician", but the word is alien to Korean ears. However that may be, it is a dignified job, having an expertise of its own. Of course, all jobs have a certain dignity when the workers become experts, but the disc jockey ideally should have more dignity than other workers. Thanks to the invention of the record player, performers do not have to come before the audience to give them music. The disc jockey performs this function. Therefore, since the disc jockey takes the place of hundreds of great musicians, he or she has to be dignified. But with the emergence of pop music, dignity has collapsed and the disc jockeys have degenerated into mere wage earners. Perhaps inevitably, as pop music has fallen into the hands of uncultured people and become a commodity instead of an art, the disc jockey booths of tea-rooms have become quite like box offices of cinema houses. Because the masses do not know much about dignity, they do not demand it of disc jockeys. Disc jockeying is a job, and that suffices.

The jockey's booth in this tea-room has quite a number of records, including a decent selection of classical records; this place is rather highbrow, for a tea-room. Most of the disc jockeys in tea-rooms are men, but in this tea-room the jockey is a woman of about twenty-two or three. She did not study music in college or anything; she does her work with some slight knowledge of music. She comes to work at one o'clock in the afternoon, and from then on until eleven o'clock at night she picks out records requested, puts them on the stereo and adjusts the volume.

Records requested are ordinarily of popular music, so they are not hard to pick out. The English used for titles is not difficult. But some customers request classical orchestral music in German, and may even specify the opus number and name the orchestra too. Ordinarily, classics are not played in tea-rooms, but in early mornings or late at night such requests are granted. To handle such cases, disc jockeys must have at least some elementary knowledge of German and some basic knowledge about classical music.

It is the same with adjusting the volume. As the interior decoration of tea-rooms must change with the seasons, so the volume should be adjusted according to the time of day. Different kinds of customers patronise the tea-room at different hours. So adjusting the volume is a task that requires sensibility, because it is part of the job of beautifying a dull, frustrating day with music. This is not an easy task, whatever anybody might have to say to the contrary, just as the manager's task of changing the interior decoration is not an easy one. Whether it be hard or easy, it is not a mere job; it requires and leads to self-discipline.

The term is rarely encountered these days, but there is such a thing as "the tea way". Our ancestors practised the way of tea as a means of self-discipline. From the blending of tea flavours and selection of utensils to the brewing and drinking of tea and handling of tea sets, the mood, the arrangement of the room in which to drink tea. . . Come to think of it, tea serving is no simple matter. We say, practise the way, but it is not so much a matter of learning the rules as of awakening to the true way of life and attaining self-discovery through the simple ceremony of drinking tea. Thus, when one has mastered the decorum of tea serving one has realised the essence of life. That is to say, in current phraseology, one has become a refined man. But modern tea-rooms care very little about this tea way. They are more like market-places. The tea-room owners may not be particularly to blame for this phenomenon, for it is a trend of the times. It is like the ape putting on an apron in imitation of human beings, or people making a clumsy imitation of picking up the load left behind by others, not knowing its real purpose.

Coming back to our Miss B, she is, anyway, burdened with this load. It is a pity she is so thin, but her profile, seen through the window of the jockey's booth, is impressive, consisting of sharply defined features. She is always sitting before the table with a somber expression—something unusual in girls of her age. One might say she is past the easily excitable age, but her somberness is not entirely due to maturity.

She has been occupying this same post for about three years now, long enough to make her feel bored. The cause of her gloom may be attributed to this boredom more than to anything else. She is a disc jockey, just as other people are other things according to their work. The obligatory adjustment of volume, the invariable record rack like a dust-coated bookcase, the request notes with the names of some silly popular songs in childish hands submitted by immature teenagers. So she often feels like the shopkeeper of a small sweet-shop. Just as at the thrusting of pennies, at the presentation of request notes she dispenses the commodity on the stereo mechanically. It is like selling sweets. But music is not for selling, at least originally it was not. What is most precious to men they keep or give to others without fee.

Music is priceless. You give music freely, and wait for the spiritual transformation in the hearer till he or she is completely of one mind with you. But in this upside-down age art has become a commercial item, and therefore its original function as the soul's tonic has been negated. Anyway, disc jockeys are not responsible for this. But the phenomenon furnishes an important factor in making Miss B bored and depressed. In the end, you might say that she has no firm principles to live by. Usually most people, whether they live entirely apart from or completely involved in the affairs of the world, rely on other people's opinions rather than on their own for value judgments. It is the same in Miss B's case. Although she is a disc jockey, she really doesn't know what to think of classical and pop music. Since most cultured people value the classics highly, she thinks that classics are valuable, and since frivolous people tend to like pop music, she takes pop music to be of trifling value.

In this regard, Miss B is not an exception. Even though her financial circumstances would not allow her to be aristocratic, she has inherited the feminine rules of conduct of the nobility; but she does not know the meaning of the whole set of virtues of aristocratic women. Miss B sits at her desk in the jockey's box. As moneyed commoners try to buy knighthood, so ignorant common men outside the box ogle her. Notes requesting a rendezvous; notes saying "I love you"; notes praising her beauty; notes saying the writers want to be her friends; notes expressing respect; all sorts of trash keep invading her section of the tea-room. On receiving these notes, she hesitates, as a nobleman hesitates about whether to sell his title for money or not.

Music originally had been the home entertainment of Western noblemen. It could be heard only on court stages and in the salons of titled ladies. Through that music, the Western noblemen reflected on life and discovered themselves. Then, with the decline of aristocracy and the rise of commoners, music was taken out of the chambers of lordly manor houses. The uncultured people did not know how to use this thing, although they took it over from the nobility; they just dragged it here and there and let it tear apart. Just as common men do not know what to do with a title of nobility, music was of no use to common men. If there was music, it was no longer music reflecting life, but music taking our thoughts away from life. No, they cannot think deeply about life. Therefore, they evade life. It is the same with Miss B. Like the commoner in the "Tale of a Nobleman", she abides by aristocratic rules of conduct, but it is without enthusiasm, without a feeling of inner reward. That means that men are, after all, slaves of the loads they have inherited. Although invisible, the knot is tight that binds her to her inherited burden. She does not comprehend the meaning of her burden, nor the reason for her enslavement to it.

When baffled by such a mystery, men usually resort to liquor, gambling and sex; but in the case of women, especially unmarried girls like Miss B, when trapped in labyrinths like this, they look for a thread called marriage. In such circumstances, a girl is likely to marry before she knows exactly what she is doing. But anything done as an escape from something is likely to bring regret and grief afterwards. It is a different question if one is prepared to meet this sorrow and regret. Anyway, this was how Miss B felt at about that time. That was why she was always so gloomy.

Then, one spring day, she became interested in a regular male customer of her tea-room. He looked about thirty, and he had been a patron of this tea-room for a couple of years now. But it was only recently that she came to feel any interest in him. Oh, it was not that she had been entirely unaware of his existence until now. She just thought that he used this tea-room like anyone else—for appointments or relaxation. But, recently, she had begun to sense something unusual about him. First of all, he was always alone. He sometimes came in the late afternoon, around the end of office hours, and sometimes dropped in for an hour or two in the late evening. For days he would come every day, but at other times he would come at intervals of several days.

Most of the people who come to tea-rooms have definite purposes of their own. Apart from those who come to meet people by appointment, many come to listen to music or to flirt with waitresses and hostesses. There are some people, too, who have no definite occupation and come to tea-rooms to kill time. At first she thought he was one of these types. But however you might look at it, he could not be classified into any of these types. Since he spent an hour or two by himself every time, he was definitely not coming to meet somebody. Neither did he have any close contacts with the hostess or the waitresses; he never talked to anybody from the time he stepped into the tea-room till he left, except to order tea. Sometimes he looked like someone who came to this tea-room in order to avoid talking to people.

Or was he out of work? But most jobless people visit tea-rooms in the daytime. Well then, finally, did he come to this tea-room to listen to music? That seemed most likely. But not quite. Music lovers usually request classical music. There had never been a request for classical music made during the hours he stayed in this tea-room. In Miss B's judgment, one cannot call anyone who does not ask for classical music a music lover.

One might say he just sat there. His profile, when he smoked, looked very lonely. But when he was not smoking, his eyes seemed to be pondering over something very deeply, so that one felt a certain isolating intensity in his eyes. The eyes of a police detective intent on a case? But his eyes were not that insistent. What did he do? Anyway, he did not look like an ordinary man. But she began to feel more keenly interested in him once she recognised the songs he requested—or, rather, his handwriting.

Having worked in the record booth several years, she came to discern most of the hands of regular patrons. But, long since, there had been requests written in an uncommonly handsome script. In most cases one can guess at the degree of learning of a man by his handwriting. But, unfortunately, the music requested in that handsome script was not elegant classical music but frivolous pop songs or cinema theme music. So she had been feeling sorry for a man who must be very learned but had very little appreciation of music. Then one day she found that the hand belonged to none other than this man. The music he requested included:

The Lost Sun (theme music of a local film)
Exodus (theme song of the film)
One Fine Day (from Puccini's *Madame Butterfly*)
Go Down, Moses (Negro spiritual)
Phaedra (theme music of the film)
He's Got the Whole World in His Hand (spiritual)
Guitar Twist (jazz)
Let's Go (jazz)
Autumn Leaves (pop song)
El Cid (theme music of the film)
Theme of Love (theme music of *Ben Hur*)

One evening she picked out all the records he had requested and played them consecutively. As the second song started, he suddenly poured out a look toward Miss B. She could not describe it even to herself, but they were such impressive eyes. They looked grateful, puzzled, no—anyway it was an expression that one could come up with only in moments of truth. As she went on playing records, his expression grew more somber and he looked away. When all the music had been played, his eyes became lustrous again and he stared at her. Miss B did not know how to deal with a moment like that, so she became flustered and dropped her glance. Then he smiled at Miss B and bowed his head slightly. Confused, Miss B also nodded in response.

Thereafter, whenever the man came in Miss B played several songs from his earlier requests before he even asked for them, upon which he would pay silent regard with his eyes. His face and manner testified that he was an unusual man, but she could not comprehend why he patronised this noisy tea-room. And why did he request pop music such as teenagers choose? What did he do for a living? Was he married? The more interested she became in him, the more enveloped in mystery did he seem. Then, early one summer evening, she received a note in his hand. It was not a request for music. It was a personal note.

"I'll be waiting for you in front of the Duksoo Palace tomorrow morning at ten."

On receiving this note, she lost her composure. It was not the first time she had received notes of this kind from patrons, but she always thought them ridiculous and threw them into the rubbish bin, because they were written by people who seemed as though they'd do such childish things. But this kind of note from this man was utterly unexpected. She had never imagined it could happen. So she was confused, but maybe she was also bemused with delight, as if something long awaited had at last arrived.

The next morning there was a slight rain. After much hesitation, Miss B set out from her house carrying an umbrella and wearing rain boots. Somehow she felt that an appointment with him was sacred, unbreakable. When she got off the bus in front of the palace grounds he was standing at the gate already, and he watched her approach. Perhaps because of the rain, his garments looked shabby. The worn and torn plastic umbrella with which he was protecting himself from the rain did not help his appearance much. They did not exchange any overt greetings when they met. He just gave Miss B a silent smile.

"Let's go in," he suggested.

What does he want to do in the ancient palace on a rainy day? But Miss B had no choice but to follow him. All of a sudden thunder struck and rain began to come down in torrents. The pouring rain splashed their legs, and through the tear in the plastic dome of his umbrella water leaked on to his face. Miss B looked at him anxiously, but they were not sufficiently acquainted yet for Miss B to remark on it. He seemed slightly embarrassed, too, for he kept turning his umbrella to prevent the tear from letting rain fall on to his face. The morning was still early; there weren't many people in the well-swept palace grounds. Only the two people were walking in the rain. They had reached the National Museum building.

"Shall we go into the museum?" he asked. Miss B nodded. Stepping into the museum, he asked again, "Shall I act as commentator?"

Miss B nodded again. Then the man, as if they had been long-time friends or old sweethearts, or rather as if they were teacher and student, began to explain about the relics, utterly unabashed. From pottery to paintings, Buddha images and decorative jewellery of royalty, his explanation was fluent. His commentary was concise and systematic, too. He divided history into dynastic periods and then wittily explained the transition of thoughts and ideas. Also, he drew freely from the East and West and ancient and modern worlds in interpreting the pattern on a piece of pottery. Moreover, his explanation was enthusiastic, unlike the mechanical commentaries of tourist guides. That made Miss B feel a little displeased. What kind of man is this? Isn't he being boastful of his knowledge? Perhaps he looked to Miss B like one of those streetcorner missionaries who wail phrases from the Bible.

When they stepped out of the exit on to the stairs, after spending quite some time inside, they saw a young American man and woman who looked like tourists taking shelter from the rain. They were people they had passed inside the museum a while ago. Maybe they had found nothing to interest them particularly. They had come out soon. The rain was pouring down more fiercely than before. The ditch below was overflowing with muddy yellow water. A pair of blue-eyed people. They looked like the incarnation of vitality to Miss B and the man. The rain pouring down cruelly. And the muddy ditch-water overflowing noisily. The trees and lawns and flowers that brave, nay, that enjoy the fierce rain; everything seemed so youthful. The man, who had been silent for some time, asked abruptly,

'Do you know today is a special day?'

She kept silent to indicate her ignorance. She looked at him in surprise. She couldn't recall that it was any kind of a special day.

"This is the seventh day of the seventh month, by the lunar calendar."[1]

It was only then that she said,

"Oh, today's the day the two heavenly lovers meet—the two stars in the old legend."

He smiled significantly.

"Well, here we have rain, sure enough," the woman remarked.

"Yes. Tears of too much joy, too much joy!" he repeated, his cheeks flushed red as if with the reflected delight of the heavenly lovers.

They parted like that that day. It was really a stupid

---

1. The seventh day of the seventh month by the lunar calendar is the day on which, legend has it, the two stars who are heavenly lovers are granted their once-a-year rendezvous. The lovers, who were a shepherd and a weaving girl, were separated by the order of the king of the sky because they neglected their work from being too deeply engrossed in love. They were exiled separately to stars located far apart, and the legend also has it that on the day of their meeting, magpies build a bridge across the sky for the lovers to meet, and it rains on that day because the reunited lovers shed tears of joy. The day is not a folk holiday and often goes by unnoticed in modern city life.

encounter, come to think of it. When a man and a woman meet, they ordinarily go to drink tea, have lunch, or see films and thus try to avoid any serious conversation. From this conventional viewpoint, their date had been very silly indeed. But the more Miss B puzzled over what kind of a man he was, the more interested she became in him.

There arose a great confusion in her world of common sense after the day of her visit to the museum. The image of that man in the museum, the image of that man listening to pop music in this tea-room, the two images she could not harmonise into one, however hard she tried.

"Does he work at the museum?" she wondered, but she discarded the idea at once. That he did not was evident from the way the ticket man talked to him.

"Then, is he a researcher in archaeology? A professor of archaeology?" But the next moment she brushed aside that idea, too. Would a cultured archaeology professor listen to pop songs? She simply could not make him out. He continued to come to the tea-room after their visit to the museum. But his attitude had not changed a bit from before that meeting. He would be sitting there, smoking and staring into space, and even when his request music was played he made no sign of recognition. But then, after the piece was finished, he would turn his head toward Miss B and nod. That was all.

A month after that, they met again at the Duksoo Palace. A sunny day in the Duksoo Palace is very pleasant. After the bustle in the streets, it is an entirely new environment when you step into the palace. Coming out of the art gallery, they took shelter from the hot sun on the shaded benches. In front of them, thin streams of water spouted from the mouths of stone seals. This fountain is a mere toy compared with the more sumptuous ones in the West, but to the young people on the bench it gave the joy of youth. Somewhere a cicada chirped, as if unaware of the fact that it was in the heart of the city. At last the man, who had been looking around the royal courtyard, began a conversation.

"Here in this palace is modern history."

Miss B, puzzled at this unexpected topic, asked,

"What do you mean?"

Then he began explaining about the two different styles of

architecture on either side of them—the stone museum building on the one hand and the ancient wooden royal audience
hall on the other. He called the Western-style stone building
the male and the traditional Korean-style building the female.
It made Miss B laugh. Then he began to explain heatedly why
they were male and female respectively. First of all, the stone
building is made of heavy material, so it gives a feeling of
massiveness and we feel a strength as of muscles in it. When
you quarry stones, you dig them with rough equipment from
steep mountains. And the lines of stone structures are all
straight lines. Straight lines are sharp and therefore challenging, looking as if they were about to pierce you. Moreover,
there is always something incomplete about straight lines; it
is expected that straight lines will act unceasingly, to comple-
ment their incompleteness. That is to say, Western architecture embodies the element of the progressive and the
innovative, which are masculine attributes.

In contrast, the ancient palace is built of wood, so massiveness is absent from it. Instead, the softness of wood reminds
one of the soft flesh of females. Besides, in dealing with the
wooden materials, their natural pattern is utilised to the
fullest; and they are gathered not from steep dangerous
cliffs, but from verdant forests. And then the curve of the
eaves bends so softly that, unlike the challenging straight line,
it is almost too perfect and complete. So, unlike the stone
structure, these elements suggest peace, timelessness, and
conservatism, which are feminine characteristics.

Then there are other elements like colour, and use of
accessories such as nails, and other matters pertaining to
construction technique; but these are the most important
factors.

"So modern history is how the male came to wed the
female."

Then the woman laughed and said,

"Oh, do males come to wed females? I thought females
married into the males' houses."

He laughed also.

"Oh, because the female is so shy and dignified, the male,
being too impatient, just jumped in."

"Isn't that like a thief?"

"Well, women often call men thieves."

"Oh, what an awful thing to say!" She laughed at the absurdity of his remark. Sobering, she said, as if to score after a lost point, "But modern girls aren't like that."

"How do you mean?"

"They aren't so shy as to wait for the men to take the initiative. Far from it, they are aggressive like men."

Then he suddenly became very excited and said,

"Are they, really?"

"Yes. Really."

"Then that's our future."

He seemed intoxicated, as if he was picturing something exhilarating before his eyes. But Miss B became gloomy because of the sudden change of subject. Rather, his tirade from the first was not of any keen interest to her. People ordinarily are not strongly interested in anything that does not directly concern them, even an urgent problem of the times. So Miss B turned to a topic that she had been anxious to explore.

"Do you like jazz?"

He looked uneasy, like one awakened from a revery and, turning a little toward Miss B, said,

"No, I like classical music."

"Classical music?" she retorted in surprise.

"Yes. In music, the most important thing is the tradition from Bach to Beethoven. After that everything is mere variations of what had already been written."

"But you always request pop music?" she inquired, at a loss.

He smiled queerly and said,

"No, I always requested classical music."

"What? You requested classical music? Then what about *Let's Go* and *Guitar Twist*?"

"Oh, those are jazz, to be sure, but when I request them, each of them becomes a movement in a classical symphony. There is a phrase, you know, like 'eight chords making up the universe'. That is to say, the pop songs are each a chord. Well, what shall I say the universe is? For me, I would say it is the *Eroica Symphony*, maybe?"

"*Eroica Symphony*? Beethoven's?"

"Yes. *Eroica Symphony*. Hahaha."

He laughed a bold laugh like a boastful, middle-aged libertine. But it seemed to Miss B that behind the laughter there lurked the truth of the man. Miss B, affected by his hearty laughter, was drawn into it and found herself laughing, unawares, forgetting her original intention in bringing up the topic.

A man's and a woman's feelings become a shade more delicate when they part without any promise of a next meeting. Miss B was not an exception, so she felt strangely emotional now and then. But, just as his reasons for frequenting this tea-room had been uncertain, Miss B's reasons for meeting the man were also obscure. They were not sweethearts, they had no definite business to discuss, and of course they were not instructor and pupil. Maybe we could call them apprentice sweethearts. But that might be the secret thought of Miss B alone. When people meet, especially when a man and a woman meet, there has to be a plausible reason. Modern people, especially, need rational reasons. To be sure, there must be a reason for Miss B's meeting that man. But she couldn't put into words her reasons for seeing that man especially.

So the feeling of boredom she had been experiencing up till now changed into one of misgiving. When one is unsure about the true character of another person, one has such anxious feelings. That is to say, when a person one is dealing with is not comprehended, the person becomes a burden. We might say that Miss B had now acquired a burden in addition to all the burdens she already bore. People try to understand one another in order that the other party will not become an added burden to them. When they have comprehended one another, people say they "saw each other".

To "see each other" means that the two people's consciousness takes one seat. The place where the consciousness of one and the other can sit together—when they find that common seat, the two cease to be burdens to each other. In the case of Miss B, she had not yet found that common seat for herself and the man. When they have not found that seat people become anxious, and in order to get away from the anxiety they unceasingly challenge the other party and search for the common seat.

So with Miss B. She wanted to know all about the man. But what really is this thing called knowing? Is it knowing his social status? His living environment? His appearance? His income? His propensity for spending? His hobby? His taste? The knowledge of these things is not enough to enable one to find the human being's ultimate seat. Or rather, the seat must exist somewhere underneath all these. Anyway, Miss B wanted to discover this man's final seat. So she diligently thought about him.

He did not appear in the tea-room again after their last date, but she kept thinking of him. As days went by, the thought of the Eroica Symphony occupied her more persistently. Most people who request music do so for the sake of a memory connected with the music. That means that by hearing a piece of music they bring to mind the specific person, event, or place connected with the melody. But when a man requests pop music as a portion of a symphony, one would have to think of the meaning of the music itself. So she thought about the meaning of the pieces on his request notes one by one. For example, Puccini's "One Fine Day" is an aria from the opera *Madame Butterfly*, in which a Japanese girl is betrayed by an American sailor. Then, what on earth was that man looking for in this music? In this manner, Miss B kept pondering.

Perhaps summer is the best season for tea-rooms. However scorching hot it may be outside, inside the tea-room the air conditioner cools the air and there are cold beverages in plenty. The waves foaming with white teeth, the wind that sweeps up the waves that break with a roar, and the young naked bodies jumping into the blue water—if this is the seashore in summer, then tea-rooms are beaches inside the city. Even so, the small disc jockey's room, walled by glass on all sides, looks enclosed. Moreover, as the man who constantly occupies her mind has not given a hint of his existence for over a month, there is nothing noteworthy about her life these days.

One early autumn evening, when the fierce heat began to subside, the long-awaited man made his appearance suddenly. Miss B's gladness was expressed in her reproachful look, but she *was* glad, to be sure. But the man, without even ordering a cup of tea, hurriedly scribbled a note, sent it to the record booth, and disappeared immediately. The note said simply, "Ten o'clock tomorrow morning at the front gate of Duksoo Palace."

Sometimes meeting people can be a bothersome affair, but really there is no greater pleasure on earth. Our pleasure in meeting people is numbed by our being surrounded by people on all sides from birth. It can easily be imagined, the delight of meeting a fellow human being on a desert island. Our feeling when we meet strangers in daily life may be anxiety, expectation, or impatience. At any rate, meeting people can be a greatly rewarding experience. We often feel unsettled when we step into a shop to have a suit made, to buy a pair of shoes, or purchase a daily commodity or fancy goods; but these moments are not unsettling because we are going to meet things. They are so because we are going to acquire things using or wearing which we will meet people. One need not describe in words the anxious, heart-throbbing expectation of two young people meeting!

Miss B stepped into the open air with a pounding heart. Continuously feeling a thrill running through her body, she hastened to the place of appointment. The sky was high and there wasn't a speck of cloud visible. When she stepped onto Taepyongro Avenue, she saw a bustling crowd densely lining both sides of the street. What had happened? But such a thing was far from having any importance to her at the moment. When she had come near Duksoo Palace, though, she was made aware that this noisy crowd had something to do with her own personal affairs. Nothing was on the road, but people were struggling against each other for a better view. And she became aware that she could not cross the road lined by crowds on both sides.

In front of the crowd, policemen and military police were strictly forbidding crossing, and mounted policemen could be seen riding about blowing whistles. Miss B became hot with impatience. But there was nothing she could do. Across the street was the Duksoo Palace. He must be there waiting for her now. The long hand of her watch ticked past the hour mark. When she recalled that it was Armed Forces Day, she was dismayed.

"For heaven's sake!" she muttered to herself, and stood there behind the crowd, as if lost. The pushing and pushed crowd. The noisy talk, the sound of the whistle; time ticked past.

In the clear blue autumn sky, a bunch of clouds came from nowhere to brood over the City Hall. At long last, with splitting metallic sounds, jet airplanes began to confound the sky with swallow swoops, and band music could be heard. With the appearance of the army band with an honour guard in front, the crowd became still more noisy and disorderly. The copper-skinned soldiers, the helmets and rucksacks and the guns looking heavy, even cumbersome, to the soldiers with their gloomy expressions, their uniformly angular, under-nourished faces—all seemed part of a loaded-down herd of animals. Trucks, combat vehicles, armoured cars, guns, mounted soldiers, and military equipment she did not know the names of. Over the heads of the dull, slow procession of the herd, balloons of all colours let loose by bored people soared to the sky, as if fleeing for freedom. Rather, they were shouting for freedom, escaping, soaring into the sky far above the City Hall plaza.

It was too painful a trial for Miss B to shrug off as the bad luck of a day. She came back home tired, and unfortunately he did not appear in the tea-room again, so there is no further progress in our story of their romance. But then one day, about a fortnight afterwards, Miss B happened to open an evening paper in her booth. There was a small article under the headline: "—Arrested for Violation of National Security Law." And there was a picture, beside the article, of the man. She looked at it again, unbelieving, but it was undoubtedly his picture. There was no mistake, although she looked at it again and again.

Most women are more shocked by an event itself than at the true and detailed facts about an event. Miss B is not an exception. She was experiencing unspeakable agitation while holding the paper in her hands. With the passing of time, that agitation changed into frustration. She was overwhelmed with a feeling, a conviction that everything had gone wrong. For some time after that she kept falling deeper into a pit of gloom. But every pit has a bottom. When hitting the bottom, one begins to ask questions. Has everything gone wrong now, irrevocably? Why was he arrested? What is this National Security law? Question after question arose in her mind. And then, after that, a person can't help wandering in a world of ratiocination, searching for the villain. It was during this stage, while ruminating through the peculiar impressions and memories of him, that she had a sudden flash of insight. A strange ray passed through her brain, making it seem a resonant chamber. Then came the ecstasy of revelation.

"That's it!" she exulted, but if you asked "What's it?" she wouldn't have been able to tell you in well-defined phrases. Still, in her mind, she saw all too clearly the thing which had been vague. The two consciousnesses found their common seat. She had striven and found the common seat for both of them. Then it became clear to her—the feeling with which he had listened to pop music, and also what is pop music and what is classical music.

Indeed, everything—the tea-room, the player booth, the ranged records—all looked vitalised as new spring plants. Moreover, all these, instead of being tiresome burdens to her, became her wings.

Our story has to come to an end here. Of course such an extraordinary experience as Miss B's provided the moment for her to love the man truly, and also began a new life for her in which she came to love all human beings; but to tell that story, we would have to go into this case under the National Security law. That would make a long, tedious story, so as we originally intended we are going to close with the account of Miss B's discovery. For reference, we record here how Miss B in her own way arranged and inter-preted the music he requested and made the whole into an Eroica Symphony. /

    1. The Lost Sun—the sorrow of the loss of one's father-land and leader.

2. Guitar Twist—chaos, disorder, incoherence.
3. One Fine Day—the breach of faith by Westerners.
4. Phaedra—Fate's stubborn pursuit.
5. Exodus—Escape from repression.
6. Go Down, Moses—the awakening to leadership, the will of the hero.
7. He's Got the Whole World in His Hand—the sense of unity, the will toward synthesis.
8. Autumn Leaves—the sorrow of estrangement.
9. The Theme of Love—self-discipline of the hero to purify love.
10. El Cid—the messiah and the cross.
11. Let's Go—everything's over.

Choi In-hoon

Born in 1936, Choi In-hoon began his writing career early, in 1959. The young writer greatly impressed a few critics and readers from the first with his firm intelligence, keen psychological insight and bold indictment of the irrationalities of society. But he had to wait quite a few years for general recognition, and even now has a more intellectual than general readership.

The writer's main probe is into the meaning of life and the human personality, and the relationship between individuals. His principal lifelong quest may be defined as a search for a spiritual home. 'My Idol's Abode' (1960), an early work, records the failure of a meeting of two souls, a typical encounter of spiritually homeless modern man.

Choi In-hoon has many remarkable gifts, not least among them his keen satirical wit which he employs for scathing attacks on the shams and subterfuges of modern society and institutions. When Choi In-hoon engages in his relentless analysis and exposure he sounds embittered and angry, but we are never made to feel he is angry without cause. He is one of the most poignant spokesmen of this generation's anguish of alienation.

The author also shows a deep concern with the national heritage, and has 'rewritten' many Korean classical works, to re-examine thoroughly the values of Korea's past and their effects on Korean people today. Of late he has tried his hand at writing dramas, and has produced daring experimental pieces which have earned him high acclaim. All in all, Choi In-hoon is a writer for those prepared to face the naked truth about life and human beings.

My Idol's Abode

Choi In-hoon

I t was shortly after Seoul was recaptured and the government moved back from Pusan. In Myongdong,[1] damaged by bombs and deserted by the pre-war crowd, there was a tea-room named "Arisa". We fledgling men of letters used a corner of the tea-room, which was very snugly recessed and which we had fondly named "Venus's bosom", as a kind of a private drawing-room, talking spiritedly or just staring at the ceiling for hours. Mr K was our respected mentor and the centre of the group. Like other tea-rooms of that time, coffee at Arisa tasted rather funny and we jokingly called it "simulated coffee", but in fact we could not very well afford to order that beverage as rent for occupying the space there.

However, we were nothing daunted by the disapproving glances from the counter; and in effect, the proprietress for the most part generously overlooked our occupying so much space every day without adding much to the income, and even hospitably attended to us. Thus, the tea-room became our haunt. Mr K was an established author at the time, and therefore many renowned figures of the literary circle of that time came by to the tea-room to talk with him and make requests for his contributions, much to our envy and admiration. And of course there were many nameless would-be authors who came for the benefit of his opinions and advice.

1. Myongdong is a busy fashion and entertainment district in the heart of Seoul.

One day I happened to notice among those who came to the tea-room on account of Mr K, one young man who belonged to neither of those two groups. It was plain that he was not there for business. Neither was he there for sociable purposes. It was one drizzly July afternoon when he first appeared in the tea-room. I distinctly remember the date, because something very depressing had occurred that day and my diary bears a record of the day.

He paid silent regard to Mr K with his eyes, strode off to a table a few yards away and sat obliquely on the chair, facing Mr K. His movement was so mechanical that it affected me strangely. When I heard later that that was the first time in many years he and Mr K had met, I did not know what to think of such deportment as his. Since Mr K was of a tactiturn disposition and treated everyone more or less equally, I had got into the habit of observing his conversation narrowly and figuring out the degree of familiarity and the nature of the relationship between him and his various acquaintances. It gave me childish amusement to whisper my inferences into Mr K's ears. Mr K usually simply smiled or chuckled at my observations.

Well, one more surprising thing about this stranger was that Mr K, who is usually imperturbable, evinced a great change of emotion on his face and, walking over to the new-comer, sat down beside him and talked to him earnestly, taking his arm. It was the first time Mr K had received anyone thus. That could not fail to excite my curiosity.

Who could the stranger be? Although he was one of those who look more mature than his age, it was not difficult to see that he was twenty or more years Mr K's junior, and although the young man seemed noticeably lacking in diffidence, I could see that he looked up to Mr K. But that was all that I could figure out about him. I could not suppress my interest and curiosity, and my attention would of itself wander to where they were, even while I was carrying on a conversation with pals at my table. Well, I was somewhat embarrassed by my intense curiosity, as it is not very flattering to one's ego to be so strongly attracted to another, and especially as the members of my group seemed hardly to notice him. But there was no help for it—he seemed such an extraordinary character.

After that, he came to the tea-room quite frequently. As Mr K had simply said, in response to my inquiry, "Well, it's someone I know," I remained totally ignorant about him, but I was beginning to think that knowing in the ordinary sense—the usual data about a person implied in the word "knowing"—was unnecessary and irrelevant in the case of that man. I blush to confess this, as it means that I had made of him in my mind a figure of mystery—like perhaps the Count of Monte Cristo in the work by Dumas *père*. However, it was not as if I was a naive idoliser. I had sensibility and discrimination enough to perceive subtle shades of character and nuances of personality, and prided myself on my acuteness in this regard. Well, he may not have been a Count of Monte Cristo, but he was certainly above my measurement, or too complex for my analysis.

When he came into the tea-room he always took a seat a table or two away from us, and then Mr K went up to him. He did not take notice of the others in the group in any way. That displeased me. I decided to take no notice of him myself, but then felt ashamed of myself—his eyes, when they met mine by chance, had no pride or arrogance in them. I discovered that I was carrying on an entirely one-sided contention. I suppose the following account will prove to the reader that my hostility or spite was entirely meaningless and that he defied hasty judgment.

From what I have said so far the reader may have imagined a human being who had become corrupt inside and callous on the surface. I was drawing towards roughly that conclusion myself. But it was a misconception. His closed lips, as he turned his eyes quietly towards the window in the middle of a conversation with Mr K, were never those of one who prides himself on having penetrated the last secret of the universe. In other words, had he been an abstract painter, he would not have been one of those who shallowly laugh at the traditional pencil sketch. Oh, yes, he's not the fossil remains of an ardent poetic aspiration gone sour, I said to myself, and decided to give up the psychological combat. Once I gave up the struggle I found that I was in a much better position for observing him. Eyes not stained by the ego—I gained that necessary condition for observation through humility. On my stage there were only two actors— him and Mr K.

When I beheld the stage as a spectator I was surprised once again by a new discovery. Of the two actors Mr K seemed to be in the minor role. In worldly terms it was certainly Mr K whose position was the weightier; but in terms of the mental currents being exchanged between the two, his was the stronger and seemed to tax Mr K's strength in the reception of it. Having got rid of personal pride, I felt a genuine artistic interest in the relationship between them. Of course, the immaturity of my view prevented my taking into considera- tion the factor that Mr K had the handicap of being so many years the young man's senior and so superior in social status that he could not take the aggressive part, and I noted only the surface phenomena. At that time at any rate my whole concern was on the shift in the uncertain balance between the two as they appeared on my stage.

One day he came to the tea-room on a very dull afternoon. Only Mr K and I were at our table. Surprisingly, the man threw himself into our "Venus's bosom". He seemed very pleased with something. He sat obliquely in a chair and tapped the floor with his feet, or playfully yawned, making a small O with his mouth in a simulated rabbit's yawn. As was their wont, neither Mr K nor the young man took any pains to carry on a conversation. But after a while the young man suddenly straightened up, moved close up to Mr K and, slipping a hand under Mr K's armpit, said,

"Your eyes are as impressively clear as in the old days. They aren't at all a middle-aged man's. Does that mean you haven't found a woman who'd buy those eyes?"

Then he chuckled. In his chuckle I thought I sensed some- thing unmistakeable—something wounded, I was convinced.

After that, he made his appearance in the tea-room only after a good month's absence. Mr K was not there then. He sat himself down at a table, apparently to wait for Mr K's appearance, looked out at the darkening streets for a good while, then got up and left the room with a barely percept- ible nod to me. My heart bade me "follow, and I hastened out after him. He was standing in the doorway vacantly, stroking his chin with one hand. I went up to him and extended my hand.

The handshake was carried out in silence, and I realised that I was admitted into the company of the actors on stage. I was ecstatic, like when a woman one fell in love with at first sight accepts one's approach.

"Haven't we been friends already? I've been convinced of it for a long time now," I said rapturously, but there was no response on his part. We walked together shoulder to shoulder, and without any explicit agreement both of us were walking into the Catholic chapel. After sitting down on the bench he spoke for the first time.

"In my opinion, those who feel drawn to each other must strive at all costs to prevent becoming friends or lovers."

I smiled, "You mean so as not to become disillusioned?"

"Disillusioned? Well, maybe that's it."

I unfolded to him my impression of him since his first appearance, and the reasons for my being drawn to him. As he listened to me his face became overcast with gloom—or, rather, torment. I became confused.

"I am an accursed man. I am fated to ruin all those who come near me."

But on his face as he said this hovered a quiet smile. His words did not make me run away from him. On the contrary, they made me trust in him the more deeply.

"If ruin is my fate, then I'll gladly accept it," I said. The dramatic declaration made me excited, and satisfied my yearning for dramatic intensity. I wanted to believe that conversation with him at least was not exchange of dead words for form's sake, but a matter of two souls comparing their call signs. Contemplating his face, on which the thickly leaved trees threw patterns of light and shade intercepting the afternoon sun, I sat bemused. Had I ever met anyone who was so keenly alive to human beings?

My religion at that time was hero-worship. Only, my hero did not wear conventional diadems or medals. My hero was rather a man of depth of character and humane attractiveness. Well, I had no definite doctrines of hero-worship, but it was a faith and a mental disposition. A man possessed by a dark, naked force; a man who failed repeatedly in worldly affairs but who never compromised, and whose intelligence and common sense shielded all the turbulence of emotion inside—such was roughly the portrait of my hero. The young man's face and mood seemed to satisfy the outlines of this portrait, and so, summoning my courage, I approached him aggressively. Thus we became friends.

He appeared in the tea-room every Wednesday between six and seven o'clock. But Mr K did not know that we had become friends. The man did not show any marks of intimacy with me before the others, and thus Mr K had failed to notice the development of our acquaintance. Neither did I take any particular notice of him in front of others. Like lovers who choose to remain unacknowledged before the public, we feigned indifference before the others.

Since the development of my acquaintance with him I had discovered many unusual things about him. When we met, we always used to come out of the tea-room and head toward a bench in the Catholic chapel. One day, as we were rounding a corner and heading up the hill, I found I was out of cigarettes, and retraced a few steps to stop at a cigarette stall. I tarried a few minutes, to wait for my change, and then headed up the hill once more, looking for him on the spot where we parted. He was not there. I walked quickly to the bench in the Catholic chapel he and I always took, but he was not there either. I waited for a long time but he did not appear.

When we met the next time I did not say a word in reproach, and he did not say a word in apology, either. This is a trivial instance, but typical of his ways. Far from seeming a defect, such personal habits seemed to me the eccentricity of a genuine artist. Well, that proves how complete his conquest of me was,

One day he became serious and said, "I really must confess."

"What is it?" was all I could say, in anxious expectation.

"I'm going to tell you something that will make you want to flee from me at all costs."

"You want to wean me away? Well, go ahead. There's no telling the consequences without having the event first."

He was silent for a long time. It almost seemed as if he was going to remain silent till the end of his life. But he began, and told me the following story:

"My home is W— city, way up north on the west coast. I was in the fifth form the year the Korean War broke out. My father was a surgeon, and had a private practice before the liberation, but after the liberation the communist government pressured him into closing his private clinic and becoming a salaried doctor in the provincial hospital. The air was always gloomy at our home, and I think it was because of my father's gloom arising from his dissatisfaction with a lot of the things he had to endure at work. But my father's ideological anguish did not draw my concern, as I was besieged with a problem of my own.

"I was at an age when Zola's 'Nana' could absolutely enthrall me. Because the repressive policy which is characteristic of controlled societies extended to the area of publication also, there were very few books from which a boy my age, just beginning to be awakened to sex, could get enlightenment on the subject. The 'Nana' that cast such a thrall on me was of course not a publication of North Korea but a Japanese translation published by Japan's 'New Wave' publisher. I found the book in a secondhand bookshop and purchased it with money coaxed out of my mother. The used book was very expensive. The night I made the book mine I stayed up all night to read it through. The reason I bought the book was a passage that caught my eyes and made my heart leap when I was leafing through it casually in the bookshop. Come to think of it, one may say that the eroticism in 'Nana' is mild compared with the eroticism in such works as 'Lady Chatterley's Lover', but to me at that time it was a dream world that surpassed my imaginative capacity. The prostitute's eroticism in the book was to me not sex but song. My knowledge of carnal transactions had been almost blank, as it was impossible to hope to be instructed by books, and as I had no friends who could supply me with so-called dirty sexual knowledge. For me, it was the summit of ecstasy to read that Nana stripped herself naked before the man in front of the mantlepiece. I caressed Nana's entire body delineated in print. When I closed my eyes her naked body loomed before me. I was intoxicated in that dream, and I walked on clouds. It was a mind's eye caress of an imagined body, in which biological desire had no part. I believe that it was the purest love of a man for a woman.

"Then there appeared before me a real live woman. There was a half-Korean and half-western style wooden house in the residential area on the slope of a hill that I had to pass on my way to school every day. One morning I saw a woman coming out of the house. I just walked past her, but when I rounded a corner of the street a hot lump shot up from my heart and exploded in my throat. I stretched my neck and looked at the gate of the house. The woman was not there. But on my retina was inscribed a distinct outline of her face, which resembled a sweet briar. A nameless grief assaulted me and I turned my gaze toward the sea quickly. In the sky above the sea were huge lumps of dark cloud which gleamed ominously with the reflected glare of the sea.

"I saw the woman a few times after that. I think she was about twenty or slightly older. The woman became one in my imagination with Nana, and I was Georges. She sometimes came out of her house wearing a light one-piece suit and carrying a parasol, or sometimes she wore a wide-brimmed summer hat.

"I did not dream that I could ever become personally acquainted with her. My only hope was that she would not disappear, but stay where my eyes could sometimes light on her. One day I saw the woman walking with a stalwart young man. Perhaps taking courage at the fact that the street was deserted, the woman halted to pick some lint off his hair. It did not seem as if the lint was important, but rather that the gesture was an expression of fondness. I felt a sorrow like one betrayed. I resolved never to pass that house again. From the next day I picked a much longer road to school.

"The war broke out about a week after that event. Before people had had time to worry about the gravity of danger, bombing began. The townspeople hastily fled to a suburb to escape the bombing, and life had become completely topsy-turvy. Huge bombers flew across the cobalt-blue sky and flew away after smoothly letting loose bombs. The silver-grey aeroplanes flying through the light, cottonwool clouds, sending reverberations through the sky, presented a languorous beauty, like silver-grey fishes swimming in a crystal-clear lake. To me at least they presented such beauty. I did not dislike the war. And there was a very good reason for it, too. The war released me from school. School had been my prison for a long time. School meant the distasteful lessons in ideology and rigorous physical training.

"The war had chased people away from the city. I, who had till then been indifferent to the city, felt a sudden friendliness and freedom in it, as if it had become mine and only mine—our family could not flee, because my father had to treat the wounded. I sauntered around the courtyard of the Catholic chapel with leisurely steps, frowned or smiled or folded my arms, all quite as I liked, and there was no one to say anything about it. I strolled the streets, in imagination crowding buildings and squares with people and events of my own creation and delighting in or mourning their imagined happiness or sorrow. It was an indescribably sweet exercise. I steered myself to the woman's house. The gate was locked, an empty basket lay a little way from it, and only silence could be heard from the house. I hid myself in a recess and watched for nearly two hours, but no one either entered or left the house. It was the same the next day. I retraced my steps home heavily.

" 'You mustn't wander around in this dangerous city. You must stay quietly at home and go into the dug-out shelter when the air raid signal sounds,' Father warned me, and scolded Mother for not keeping me at home, but there was nothing Mother could do short of literally tying me down to make me stay at home.

"The next day there was the largest-scale air raid since the outbreak of the war. Bombers, which came in sets of four, came and went and dropped bombs. The neighbourhood of my home and the woman's house had escaped bombing till then, but we were not spared that day. After the raid ceased I slipped out of the air-raid shelter and searched in the direction of her house, but I saw the entire area thereabouts befogged with black smoke. I found myself frantically running toward her house. Tears were streaming down my cheeks as I ran. Arriving there, I saw that half of her house had disappeared, and flames were rising from what must be the kitchen. Looking carefully, I saw that the house was not on fire but that the flames came from the house next to it, which was on fire. Courage rose in me and I jumped on to the porch of that house. Where the hall ended, there was a woman lying on her back, pressed under a huge column.

"I could not help screaming when I saw her face. It was a terrible face, all besmirched with blood, and gaping. Her hand waved to me in supplication. I shot out of the house like lightning, ran all the way home, and jumped into my bed to forget everything. I lay still until sundown, racked by chill and headache, but jumped out of bed after dark. When I reached the spot again I saw corpses being carried out of the house on stretchers.

" 'A column fell on her. She could've lived if only she'd been discovered earlier.' I heard the words dimly, and fainted away."

He paused when he got that far in the story. The he resumed. "I didn't realise what it meant for me then. My family all escaped south safely. But from then on there grew in my heart a secret torment. Had I removed the column, or summoned people, she would have lived. The men's words, 'she could've lived if discovered earlier', haunted me like a curse. I don't know why I did such a foolish thing at that time. But the fact remains that I knowingly left a human being to writhe with pain for hours and to die. And that human being was my beloved. The woman still lives in my heart and accuses me of cruelty. Ah, I'm a murderer, a murderer!"

He sobbed, pressing his forehead on the back of the bench.

All my questions were answered.

I sat there speechlessly, with my hand upon his shoulder, feeling the veil of mystery lifting from around him. He was tormented by this secret sorrow! Compassion welled up in my heart, and I added pressure to my hand on his shoulder, cursing life for its cruel tricks.

From that day till the next time we met I racked my brains trying to think of a way of relieving him from the burden of that memory. But I could think of nothing more original than a few days' trip. When I suggested it to him, he looked thoughtful for quite a while and then accepted my invitation, saying that I might pick him up at his home on the day we were to leave.

I set out in search of his house with a small suitcase in one hand and the sketch map of his home in the other. After wandering for quite a while I found the house which bore the address he had inscribed on the map. I was much taken aback by the sign on the brick house which said "St Mary's Neuropsychiatric Clinic". I recalled that he had said his father was a doctor. At the reception desk sat a thin, bespectacled man who looked up at me when I went in, putting down the balance in his hand. I put my suitcase down beside the sofa in the hall and said,

"I've come to see somebody."

"Yes? Is it a patient?"

"No."

"Then an employee? Who?"

"No, I came to see the director's. . ."

"The director's away."

"No, it's not the director."

I realised how foolishly I had been stammering and gave his name, adding that I believed he was the director's son. The clerk grinned at once.

"I see. Well, I suppose you add one more to the list of his dupes. He's an in-patient. If you want to see him you must see his doctor first."

The clerk led me to the room with a "Consultation" sign on it and opened the door for me. A doctor who looked about forty glanced up from a thick book he was reading. I was completely at a loss.

"I'm in charge of everything concerning the patients while the director's away," the doctor told me.

I told the doctor that I was a friend of the young man, and that I had decided to go on a trip with him to help relieve him of a tormenting memory.

"We do sometimes permit patients to take trips, but first

tell me what kind of acquaintance you have with him," was the doctor's response.

After briefly narrating the history of my friendship with his patient, I asked, "But how did he come to be hospitalised so suddenly?" and then felt surprised as I remembered that the hospital address was what my friend had given me as his home address.

"Well, he became an in-patient about three months ago."

"What?"

I was astonished. It was less than three months since I first met him. The doctor sighed and said, "I see you're one of his victims."

"What do you mean, victims?"

There was nothing I could do but grow more and more amazed at every utterance of the doctor's. The doctor explained, "I mean that story about the woman who died during the bombing."

"Yes, I know that story. Well, it's no wonder you know it, as data concerning your patient."

"Well, it's not something I detected as a doctor. To tell you the truth, I'm one of his dupes myself."

"You?" I exclaimed in confusion, and pursued, "I don't understand. Please explain."

The doctor nodded and offered me a cigarette, lighting one up himself.

"I will. I'll begin with the conclusion. That story is a complete fiction. He's never been anywhere north of Seoul. He was born and raised in Seoul throughout his life."

Something exploded in my head. I could not believe it. His tormented expression as he recounted the story, and the faultless narrative! Why should he unfold such fiction to everyone he met, and why should he feign such preposterous grief?

"His illness is a very intricate mixture of many complexes. There is no single name for it, but it is a kind of exhibition-ism. Megalomania, Oedipal complex, delusions of heroism and other disorders are very complexly woven in his psyche. That imaginary tale is a manifestation of that illness. He thinks that fiction solves his many problems."

"But he looks perfectly normal, except for the invention

of that story."

"That's exactly why his is a difficult case. He is one of the almost incurable cases."

The doctor told me further that Mr K also sometimes came by the hospital, and that the hospital had been permitting him to seek out Mr K in town, as Mr K had a great deal of influence on him.

I kept on smoking. My chest tightened up. I felt like one kicked hard in the behind after being dragged around by a cunning, invisible foe.

"Would you like to see him?"

I still had too much lingering attachment to resist the offer. I nodded. The door opened after a while and he walked in. He was completely unperturbed to see me. I exclaimed to myself, "So this was it!" I realised at last that I had mistaken the meaningless unconcern of a man out of his right mind for the lofty indifference of a true artist.

He smiled generously at me and said, "I suppose you've been given an introduction to Freud by our revered doctor. That story, I admit, is a fiction. But what if it is? Are you, too, one of those who think it's a harmless joke to make friends love-sick by writing sham love letters, but it's insanity to create a fiction to show what damage the war has done to us? Do you also think I am a mental case? Have I done anything till the other day that made me look suspicious in your eyes? Wasn't it I myself who gave you the address of this hospital? Have you ever heard of a criminal giving his address to a detective?"

As I remained speechless with confusion at his eloquent outburst, the doctor replied for me, "Doesn't it prove the criminal to be abnormal, that he gave his address to the detective?"

That logical answer was a truly incisive surprise attack. The man's dignified face blanched instantly and then became flushed. Glaring at the doctor, he shouted, "What, you cunning swindler! You dare pretend to correct human minds with your bits of Freud? Let me out of here at once! And refund all the money you squeezed out of me! You dare say I'm mad? Make me a university professor, and I'll explain Hegel's logic for hours on end. And you!" He turned to me.

"Is this all your friendship means? You bow to the diagnosis of a quack doctor like that? It's you who are to be pitied. I pity you! Please get out of here. I don't want any pity or affection from fools."

The solid friendship between him and me in which I had such complete faith evaporated before my eyes like a mist and he became a total stranger again. I saw an impassable gulf gaping between us. I wasn't sure any more who was sane and who insane. I was afraid I was going mad. A berserk desire to kick and smash up everything swirled inside me. I could not stay still any more. I pushed open the door and ran outside. I swept past Mr K's surprised face which I glimpsed as he was coming in the gate as I went out, and I heard my former friend's guffaw and derision, "There, look at that! A self-styled first-rate intellectual of this country making a hasty retreat before the divine authority of common sense! My friend, my old pal!"

I ran, not knowing where to go, with the suitcase in my hand. Passersby who saw me must have thought me a mental patient escaping from the hospital. As I ran, in the endless desert of my brain only sands swirled up in a whirlwind.

Yun Heung-gil

Born in 1942, Yun Heung-gil is one of the most important rising authors on the literary scene today. When most young writers are increasingly turning toward naturalistic social protest or psychological analysis novels, Yun Heung-gil continues to cultivate an individual path with his adherence to the conventional story-telling mode and his quiet but earnest investigation into how people can live worthily as individuals and coexist harmoniously with fellow human beings.

While his predominant concern, like most of the other writers of his generation, is with underprivileged people and the various irrationalities of the social structure, there is always a greater fullness in his stories owing to his ability to be fair to all the characters, and because his people are never stereotypes and rarely sentimantalised. This is the more remarkable in view of the fact that he struggled with extreme poverty throughout his childhood and youth, and has many reasons to be bitter. Yun Heung-gil can see both the large misfortunes and the small but nagging grievances that harass people, and can also perceive the manifold sources of human strength and resiliency that enable them to withstand their fates. His stories, therefore, are not mere chronicles of survival but sincere quests into the problem of how life can be lived at all, and how it can be lived meaningfully.

His sure control of the narrative medium and his thoughtful but lively style are his other strengths. 'The Rainy Spell', which records a momentous encounter between two mothers with sons in opposing war camps, is unpretentiously told by a child who is himself a victim of the historical situation.

185

The Rainy Spell

Yun Heung-gil

1

The rain that started to pour from the day after we reaped the last pea-pods showed no sign of lifting even after many days. The rain came sometimes in fine powdery drops, or in hard, fierce balls, threatening to pierce the roof. Tonight, rain enveloped the pitch darkness like a dripping-wet mop.

It must have been somewhere right outside the village. My guess was that it was from somewhere around the empty house beside the bank which was used for storing funeral palanquins. The house always struck me as an eerie place, and I thought that near it even ordinary dogs would bark in long, dismal, fox-like howls. But it might have been in reality a place much further than the empty house. The relative silence allowed by the thinning rain was being filled by the distant howling of dogs. As if that far-off wail had been a military signal, all the village dogs that had managed to survive the war began to bark in turn. The dogs were unusually fierce that night.

That evening we were gathered in the guest room occupied by my maternal grandmother, because she was greatly disturbed by something, and we all had to comfort and reassure her. But Mother and Maternal Aunt ceased trying to say comforting things after the dogs began to bark fiercely. Stealing glances at Grandmother, Mother and Aunt were repeatedly turning their eyes towards the darkness beyond, separated from the room only by the door panelled with gauze mosquito net. A nameless moth had been crawling up and down the doorpost with tremulous wings for a long time now.

"Just wait and see. It won't be long till we'll know for sure. Just wait and see if I'm ever wrong," Grandmother murmured in her sunken voice. She was shelling peas from the pods. The peas were to be cooked with the rice for breakfast the next day. Sitting with the lap of her skirt full of damp pea-pods, she shelled the peas with sure, experienced hands—first breaking off the tip and slitting open the pod, then running her finger through it. When the bright green peas slid out to one side, Grandmother cupped them in her palm and poured them into the bamboo basket at her knee, and let the empty pod fall back into her lap.

Mother and Aunt, who lost the chance to make a rejoinder to Grandmother's words, exchanged awkward glances. The rain grew roughly noisy again outside, and the dogs barked more fiercely, as if in competition. The night grew still more stormy, and there came from the direction of the storage platform a clattering of metal hitting the cement floor. It must have been the tin pail hung on the wall. A sudden gust of wind and rain rushed into the room, rattling the door, and blew out the kerosene lamp that had been shivering precariously. The room sank under the sudden flood of darkness and sticky humidity, and the tremor of the moth's wings also stopped. The dog began to bark three or four houses beyond ours in the alley. Our dog Wolly, who had kept silent till then, emitted a growl. The fierce barking of dogs, which began at the entrance of the village, was coming nearer and nearer our house.

"Light that lamp," Grandmother said. "Light the lamp, I said. Didn't you hear me?" Grandmother made a rustle, feeling about the room in the darkness. "What evil weather!"

I groped about the room, found a match, and lit the kerosene lamp. Mother trimmed the wick. A strip of sooty smoke curled upward and drew a round shadow on the ceiling.

"It's always wet like this around this time of the year." Mother spoke in an effort to lessen the unease created by the weather.

"It's all because of the weather. It's because of this weather that you're worrying yourself sick for no reason," Aunt also put in. Aunt had graduated from a high school in Seoul before the war broke out, while my mother's family lived in Seoul.

"No. It isn't for no reason. You don't know. When has my dream ever predicted wrong?" Grandmother shook her head left and right. But even when her head shook, her hands did their work surely and steadily.

"I don't believe in dreams. It was only the day before yesterday we received Kiljun's letter saying he's well and strong."

"That's right. You read yourself where Kiljun said he's bored these days because there aren't any battles."

"All that's of no use. I knew three or four days beforehand when your father died. Only, that time, it was a thumb instead of a tooth. I'd dreamed that time my thumb just came loose and disappeared."

Oh, the hateful account of that dream again! Doesn't Grandmother ever get fed up with talking about that dream? Ever since she woke up from the dream at dawn, Grandmother had kept murmuring about her dream, her eyes vague and clouded. Continually moving her sunken, almost-toothless mouth, she kept hinting that there was an inauspicious force rushing towards her. She had only seven teeth left in all; she had dreamed that a large iron pincer from out of nowhere forced itself into her mouth, yanked the strongest of the seven, and fled. The first thing Grandmother did as soon as she woke up from the dream and collected her wits was to feel in her mouth and check the number of her teeth. Then she ordered Aunt to bring a mirror and checked the number again with her eyes. Not content, she made me come right up to her face and gained from me repeated assurances. No matter how often anybody looked in, there were seven teeth in her mouth, just as before. Moreover, the lower canine tooth that she cherished as a substitute for a grinder was as soundly in its place as ever.

But Grandmother wouldn't give credence to anybody's testimony. It seemed that to her it was out of the question that the canine tooth could remain there as if nothing had happened. Her thoughts were not in reality anymore, but dwelling in her dream. She refused to believe that her daughters and her son-in-law were telling her the truth, and she even doubted the eyesight of her grandson, whom she always praised highly for being good at threading needles. To say nothing of disbelieving the mirror, she even disbelieved her own fingers, which had made a survey of her teeth through physical contact inside her mouth.

Grandmother had spent the whole long summer's day murmuring about her dream. It taxed all of our nerves to distraction. The first one to break down and mention my maternal uncle's name was my mother. When Mother incautiously mentioned the name of her brother, who is at the front as a major and commander of a platoon in the Republic's army, Grandmother's flabby cheeks convulsed in a spasm. Aunt cast a reproachful look toward her incautious elder sister. Grandmother, however, ignored Mother's words. Before long Aunt also began talking of Uncle, judging that there was no other way of setting the old woman's mind at ease. But Grandmother never uttered her only son's name even once. She kept on talking about that hateful dream nonetheless.

From the time darkness began to set in, it became difficult to tell who was being comforted and who giving comfort. As night deepened, Grandmother's words became more and more darkly suggestive, as if she were under a spell, and her face even took on an expression of triumphant self-confidence. Mother and Aunt, on the other hand, fidgeted uneasily, and gazed vacantly at the pea-pods they had brought in to shell. In the end, all work was handed over to Grandmother, and Mother and Aunt could do nothing but listen to the endless incantatory mutterings of the old woman.

The dripping rain was wetting the whole surface of the village like a soaking wet mop. The three or four dogs that were lucky enough to survive the war mercilessly tore the shroud of darkness, enveloping the village with their shrill howls. Grandmother kept shelling the peas with expert hands, putting the peas into the bamboo basket and the empty pods back into her lap. Our dog Wolly, who received no kindly attention from anybody these difficult, gloomy days, began barking in surprisingly fierce and ringing tones. Just then we could hear footsteps rounding the walls of the house next door. They were not the footsteps of just one person. There seemed to be three, or two at least. A foot must have stepped in a puddle; there was a splashing sound, and hard upon it came a grumbling about the evil weather.

Who could those people be, who would dare trudge through the village in this pouring rain in the depth of the night? It was still a dangerous time, even though the war front had receded north, what with the communist partisans still occasionally invading and setting fire to the town police station. No one with any sense of propriety ever visited other people's houses after dark, unless on some emergency. To which house, then, could those people be going at this time of the night? What mischief might they be brewing, tramping the night streets in a group?

Mother grabbed hold of Aunt's hand. Aunt, leaving her hand to her sister's disposal, was staring into the darkness beyond, thinly veiled by the gauze panels of the door. Underneath the wooden porch adjoining the inner room Wolly was vomiting desperate barks. Even Grandmother, whose hearing was not very good, had already realised that the band of men had stopped in front of the twig gate of our house and was hesitating there.

"Here they are at last. Here they are," Grandmother murmured in a parched voice.

"Soonku!" Someone called Father's name from beyond the twig gate. "Soonku, are you at home?"

In the inner room Paternal Grandmother coughed short-breathed coughs. We could hear Father stirring to go out. Hearing that, Mother whispered frightenedly towards the inner room, "I'll slip out and see what's going on. You stay where you are like a dead body."

But Father was already in the hall. Putting on his shoes, Father bade us the same thing Mother had told him to do. We were ordered by Father never to stir a step from where we were. Wolly, who had been yelping frantically, suddenly ceased barking with a sharp groan. Father must have done something to him. Crossing the yard, Father spoke cautiously,

"Who is it?"

"It's me, the village head."

"Why, what brings you here in the middle of the night?"

The bell attached to the twig gate tinkled. We could hear the men exchanging a few words. Then there was silence again outside, and only the vigorous dripping of rain filled our ears. Mother, who had been standing irresolutely in the room, could stand it no longer and threw open the door. She rushed outside, and Aunt followed hurriedly. In the inner room Paternal Grandmother was retching a few short-breathed coughs. Right beside me Maternal Grandmother was shelling peas steadily, completely absorbed in the work. Running her finger through the pod, she murmured, "It won't shake me a bit. I knew we were going to have some tidings today or tomorrow. I knew from long before. I'm all prepared."

I couldn't sit still. After some inner struggle, I left Maternal Grandmother alone and stole out of the room. I could hear her parched voice even on the dirt verandah, "I'm not shaken, not I."

It was much darker outside than I had thought when inside. Each time I moved my legs, Wolly's wet, furry, smelly body hit my inner thighs. The dog kept groaning and licking my hand. The rain was thicker than I had expected when indoors. It bathed my face and soaked my hemp shirt, and made me drenched as a rat that has fallen into a water-jar. Wolly gave up following me any further and retreated, growling fearfully. The grown-ups revealed their outline only when I approached quite close to the twig gate. It looked as if whatever information had to be exchanged was exchanged. The grown-ups just stood still, in spite of the pouring rain. I could dimly see the heads of two men covered with military waterproof cloth and the familiar face of the village head who was standing facing us. Father and Aunt were supporting from either side Mother's trembling, sinking body. After a long silence the village head spoke.

"Please give your mother-in-law my sincere condolences."

Then one of the two men shrouded under the military waterproof cloth spoke. He hesitated a great deal, as if extremely reluctant to speak. His voice, therefore, sounded very shy.

"I really don't know what to say. We're just as grieved as any of his family. It was an errand we'd have been glad to be spared. Goodbye, then, sir. We'll have to go back now."

"Thank you. Be careful in the dark," Father said.

They slid through the twig gate, picking their way with their flashlights. A sob escaped from Mother. Aunt reproached Mother for it. Then Mother began to cry a little louder. Without saying a word, Father walked ahead towards the house. Also walking towards the house supporting Mother, Aunt whispered repeatedly,

"Please collect yourself. What would Mother do, if you cry like this? Try to think of Mother, Mother!"

My mother stopped her own mouth with her fist. She thus managed to control her sobs when she stepped into the room.

Father, who had reached the room before any of us, was kneeling awkwardly before Maternal Grandmother, like one guilty, and was turning something over in his hand. It was the wet piece of paper that the village head must have handed over to him. Father was dripping water like just-hung laundry. But it was not only Father. All of us who had been outside, including myself, were making puddles on the floor with water dripping from our bodies. The thin summer clothes of Mother and Aunt were pasted to their skin, and revealed their bodies inside as if they were naked.

"I told you," Maternal Grandmother murmured, again as if to herself. "See?"

I had been watching Grandmother's moves for some time now with great uneasiness. I was paying more attention now to her working hands than to her incessantly moving sunken mouth. I noticed a change in the movement of her hands. It seemed that no one except me noticed the change. Even though she was preoccupied with her work with lowered eyes, as before, after we returned to the room from outside Grandmother's two gaunt arms were trembling slightly. Moreover, she was unconsciously dropping the fresh shelled pale-green peas into her lap filled with empty pods. I was afraid she would keep on making the mistake, and repeatedly looked out for a chance to give a hint to Grandmother, but each time I tried I could not open my mouth, so heavily oppressive was the silence of the room. I could do nothing but watch her shaking, wrinkled fingertips even though I knew she would be dropping the empty pods good only for fuel into the bamboo basket that ought to collect shelled peas.

"Haven't I been telling you all along we'd have some tidings today, for sure?" Grandmother, whose hitherto pale face was momentarily flushed and looked ten years younger, murmured again. But as she broke the tip of another pod again and ran her finger through it, she instantly became ashen pale like a corpse, and aged ten years more in the self-same posture. Grandmother was in a strange state of excitement. We could feel it from the way she breathed hard between words and the way she swallowed till her entire throat trembled.

"I knew several days in advance when your father died. I suppose you resented me, thinking this old woman mutters sinister words as a pastime, having nothing to do besides eat. But what do you say now? I'd like to know what you think of my premonitions. Do they still sound to you like the stupid words of an old woman? You mustn't think that of me, you mustn't. Even though I can't see and hear as well as you, I don't go around jabbering empty words. You're greatly mistaken if you think old women have nothing to do but waste precious food and murmur empty words. To this day my dreams have never predicted wrong. Whenever there was any calamity coming, my dreams have always predicted it."

Sitting erect at full height, with her head upright, she reproached her daughters for not having acknowledged her prescience. Her face was again flushed red. What filled her bloodshot eyes as she looked at her daughters was akin to triumph. She seemed besieged with an irresistible desire to brag about the realisation of her prophesy. As I gazed at her ridiculously triumphant expression, something like a spell hit me and my maternal grandmother suddenly looked to me like a weird, dreadful being. I could not help giving credence to her assertion that she had always, like an inspired prophet, unerringly predicted the approach of a tragedy. Grandmother had gained her victory in the battle declared by herself, and

she seemed still to have abundant energy left over after the
battle to upbraid us for any imagined slight to her authority.
To me, such an aspect of Grandmother gave me a deep,
ineradicable impression, as if she had been a being of in-
scrutable, unapproachable power.

Mother was raising her sobbing voice by imperceptible
degrees. It began as thin as a thread, so that the other people
in the room hardly perceived it at first. But as no one
checked her, even when she had considerably raised her
voice, she began at last to cry at full force. A mosquito had
alighted on the nape of Aunt's bloodlessly pale neck and was
sucking blood. But Aunt did not stir, sitting there like one
out of her wits, even though the mosquito sucked until its
belly was round and pink as a cherry. The door of the room
was standing open. Even though mosquitoes swarmed in
through the open door, nobody bothered to close it.

One could clearly guess at the progress of the people
covered with military waterproof cloth by the shifting
location of the dogs' barking. Receding from the moment
the men left, the barking of the dogs diminished further and
further to the end of the village, and at last entirely died
down. A black flying insect that had come in without my
noticing it was disturbing the air of the room, flying around
quite at its liberty. At last, after zooming through the room
several times and almost putting out the lamp, it was caught
in my hand. It was a mole-cricket. It writhed between my
thumb and forefinger and tried to get loose. Thrusting out
its strong forelegs which it used to dig up earth, it tried to
break my grip. But what use were all its desperate struggles?
Its life and death were completely at my mercy. I could kill
it or let it live just as I liked. I began to put more and more
pressure into my two fingers holding the insect. Just then
I heard Grandmother murmur again.

"I'm not shaken. I knew all along this would happen.
I'm all right."

Then, Mother's sobs reached their peak, and the whole
room was filled with the painful, drawn-out lament that
seemed to gnaw into our very bones.

"Poor Jun, poor Jun, what a fool you were to volunteer
when others went into hiding to dodge conscription! Poor

Jun, poor Jun, why didn't you listen to me when I told you not to become an officer? Now, what are we to do? What are we to do?" Her voice prolonged the words and trailed off into moans whenever the name of the dead man was pronounced.

The crimson-coloured sobs of Mother, which filled the room in no time, soon spread into the yard steeped in the dark, and on the blanket of her sobs piled, layer upon layer, the shrieking rain of the long rainy season.

2

Gunjissan Mountain, which stood erect, piercing the sky with the tip of its peak, surrounded by a host of lesser mountains and hills, always looked dignified. There was a time, however, when this dignified Gunjisan Mountain took on a ridiculous aspect. For a time Gunjisan became a place where grown-ups gathered at night to play with fire. Sometimes we could see mist rising from the top of the mountain even in broad daylight. What an enormous amount of water must have been made on it by the grown-ups at night! Having experienced the bitter humiliation of making the round of the village wearing a rice winnowing basket over my head as punishment for bed-wetting, I could not help looking at the running brook in the village that started from the mountain with suspicious eyes. The rustic, taciturn and dignified mountain looked absurd, suddenly sending up smoke and fire. For grown-ups' play, it was childish and silly, but peaceful and tranquil. I had not then realised the relationship between the signal fire and the massacres. I could not have understood why, time after time, immediately after flames rose up from the mountain, there was a street battle in town and one of the villages was laid waste. But even had I understood such points, the result would have been the same. In spite of my ridiculous imaginings when first beholding the signal fire, Gunjisan Mountain shortly regained its dignified repose in my eyes and came to be even more dear to me.

One day, waking up I found that thick black clouds had coiled around the mountain from the waist up. The rain had halted, but anyone could see from the dark cloud completely covering the eastern sky around Gunjisan that a bigger batch of rain than any we'd had yet was making preparations for an assault. From time to time, from the dark corner of the sky, lightning darted out and pierced Gunjisan as sharply as the bamboo lance that I once saw being thrust into a man's chest on the village road beside the dike. And each time, thunder shook heaven and earth, like a scream sent out by the pierced mountain. I could very well imagine what the pain of being impaled by darting lightning must be like, and did not at all think the mountain cowardly for sending out such a miserable scream. It was clear that Gunjisan was being tortured by the sky from early morning.

I could tell Maternal Grandmother's approach even with my eyes closed. When she walked, there was no sound of footsteps but only the rustle of her skirt, so lightly and carefully did she walk, like a weightless person. Having approached so carefully, she emitted a strange smell. It was a very strange smell, such as one can sniff in the corners of an old, old chest, or an antique, or a deep pond of stagnant water. I vaguely felt the careful approach of my grandmother, who could be distinguished by a smell like that of ancient dust and the rustle of her skirt.

I was lying in the side room, pretending to be asleep. From the time I began to regard my grandmother as an awesome being, I had got into the habit of pretending to be asleep when she came near. Grandmother seemed to be taking twice her usual care so as not to awake her grandson from his nap. But I had already smelt my distasteful fill of that peculiar smell, and had already guessed what she was going to do. And I was not wrong, either. Maternal Grandmother's gaunt hand fumbled into my underpants. "Now, let me feel my jewel," Grandmother would have said at other times. She would also have said, "This one's round as an apple, just like his maternal uncle's." But today, Grandmother did not say a word. She only silently moved her fingers, and felt my groin. This nameless act, which began from the time Mother's family came to live with us as refugees, was a big trial for me, and a very insulting experience. I'd dare anybody to claim I'm not telling the truth when I say I have never admitted my maternal grandmother's encroaching hand into my underpants without great displeasure. I don't know whether there may be any seven-year-old who would willingly consent to be treated like a baby; for my part, as I had great pride in myself as a big boy with as sound a judgment as any grown-up, such an act by Grandmother was a severe blow to my self esteem. But there was no shaking her off, as I knew such a refusal would grieve her deeply, and there was nothing I could do but endure the insult.

Grandmother's hand left my groin with a deep sigh. I could feel her gaze lingering on my face for a long time after her hand left my body.

"Poor thing!"

Leaving the two muttered words behind, she left my side. I opened my eyes a slit and peeped at Grandmother's back as she receded noiselessly, trailing her wrinkled cotton skirt. I don't know whom she may have meant in her lamentation just now. There were too many poor things around me. There was, of course, my maternal uncle who had just been killed in battle at the front. And, to speak the truth, I myself was also very much of a poor thing in those days. Since the incident of having accepted the bribe of a western sweet from a police detective, I had been cooped up inside the house for over a month now in penance, anxiously watching the moods of my father, who held command of housebound penance, and of Paternal Grandmother, in whose hand and in whose hand alone rested the power of forgiveness. But maybe the poorest thing of all was Maternal Grandmother herself. Maternal Grandmother, as she sat on the edge of the living-room floor, looked completely worn out. There was not a trace of the stubborn, awesome being glimpsed on the night we received the notification from the front. There simply sat a shabby, withered old woman gazing vacantly at the distant mountain. My joy at being freed of her unwelcome hand sank back to gloom at the sight of her pitiful figure.

For a few days after we learned of the death of my maternal uncle, the house was in a complete mess. Everyone was in grief, but my mother's grief was the most uncontrolled.

Mother had her forehead tied with a white cloth strip like we children did on school sports-days, and was quite bedridden with grief. She sat up from time to time to cry for a while, striking the floor with her palm amid loud lamentations, and then collapsed back on the bedding. At mealtimes, however, she sat up to eat hurriedly the bowl of barley Aunt brought in to her, and as soon as she finished eating she cried out with loud lamentations, thrusting away the meal tray, and sank back again on her bedding. Lying on her back, she would repeatedly mutter that her family ought to adopt a son and so continue the line.

Aunt's behaviour was in sharp contrast to Mother's. From first to last, she did not show a drop of tears, nor did she exchange a word with anybody, nor did she eat a thing. Moreover, she silently took over all of Mother's work, and cooked, washed dishes, and did the laundry. Until I saw her flop backwards on the third day while trying to lift up a water pail beside the well in the backyard, I had been thinking that Aunt must surely be eating something secretly inside the bamboo grove behind the house or in the dark kitchen. I had made myself easy on that point, thinking that Aunt, who had unbelievably strong will-power and sometimes completely confounded our expectations, would surely not go three days without eating a morsel.

But Mother and Aunt were not our greatest worry. What made us most uneasy was the discord between my paternal and maternal grandmothers. When my mother's family, which had moved to Seoul to give my uncle and aunt the benefit of education in the capital, suddenly appeared before us one day as refugees carrying bundles, it was my paternal grandmother who welcomed the family warmly and emptied the guest room for them to move in. We often heard my paternal grandmother express to her in-law counterpart her wish that the two old women could be each other's companion and support in the harsh times; and in fact the two old ladies got along perfectly well, without even a single discord, until that unfortunate day. They got along well even after the Republic's army recovered dominion over the South and my paternal uncle, who had till then been going around flourishing his arm-band as an officer of the People's Army, fled with the retreating communist forces, and my maternal uncle, who had till then kept in hiding in a dug-out cave in the bamboo grove, joined the Republic's Army, and thus made each victory or defeat in the war a matter of conflicting emotion to the two old ladies.

The discord between the two old ladies began with that incident of my accepting the gift of a western sweet from a stranger, and thus earning the fury of Paternal Grandmother, who branded me a butcher of men who sold his uncle for a sweet, and therefore one not worthy to be treated as a human being. Maternal Grandmother earned the displeasure of her counterpart by protecting and defending me. The decisive rupture between the two grandmothers came on the day after we received the death notice of my maternal uncle. It was my maternal grandmother who made the provocation. On that afternoon also the weather was sinister, and forked lightning darted out of the clouds, repeatedly impaling the crown of Gunjisan Mountain. Maternal Grandmother, who had been watching the sky, standing on the edge of the living-room floor, suddenly began to utter dreadful curses.

"Pour on! Pour on! Pour on and sweep clean away all the red particles hiding between the rocks! Strike on, and burn to soot all the red particles clinging to trees! Pour on, strike on! That's right! Thank you, God!"

All the family rushed into the living-room, but everyone was so stupefied that no one could say a word to check Grandmother's torrential curses. She continued to pour out vehement curses towards Gunjisan Mountain, which was said to be teeming with communist partisans, as if she could distinctly visualise red partisans being struck dead one after another by lightning.

"Has that old hag gone stark mad, or turned into a devil?"

The door of the inner room opened with a clatter and out came Paternal Grandmother, face distorted with fury. I realised belatedly that there was a person in the house who could be Maternal Grandmother's match, and became tense.

"Whose house does she think this is, that she dares put on such horseplay?"

Maternal Grandmother looked around with vague eyes, like one awakened from sleepwalking by a violent shake.

"This is too good a spectacle for only a family audience, isn't it? I've heard of grace repaid with poison, and I'm seeing a case today. Fine coquetry this is, to one who gave you shelter from the bombs! If you mean to go crazy, do so at least with a clean conscience. If you harbour such base ingratitude, lightning will fall on you!"

After thus subduing the other with imperious reproof, Paternal Grandmother continued her serious upbraiding.

"Do you think your curses will bring your dead son back and kill living people? Don't you imagine such a thing! Life and death are meted out by Heaven, and Heaven only. One lives as long as one's allotted to live by Heaven. And it is because of one's own sins that one has a child die before oneself. It's because of sins in an earlier life that a parent has to see a child die and endure the sorrow. It's your own fate that your son died. There's nobody to blame for it. You ought to know shame by now. Aren't you in your sixties?"

"All right. Granted it's because of my sins[1] that I lost my son. It is because you're a blessed woman that you reared a son like that?"

"Listen to that! Hasn't she really gone raving mad? What do you mean, 'a son like that'? What's wrong with my son?"

"Think. You'll know if you're not a fool."

"Because you have no son left to offer you sacrifice after your death, you wish the same for everyone!"

"Stop it, both of you!" Father shouted.

"Wait and see. My Soonchul isn't such a fool! You might not rest content until something happens to him, but Soonchul can slip through showers without getting wet!"

"Stop it, please!" Father shouted again.

Mother had been pinching Maternal Grandmother's thigh

1. This is not to be taken as the maternal grandmother's admission of having committed sins needing expiation. It is rather an announcement of her resolution to accept her suffering and sorrow in resignation. According to Buddhist theory of metempsychosis, one pays for one's sins in an after-existence, and thus there is no escaping the consequences of one's acts. This theory is often used by Koreans to "justify", and to reconcile themselves to, their unmerited sufferings for which there can be no explanation in terms of universal justice of reward and punishment.

all along.

"Did you hear what your mother-in-law said? She, who's an in-law relation, after all, calls me a woman without a son to offer sacrifices after her death. Isn't it misfortune enough to have given up an only son for the country, without being despised by an in-law? What mad words can a woman not utter, a woman who's lost a son? Does she have to reproach me thus for foolish words uttered in madness of grief, and flaunt before me her possession of many sons? Answer me, if you have a mouth that can speak!"

Maternal Grandmother appealed to Mother, and Mother, with a tearful face, kept winking a pleading eye at Maternal Grandmother and pinching her leg. Paternal Grandmother, for her part, appealed to Father.

"Be careful how you judge, son! Is it wrong of me to rebuke an old woman who's praying for your brother's death? Must you, too, blame me? She may be your mother-in-law, but she's an enemy to me, and I can't live with her under the same roof! If you don't throw her out at once, I'm going to leave this house!"

"All right! I'm leaving! I spurn to live in this house any more! I'd rather die in the streets than stay a minute longer in a communist's hou. . ."

Maternal Grandmother's hoarse voice stopped dead. She slowly turned her head and vacantly gazed at my father. Finishing the word "house" weakly and at length, she looked this time at Mother. Lastly, she gazed at me intently for quite a while, and shook her head left and right. Then she suddenly dropped her head. Her downward-bent gaze sank heavily towards a bamboo basket. Silently pulling the bamboo basket toward her knee, she picked up a pea-pod with a motion as silent as if she had been a shadow. Maternal Grandmother's face was ashen grey like a corpse's, and so remained from then on.

The turmoil created by Maternal Grandmother's words shook the whole house. When the word "communist" came out of Maternal Grandmother's mouth, all the family members doubted their ears, and stood still in stupefaction. They could hardly breathe, and could only watch the slowly-moving hands of Maternal Grandmother. "Communist" was a forbidden word among us, ever since we became a marked house in the village, watched by the police on account of my paternal uncle. This taboo was as strictly observed as the taboo against pickled shrimp juice during scrofula. Oh, to trespass such a solemn taboo! Maternal Grandmother's mistake was a fatal one, not to be pardoned by any apology, and the amazement of the family members was beyond description. But the one most amazed by the utterance was none other than the one who uttered it. Maternal Grandmother did not offer any apologies. It was partly because all apologies were useless, but more because she tried to expiate her transgression by silently enduring all the censure of her in-law counterpart. No words can describe the fury of my paternal grandmother. She jumped up and down madly, foamed at the mouth, and almost fainted away. Then she tried to wrest an assurance from Father that he would expel Maternal Grandmother and Aunt from the house, or even Mother if she seemed sympathetic to them.

"You must drive them out this very day. And be sure to open their baggage before they step out of the gate. My silver hair-slide is missing, and it's not hard to guess who took it."

Aunt silently walked away to the guest room. After pouring out her fill of abuses, Paternal Grandmother lay down from exhaustion. The silence that ensued was soon shattered by the outburst of Mother's weeping. Instantly, Father's command fell like thunder.

"Shut up!"

Silence was a more unbearable torture than noisy unrest. Father strode out of the house. Maternal Grandmother remained on the living-room floor deep into the night, shelling peas with her gaunt, shaky hands. Father came back home only at dawn, dead drunk, reeking of sour alcohol.

Incandescent sparks of lightning kept piercing the crown of Gunjisan Mountain, thickly enfolded in black clouds. The signal fire which rose up almost every night from the mountain could not be seen any more since the rainy season began. Maternal Grandmother, who turned her eyes from time to time towards the mountain, looked pitifully lonely as she sat on the edge of the living-room floor. Maternal Grandmother said not a word today, even though lightning struck today just as on that other day. Ever since that unhappy quarrel with her in-law, Maternal Grandmother hardly opened her mouth at any time. She kept moving her hands incessantly, the bamboo basket at her knee, as if shelling peas were the one and only task left for her in the world till her dying day.

3

A boy who had lately come to live in our village as a refugee from the north came to where we were playing, accompanied by a man wearing a straw hat. The boy, whose face was all scabby, said a few words to the man, pointing at me with his hand that had been scratching his bare, dirt-stained belly. The man gave me an attentive stare from beneath the wide brim of the straw hat which was shading a good part of his face. The boy from the north took what the strange man gave him from out of his pocket and galloped away like a fleeing hare. The tall man with the straw hat walked up to me directly. His dark, tanned skin, his sharp, penetrating eyes, and his unhesitating stride were somehow overpowering to me.

"What a fine boy!"

The stranger's eyes seemed to narrow and, surprisingly, unlike what I expected from my first impression, a friendly smile filled his face. The man stroked my head a few times.

"You'd be a really lovely boy if you answered my questions straight."

The man's attitude made me extremely uneasy. I could not look into his eyes, so I opened and closed my hands for no reason, and kept standing there with my head lowered. In my palm was my paternal grandmother's silver hair-slide, which I had rubbed against a stone mortar into a giant nail, and which earned me victory over all the neighbourhood boys in nail fights.

"Your father's name is Kim Soon-ku, isn't it?"

The man unbuttoned his white tieless shirt.

"Then Kim Soon-chul must be your uncle, isn't he?"

The man took off his straw hat. I had not said a word till

then. But the man went on ingratiatingly. "That's right. You answer just like the clever boy you a re!"

The man shook his straw hat as if it were a fan, holding open his tieless shirt to ventilate his body.

"I'm your uncle's friend. We're very close friends, but it's been a long time since we met last. I have something very important to discuss with your uncle. Will you tell me where he is?"

The man, whom I had met for the first time in my life, used the standard Seoul dialect meticulously, like Aunt.

"Oh, isn't it hot! It's very hot in here. Shall we go over there where it's breezy and talk a little?"

He forbade the other children to follow. When we reached the shade of a tree on the hill behind the village where other children couldn't see us, the man halted and fumbled in his pocket.

"I've got a very important message to convey to your uncle. If you tell me where he is, I'll give you these," the man said, holding out in his palm five flat pieces of something wrapped in silver paper. He unwrapped one of them and proffered it in front of my nose.

"Have you ever tasted anything like this?"

The dark-brown-coloured thing gave off a delicious fragrance.

"These are chocolates. I'll give you all of them if only you answer my question straight."

I took a great deal of care not to let my eyes rest on the strange treat. But I could not suppress my swallowing.

"There's nothing to be shy about. It's natural for good boys to get rewards. Now, won't you tell me? If only you tell me what I've asked you, I'll be happy because I'll meet my friend, and you'll be happy because you'll eat these delicious chocolates."

I don't know what it was that made me hesitate. Was it because I was undecided about the ethical propriety of accepting such a gift? Or was it because of the shyness of a country boy in front of a stranger, a shyness common to most country boys my age? I don't remember distinctly. But I think I remained standing there unresponsively for quite a while.

"Don't you want them?" the man pressed me. "You're sure you don't want them?" The man made an expression of regret. "Well then, there's no helping it. I did very much want to find you acting like a good boy and give you these delicious things. I myself don't need these sweets. Here, look. I'll just have to throw them away, even though that's not what I want to do with them."

Unbelievably, the man really threw one of them on the ground carelessly. He not only threw it down but stepped on it and crushed it. Casting a glance at me, he threw one more on the ground.

"I thought you were a bright boy. I'm really sorry."

He crushed the third one under his foot. There were only two pieces of the sweet remaining on his palm. It was evident that he was quite capable of crushing the remaining two into the ground. The man suddenly chuckled loudly.

"You're crying? Poor boy! Hey, lad, it's not too late now. Think carefully. Hasn't your uncle been to the house? When was it?"

It was at that moment that I felt I was powerless to fend off sophisticated grown-ups' tactics. Then, as I thought that this man might really be a friend of my uncle, my heart felt a good deal lighter.

The first few words were the most difficult to utter. Once I began, however, I related what had happened as smoothly as reeling yarn off a spool.

My paternal aunt who lived some eight miles off came to visit us, walking the entire distance under the broiling July sun. There was no reason for me to attach any special meaning to Aunt's visit, as she had several times come to our house without announcement to stay for a day or two even in those days of unrest. But things began to look very different when Mother, who had gone into the inner room with Aunt, sprang out of the room with a yellow complexion. Instead of sending me, as was usual, she ran out herself to fetch Father. Father, who had been weeding in the rice paddies, ran directly into the inner room with his muddy clothes and feet, without stopping to wash himself at the well. Mother, who returned hard upon his heels, fastened the twig gate shut even though it was broad daylight. Everybody seemed slightly out of their right senses. In the inner room the whole family, except my Maternal Grandmother and Maternal Aunt and me, was gathered and seemed to be discussing something momentous. Around sunset, the three of us who had been left out were given a bowl of cold rice each. As I finished my meal, I saw Father had changed into clean clothes. I looked suspiciously at Father's back as he stepped out of the twig gate into the alley paved with darkness.

"You go to sleep early," Mother told me, as she spread my mattress right beside where Paternal Grandmother was sitting. It seemed that everyone was bent on pushing me into sleep, even though it was still early in the night.

"Wouldn't it be better to have him sleep in the other room?" Paternal Aunt queried of Mother, pointing her chin at me.

"I think it'll be all right," Paternal Grandmother said, "He sleeps deeply once he falls asleep."

"You must be dead tired from playing all day long. You must sleep like the dead until tomorrow morning, and not open your eyes a bit all through the night. You understand?" Mother instructed me.

I knew that Father had not gone out for a friendly visit. It was obvious that he went out on important business. I wanted to stay wide awake until Father returned. I was determined to find out what that important business of grown-ups was that I was excluded from. To that end, it was necessary to pretend to obey the grown-ups' orders to go to sleep at once. I listened attentively for the least sound in the room, fighting back the sleep that overwhelmed me as soon as I lay down and closed my eyes. But no one said anything of any significance. And, before the important event of Father's arrival, I had fallen fast asleep.

I was awakened by a dull thud on the floor of the room.

"My God! Isn't that a bomb?"

I heard Paternal Grandmother's frightened voice. The two bulks that were blocking my sight were the seated figures of Father and Mother. Dull lamplight seeped dimly through the opening between the two large bulks.

"Undo your waistband, too," Father said to someone imperiously. The person seemed to hesitate a little, but there came a rustle from beyond Father's bulk.

"*Two* pistols!"

"My God!" Mother and Grandmother softly exclaimed simultaneously. Sleep had completely deserted me, and a chill slid down my spine like a snake. Even though I knew nobody was paying any attention to me, I realised it was unsafe to let grown-ups notice my wakefulness, and so I had to take painstaking care in moving my glance inch by inch. I concentrated all my nerves on what was happening in the small space visible to me.

"Has Dongman gone to sleep without knowing I'm coming?"

As it seemed that Father was about to turn to me, I closed my eyes quickly. The shadow that had been shielding my face moved aside quickly, and lamplight pricked my eyelids.

"We kept him in the dark," Mother said proudly, as if that had been some meritorious deed.

"Don't worry. Once he falls asleep, a team of horses couldn't kick him awake," Grandmother assisted.

There was a short silence in the room. It seemed that nobody dared open his mouth. But my ears were brimming with the thick voice of the man who had sneaked into the house in the dark, carrying pistols and hand grenades. If that man is really my uncle, I thought, news of whom the whole family had been fretting about, his voice had, regrettably, become so rough as to be unrecognisable to me at first. His voice didn't use to be as rough as a clay pot that has been carelessly handled on pebbles, or so heavily gloomy that nothing seemed capable of cheering it up. As far as I can remember, my uncle chuckled heartily at the slightest joke, frown as his elders might on such manners, rarely remaining aloof from disputes, but always trying to involve many people in them. He was easily excited or moved. But, no matter how I reckoned, there was no one but my uncle who could be the owner of that voice I had just heard. I imagined my uncle's face and form, which must have become as rough as the voice. Then, suddenly, I felt an uncontrollable itch in the hollows of my knees. The itch spread instantly over my

entire body, as if I had been lying on ant-infested grass, and
I had an uncontrollable yearning to scratch such parts as the
middle of my back or my armpits or between my toes, places
I could not reach with my hand to scratch while lying flat
on my back without being noticed by the grown-ups. On top
of it, my throat itched with an imminent cough, and my
mouth filled with water.

Grandmother seemed most anxious to know what Uncle's
life on the mountain was like. She heaped question upon
question about how he fared on the mountain. To all the
questions Uncle answered barely a word or two, and seemed
irked by the necessity of saying even that much. But Grandmother seemed not to have noticed Uncle's mood, and kept
on asking questions without end.

"You say there are many others besides you, but they
must all be men. Who cooks rice and soup at each mealtime?"

"We do."

"You make preserves and season vegetables, too?"

"Yes."

"How on earth! If only I could be there beside you I'd
prepare your food with proper seasoning!"

No response.

"Do they taste all right?"

"Yes."

"I know they couldn't, but I can't help asking all the
same."

"They're all right."

"Don't you skip meals too often, because you move here
and there?"

"No."

"Promise me you won't eat raw rice, however hungry you
may get. You'd get diarrhoea. If you do, what could you do
in the depths of the mountain? You can't call a doctor or
concoct medicine. Do pay attention, won't you?"

"Don't worry."

"And since it's in the depths of the mountain, it must be
cold as January at night, even in summer like this. Do each
of you have a quilt to cover your middle at night?"

"Of course."

"Padded with cotton wool?"

No response.

"Don't stay in the cold too long. And, for frostbite, egg-plant stems are the best remedy. You boil the stems and soak your hands and feet in the fluid. That takes out the frostbite at once. If I was beside you. . ."

"Please don't worry!"

"How can I help it? It tears my heart to see your frost-bitten hands and feet. The times are rough, but for you, my darling last-born, to get so frostbitten!"

"Please, mother, stop!" Uncle sighed with impatience.

"Do, Mother, that's enough," Father chimed in cautiously.

"Do you mean I shouldn't worry, even though my son's hands are frostbitten like that?" Grandmother raised her voice angrily. Such things were to her of the utmost import-ance. But Father also raised his voice.

"It's going to be daybreak soon, and you keep wasting time with idle questions! How can you worry about pre-serves and quilts when his life's at stake?"

Grandmother was silenced. Of course she had many more questions, but a certain tone in Father's rebuke silenced her, stubborn as she was.

"What are you going to do from now on?" Father asked, after a pregnant silence. It was directed at Uncle.

"About what?"

"Are you going to go back to the mountain and stay there?"

When Uncle kept silent, Father asked him if he would consider giving himself up to the police. Father slowly began his persuasion, as if it was something he had carefully con-sidered for a long time. Father emphasised again and again the misery of a hunted existence. Citing as an example a certain young man who had delivered himself up to the police and was now living quietly on his own farm, Father recommended urgently that Uncle do the same. He repeated again and again that otherwise Uncle would die a dog's death. A dog's death, a dog's death, a dog's death, a dog's death.

"Why do you keep saying it's a dog's death?" Uncle retorted sullenly. Uncle swore that before long the People's Army would win back the South. Vowing that he had only to remain alive until that day, he even recommended that

Father should so conduct himself as not to get hurt when the government changed. Listening to his talk, I was struck once again by the great change in my uncle. His talk was fluent. In the old days, my uncle never used to be able to talk so logically. Because he had difficulty getting his points across by logical argument, he often used to resort to the aid of his fists in his sanguine impatience.

Uncle began to collect things, saying that he must go up the mountain before sunrise. It must have been his pistols and hand grenades that he gathered up. Everybody moved at once.

"I won't let you go, never, now that you're in my house!"

I opened my eyes at last. In that sudden turmoil, nobody paid any attention to me slowly raising my body and sitting up. Uncle's face was covered all over with a bushy beard. Father and Aunt were on either side almost hugging Uncle, who was sitting leaning against the wall on the warmer part of the floor. Grandmother snatched Uncle's arm from Aunt and, shaking it to and fro, entreated,

"Because your brother told me lies I thought you were staying comfortably somewhere. I thought you spent your days sitting on a chair in a town office somewhere doing things like giving hell to harsh constables. But now that I know the truth I won't let you go back to such a dreadful place! I'd die first rather than let you go!"

Grandmother wept, stroking Uncle's cheek with her palm.

"I'd let you go if I could go with you and look after you day and night, but since it seems I can't, I'll tie you down in this room and not let you out of my sight day or night. Why can't you stay at home, farm the land, get married and let me hold your children before I die?"

Aunt opened her lips for the first time in my hearing that night and talked to Uncle about the joys of married life, and Mother supported Aunt with timely assent. Father talked again persuasively. He explained minutely what the drift of the war was, and tried to make Uncle realise that he was being deceived by the empty promises of the communists. He said further that as he knew a couple of people in the police there would be ways to get Uncle released without suffering bodily hurt. But Uncle at long last opened his mouth only to say, "Are you, too, trying to trick me into it?" and shook off Father's hand.

"What do you mean, trick you?"

"I've heard all about it." Uncle said that the police slaughtered all the people who went down the mountain to surrender, decoyed by promises of pardon in printed hand-bills. Uncle said that promises of unconditional pardon and freedom were screaming lies and tricks.

"And you, too, are trying to push me into the trap?"

"What?" Father's arm shot up in the air. The next moment there was the sound of a sharp slap on Uncle's cheek. Father panted furiously and glared at Uncle, as if he would have liked to tear him apart.

"How dare you strike my poor boy!" Grandmother wept aloud, covering Uncle with her body. Father drew the tobacco box near. His hands shook as he rolled up the green tobacco. Uncle dropped his head.

A cock crowed. At the sound Uncle lifted his head in fright and looked around at the members of the family. The short summer's night was about to end.

"I've killed people," he murmured huskily, like one who had just set down a heavy load he had carried a long, long way. "Many, many people."

Thus began Uncle's wavering toward self-surrender. It was a long persuasion that Father carried out that night, and the patience he showed for it was truly remarkable. At last every-thing was settled as Father had planned, and it was agreed that Uncle was to remain in hiding for a couple of days until Father obtained assurance from the police for Uncle's safety. Uncle was to go into the dug-out cave in the bamboo grove that Maternal Uncle had used for hiding under communist occupation.

Everything was settled, and all that remained to be done was for everybody to snatch a wink of sleep before it was broad daylight. But that instant Uncle, who was about to pull off his shirt, suddenly bent forward and pressed his ear to the floor. Grandmother almost jumped from fright.

"What is it?"

"Ssh!"

Uncle put his forefinger on his lips and eyed the door of

the room. Everybody's face stiffened, and all listened
attentively for noise from outside.

"Someone's there."

My ears caught no sound. There were distant chirps of
grass insects, but I could hear nothing like a human sound.
But Uncle had his ear still glued to the floor and didn't seem
likely to straighten up. I heard for a while only the loud
pounding of my heart in that suffocating tension, but I caught
a certain sound that Uncle must have spoken of. That sound,
which distinctly was not the sound of a heart pounding, was
footsteps treading ground with long intervals in between.
They were so soft and careful that it was hard to tell whether
they were approaching or receding.

"Who's that outside?"

Father's voice was low, but the reprimand was severe.
Then the sound of movement stopped altogether. Suddenly
it occurred to me that it was a familiar tread, of someone
I know very well. I quickly ransacked my brain, trying to
work out who it might be. The footsteps began again. They
seemed to be moving a little faster this time. Uncle's body
shot up erect. Within the blinking of an eye the dark bulk
jumped over my seated form. The back door fell to the
ground with a shattering sound, and Uncle's big bulk rushed
away in the dark. He had already crossed the bamboo grove.
His motion was so swift that nobody had had a second to
say a word.

I came out through the frame of the back door that Uncle
had knocked to the ground. I ran past the kitchen into the
inner yard. I wasn't at all afraid, even though I was alone.
I surveyed everything within the twig fence from the yard
and the kitchen garden down to the gates, but I could see
nothing. When my eyes fell on the unlighted guest room,
however, I caught the half-opened door of that room closing
noiselessly, shutting out the dim, whitish glare of the morning. I savoured the discovery with rapture. It was indeed a
familiar tread, of one I knew very well.

"I'd have packed things for him to take if I'd known it
would come to this! I didn't feed him a morsel, nor give
him one clean garment! If only I'd known! How could I have
not fed him one bowl of warm rice! If only I'd known!"

Paternal Grandmother wailed, beating her chest. Paternal Aunt grasped my hand tightly and pulled me to one corner. Then she poured her hot breath into my ear.

"You mustn't tell anyone your uncle's been home. Do you understand? If you talk about such things to anybody all of us must go to jail. Do you hear? Do you hear?

Village people were surrounding my house, standing in multiple ranks in front of the gate. They were whispering things to each other and trying to look over the gate into the house. The wailing of women that I could hear from as far as the hill behind the village I now found to be coming from my house. As I approached all eyes turned on me. Villagers exchanged meaningful glances among themselves pointing their chins at me, and whispered again. The palisade of people suddenly parted in two, as if to make way. A strange man walked out ahead, and my father followed. One step behind him I could see the man with the straw hat. He was holding coiled around his hand the rope that bound both my father's hands behind his back. On seeing me, he grinned and winked. Father halted in front of me. His eyes seemed yearning to say something to me, but he silently resumed walking. At the gate Mother, Paternal Aunt and Paternal Grandmother were wailing and crying, repeatedly collapsing and sinking to the ground. Only then did pain begin to rise in me. During the entire day while I was ransacking the village in search of the boy from the north who had conducted the man with the straw hat to me, the pain assailed me sometimes with a sense of betrayal, or a terrible fury, or an unbearable sorrow that stung my eyes and stabbed my heart. The man with the straw hat had promised me on his oath that he would never tell anybody what I would tell him. It was the first mortal treachery I experienced at the hands of a grown-up.

From that night Maternal Grandmother became my sole protectress and friend. Between us there was the shared secret of sinners. It could have been that secret which gave the two of us the strength to support each other through many persecutions. My Paternal Grandmother was a woman of very strong temper. If she so much as caught sight of me, she started back as if she had stepped on a snake, and she refused not only to talk to me but even to let me have my meals in the inner room with the family.

Father returned home after spending seven full days at the police station. My mother, who made frequent trips to town to send in Father's food, sprinkled salt again and again on his head, sniffing and sobbing, as he stepped into the gate. Father's good-looking face had changed a great deal in those seven days. His eyes were sunken, his cheekbones stood out, and his face, which had become pale-bluish like newly bleached cotton, looked indescribably shabby. But what hurt me most of all was the look of pain that appeared on Father's face whenever he moved his right leg with a limping lurch. On the night of his return home, he ate no less than three cakes of raw bean curd which, along with the sprinkling of salt, was believed to be a good preventive against a second trip to the police station. Father had always been of taciturn disposition, but he uttered not a single word that day. From time to time he gazed vacantly at my face and seemed about to say something, but each time he withdrew his gaze silently. I was fully resolved never to run away should Father decide to give me a flogging, even if I were to die under his switch. And there, within his easy reach, were the wooden pillow and the lamp-pole. I felt I could not withdraw from Father's sight without receiving my due punishment. I waited, solemnly kneeling before him. But Father uttered not a word about what had passed. Only he did not forget to lay this command on me before lying down to sleep,

"Dongman, if you ever so much as step an inch out of the gate from tomorrow I'll break your legs."

Ah, how happily I'd have closed my eyes for good, if Father had wielded his switch like mad that night, leaving these as my last words, "Father, I deserve to die."

4

The rainy front stayed on. The sky sometimes feigned benevolence by suspending the rain for a morning or an afternoon, but its frown did not relax at all; rather, the pressure of the iron-grey clouds increased, and malicious showers poured down fitfully, as if suddenly remembering. Everything between the earth and the sky was so saturated with wetness that if you pressed a fingertip on any wall or floor, water seeped out in response. All the world was a puddle and a slough. Because of the rain-soaked earth, the well water was no better than slops, and you could not drink a single drop of it without boiling it for a long time.

Even amid such persistent rain there was an attack by communist partisans under cover of night. Though there was a good five miles' distance between our village and the town, we could distinctly hear the noise of bullets like corn popping. Father, who had been up on the hill behind the village in spite of the rain, said that he could see a scarlet flame shooting up in the night sky even from that distance. The detailed news of the surprise attack spread through the village in less than a day.

One villager, who had been to town to ascertain the safety of his brother's family, came by to see Father with our neighbour, Jinku's father, to give important advice. As soon as he sat down on the edge of the living-room floor, he gave a vociferous report of his survey in the town, not knowing that Paternal Grandmother was listening in the inner room beyond a paper-panelled door. He said that houses in the vicinity of the police station had suffered much damage, and that the red partisans who made the attack had been severely beaten. According to him, only a handful of partisans made the retreat to the mountains alive. What was most shocking in his report was his description of the corpses of partisans that he said lay scattered throughout town. He described in vivid detail the hideous shapes of the corpses covered by straw mats. For example, he described a corpse whose limbs were all torn apart. He also said that one corpse had sixteen or seventeen bullet holes. The incident that attracted my interest was a corpse that the man said was thrown in the ditch folded quite double, with the back inside. I was greatly surprised that a man's body could be folded double, like a pocketknife, with the back inside. I couldn't believe that was possible. Lastly, he transmitted the news that the corpses were on display in the backyard of the police station, to be

given to relatives or friends upon request. That was the point
of his visit to Father. He recommended by hints that therefore Father had better pay a prompt visit to the town police
station. Jinku's father, who came with him, urged the same.
Throughout their visit, Father had been wearing an expression of despair, and he showed great reluctance at the recom-
mendation of the two men. But when the village head, who
was Father's childhood friend, came by later and offered to
accompany him to town, he resolved to do so at last.

Paternal Grandmother did not try at all to hide her contempt of Father for leaving for town in the rain, donning an
oil-paper hat cover over his bamboo rain-hat. Paternal Grandmother had from the first opposed Father's trip to town. It
was her conviction that the trip was entirely unnecessary.
She even got furiously angry at her son, who still would not
give credence to the decree of Heaven. What Grandmother
maintained was simply this: whatever had happened in the
town had nothing to do with Uncle; it was the providence of
Heaven that Uncle would escape unharmed, no matter what
danger he may have run into; Heaven had already appointed
the date and even the hour that Uncle was to appear before
Grandmother alive and entirely sound. Thus it was utter
nonsense that Father should make the long trip to town to
wade through corpses in search of such a brother. Grandmother, if no one else, had complete faith in this. Well, she
not only had complete faith, but she had made detailed
preparations against the happy event, and was waiting with
outstretched neck. There was a reason for Grandmother's
conviction. Grandmother's days, since the unfortunate flight
of her younger son, had been a time of unbearable agony.
She couldn't sleep, she couldn't eat, and she fretted all day
long, waiting for news of her son. Then one day my paternal
aunt, who had come to pay a visit, suggested that she consult
a fortune-teller in the village next to hers. Thus, Grandmother made the trip to the fortune-teller, reputed to have
divine prescience, carrying a weighty bundle of rice on her
head as fee. Late in the evening, Grandmother returned home
with a beaming face and summoned all the family to give
highest praise to the blind man's foresight and to relate his
oracle. Well, the ardently-awaited day, the day that was fated

to bring our uncle home at a certain hour, was only a few days ahead of us now.

Father and the head of the village came back from town empty-handed. That Father's trip had been in vain as good as meant to us that Uncle would be returning alive. But it was strange that Father remained as taciturn as ever. There could be seen on Father's face two very different strands of emotion woven together. His face wore in rapid and irregular succession a look of relief, or a look of bleak despair. It seemed that Father, even if he could regard the absence of Uncle's corpse in the police station yard as meaning that Uncle was still alive, could not rest easy when he thought of the hardships and danger Uncle would have to endure in the future. But Grandmother was vexed by no such considerations. She became triumphant at once, and almost yelled that it was just as she had told us from the first, and that her son Soonchul was not an ordinary human being. Then she fell to weeping aloud and, rubbing her palms together heatedly in fervent prayer, with her old worn-out face all muddled by continuously gushing tears, she made full, deep bows in all directions, in token of her gratitude to Heaven and Earth, to Buddha and the mountain spirits, ancestors and household gods. She looked like one gone mad, but her innocent faith and boundless maternal love moved the hearts of all of us. We all decided to believe. How could we have calmed her down without believing what she believed? It ended by every member of the family repeatedly reciting, solemnly and religiously, the date and the hour that my immortan uncle was destined to return to us, in repeated confirmation of our conviction. It was only after we realised that daybreak had stolen up to just outside the room that we went ot bed, to have a preview of our happiness of that day in dreams. It was a long, long day that we lived that day.

Lying on my back in the guest room occupied by my maternal grandmother, I was dimly measuring the density of the rain outside the door by its dripping sound. The noise, which lifted and resumed and thickened and thinned, tickled my eardrums like the soft tip of a cotton swab. As I was still struggling with a heavy drowsiness on account of the fatigue from the night before, the noise of the rain sounded like a distant whisper in a land of dreams. Still under order of confinement at home, I sensed the long, tedious rain at times as a blessing. Had there been clear sunshine outside to make the fields and hills blaze with light, wind that shook the trees on the hills, and the cool chirping of cicadas, all the light and sounds of the world might have seemed like a curse to one who had to stay confined indoors without any amusement or distraction. On those occasional afternoons when the rain lifted a bit, I could hear very clearly, sitting in the room, packs of children noisily galloping through the village streets. Whenever I pictured the children gleefully drawing baskets of willow fishtraps in the weedy pools around the river or in the forks of the irrigation ditches, and the silvery-scaled, plump carp they scoop up, I couldn't help sinking under the misery of a forlorn prisoner. I seemed to have already become a long-forgotten being among my contemporaries. My friends never stopped any more at my gate to call me out, even for appearance's sake. I therefore disconsolately picked up persimmon blossoms beaten down by the rain under the old persimmon tree beside the twig fence in the hours of envy when all the world seemed to belong to my friends, thus teaching myself resignation early in my life. The opening of school was all the hope that I had to cling to. The school, which had closed down because of the war, was to reopen soon, and then Father's order of confinement would lose effect, and my nightmarish house imprisonment would eventually end.

Maternal Grandmother stretched her back, pausing from shelling peas. Thanks to Grandmother, who kept silently moving her fingers all day long without ever saying a word to anybody, the major portion of the harvested peas had been sorted. But the pods that were still in storage in a corner of the barn showed signs of germinating. The moisture-saturated pods thrust up pale yellow sprouts. The task of shelling the peas before they became inedible fell to Maternal Grandmother. For some reason, all the family seemed to take it for granted that pea shelling was solely and entirely Maternal Grandmother's charge. And she herself seemed to take it for granted also, spending all her waking hours shelling the clammy things. Well, it may be more accurate to say that, because Maternal Grandmother regarded pea shelling as her appointed task, and jealously engaged in it lest someone should take the work away from her, all the others abstained from helping. At any rate, Maternal Grandmother, once she sat down with a basket of peapods, kept quietly moving her hands, seemingly oblivious to the passing of time. From time to time she poured into the bamboo basket her heavy sighs along with the round, pale-green peas.

Even though Maternal Grandmother's patience and perseverance were truly extraordinary, sitting thus immobile in one posture seemed to cause occasional aches in her back. Thus, she now pushed the bamboo basket aside and shook the lap of her skirt. She rubbed her hands on her skirt and moved close to me. I smelt the peculiar smell of Maternal Grandmother in the lukewarm breath that descended on my forehead. I guessed what was forthcoming. Sure enough, a chilly hand that made my body shiver crept into my pants. I had never, even for once, felt pleased to lie thus under Maternal Grandmother's gaunt hands.

"It's round as an apple, just like his maternal uncle's."

I knew, without looking, that Maternal Aunt was pulling her summer quilt up to her crown. Maternal Aunt had been living for quite some days now almost continuously lying on the warmer part of the floor because something had evidently gone wrong with her respiratory system. Aunt always pulled up her quilt like that whenever Maternal Grandmother mentioned Maternal Uncle.

"Who do you like better, your maternal uncle, or your paternal uncle?"

This was the unreasonable question Maternal Grandmother had got into the habit of posing me. At first I was extremely disconcerted when asked that question. For one thing, it was a question meant for extorting one answer. It was always Maternal Uncle she mentioned first in the question. But my situation did not allow me to pick out either one as my favourite. If I were to tell the truth I would have had to say that I liked both of them. But Maternal Grandmother was demanding that I pick out one of the two.

"Do you like your maternal uncle, or your paternal uncle?"

But I knew that the important thing was neither the question nor my answer. I had long ago worked out that that question, posed without any emotion or stress, was simply an introductory remark to her long, rambling discourse. And so it was only the first couple of times that the question threw me into confusion. I thus lay there silently, pretending not to have heard the question. Then Grandmother would put on an expression of regret.

"I know. The arm always bends inward."

But it was only for a moment that the look of regret shaded her face. Her face regained equanimity soon enough, and she began her discourse.

"If you are really to be worthy of being Kwon Kiljun's nephew you must first of all know what kind of a person he was. Unless you know what kind of a person your maternal uncle was, you're not fit to claim kinship with him. No, you're not."

The maternal uncle that my maternal grandmother described always wore a football player's uniform. And he dashed about like a thoroughbred mare on the infinitely vast playground rapidly constructed in my imagination. And he kicked the ball up sky-high, with a perfectly graceful motion. Maternal Uncle excelled in studies, too, to be sure, but he was a genuis in sports. And among sports, football was his speciality, and he was the leader of his high school football team from middle school to college.

The first time Maternal Grandmother felt pride in her football-playing son was when she attended a football match for the first time in her life in the public stadium, when Maternal Uncle was in the sixth form. Maternal Grandmother, who had not wanted her only son to grow up to be a professional player, was dumbfounded when, after the game was over, hordes of schoolgirls rushed over to her and addressed her as "mother", as if she had been their mother-in-law. Even more amazingly, the girls praised her son sky-high, as if he had been their husband.

She was not one to brook such forwardness in nubile girls, and she chased them away after giving them a smart lecture, but the incident was not altogether displeasing to her. From then on, it became an important task for her to scold away with a stern lecture any schoolgirl fans who besieged her and her son.

"You should've seen your uncle that time. . . that time when the goalkeeper of the opposite team fell backward, struck by the ball your uncle had kicked. That'd have made it easier for you to answer—that you like your maternal uncle better than your paternal uncle."

Maternal Grandmother was not a woman of many words. But once she started talking of her son there was no stopping her. She was putting all her strength into her words, in an effort to implant deep into my heart the image of her splendid son. Sometimes she demanded that I describe my maternal uncle's features, as if afraid I might forget his face.

It is true that my maternal uncle was a splendid young man, worthy of any mother's pride. Even though there were some exaggerations and embellishments in Grandmother's memory, that he was an excellent football player and a much-admired figure are honest truths.

He was, in short, a brilliant and handsome man. His face was white as porcelain, and his sharp nosebridge and dark eyebrows gave him a truly distinguished look. His smiles, which revealed two neat rows of clean teeth, and his well-proportioned body gave him a look of refinement and good breeding. We had several times had him and his friends as guests for a few days. One time he came with quite a number of friends, all carrying rucksacks. The young men, who said they were on their way to Chirisan Mountain, played harmonicas and guitars all night long in the guest room. That night, one of his friends said he'd give me instructions on how to kiss girls, and rubbed his coarse jaw on mine and made me scream and flee from the room. That was when I was five years old. There was a time also when there was a beautiful young woman in the group. That was the year before the war broke out, and that time also he and his numerous friends carried on gleefully for five days, incurring the silent displeasure of my paternal grandmother, and putting Mother in an embarrassing position.

My maternal uncle's friends seemed to be treating him and the young woman like a royal couple. The group also locked themselves up in the room for hours at a stretch and seemed to be earnestly discussing something. Mother explained later on that they were in flight at the time, after a clash with leftist students with whom they were in long-standing opposition. Except for the period of about a month after the outbreak of the war, during which my maternal uncle was in hiding in a dug-out in the bamboo grove behind our house, these were about all the contacts I had had with him.

My feelings toward my uncle formed through such short contacts was closer to reverence than love as a kinsman. There were many things about him that could inspire my adoration. There was about his comely features and cultured manners and speech an almost feminine refinement; but his adroit movements and clear-cut decisiveness which had at the base his almost limitless energy bespoke manliness itself. The fact that he was a leader of an organisation at such an early age proved him to be a man of extraordinary qualities, and made him seem the more distinguished in my eyes. To me, the wondrous combination of such diverse abilities in one human being was an eternal enigma.

My paternal uncle was three years older than my maternal uncle. But, in spite of his seniority, he was much more youthful in his actions than my maternal uncle. His method of "rewarding" the labours of the supervisors of home-brewing and clandestine butchery who had earned the resentment of villagers for their harshness made him famous in the vicinity for a while. In the middle of a gathering of numerous villagers in the village square, my uncle gave each of the supervisors a large bucket of plain water to drink. He termed it their reward for their diligent labours in supervising clandestine brewing. Each of the supervisors had to gulp down the enormous amount of water, kneeling before the guns aimed at the napes of their necks. Then they were required to chant, marking time by striking their enormously swollen bellies, "I am the grandson of the yeast! I am the bairn of the cow! My father is an ox! Swine is my mother!" exactly one hundred times. Then they were asked to entertain the villagers with songs—any songs. Their hoarse singing, which sounded more like the bellowing of calves, sounded so miserable that the villagers who had been writhing with giggles all along stopped laughing in the end.

All his actions were comic and preposterous in such a way. There is also the famous anecdote of his "marriage" with the daughter of a small landowner in the neighbouring village. With a notorious hoodlum of the village officiating, he "married" the daughter of Mr Choi in a sham marriage ceremony. The ceremony also took place in the village square, and it was a completely modern, western-style ceremony, too. To the ceremony were invited, or summoned, Mr Choi and the bride's husband as guests. As soon as the ceremony was over, Uncle handed the bride over to the hoodlum who officiated and went directly up to Mr Choi. That day Mr Choi was beaten till he fainted away by the ruffian who kept calling him "father". That was in repayment for the atrocious thrashing he received at the hands of Mr Choi's servants on the moonlit night he jumped over the wall of Mr Choi's house while drunk, after yearning for his daughter for a long time.

My two uncles were thus antithetical. Whereas my paternal uncle's joining the red army was a blind and impulsive involvement in the whirlwind of events, just like his jumping over Mr Choi's wall in drunkenness, my maternal uncle's activity in the right-wing movement and his volunteering for officership in the Republic's army were decisions grounded firmly on principle and made after careful weighing and examining of the meaning and consequences. Although they had not met often, my two uncles seemed to like each other well enough. If they hadn't, it would have been impossible for my maternal uncle to remain safe in hiding for over a month under the communist rule. Saying that it was only ignorant and poor men like himself who would wear red armbands, my paternal uncle treated my maternal uncle with respectful courtesy. It may have been an expression of envy and admiration for one who had received higher education than himself. At any rate, Paternal Uncle frequently bestowed kindly attentions on his in-law relation who had to stay in hiding in a cave. To Mother, he explained his kindly attentions by saying that it was in consideration of their mutual nephew, and the position of Father and Mother.

But my maternal uncle was different. Even though inwardly he felt warmly towards my paternal uncle, who was so cheerful and frank, outwardly he always cast cold glances at his in-law relation who went around acting like a playful urchin. His intuition proved right. My paternal uncle, who seemed to have so much affection for my maternal uncle, dispatched his men to the cave in the bamboo grove on that mad dawn of the communists' retreat. It was a few hours after Maternal Uncle, after a hearty supper, had silently disappeared without saying a word to anyone in the family.

I could hear Aunt coughing. Covered with the thin quilt up to her head, and lying still on her back on the warmer part of the floor, Aunt was vomiting in coughs the pain that constricted her respiratory organs. I could hear Maternal Grandmother murmuring. And I could hear the noise of the thinning and thickening rain.

"He always disliked anything the least bit sloppy. I bet he died as neatly as he always lived. I'm sure only one bullet struck him, in the heart or in the head, so that he died instantly, without writhing or suffering pain."

It seems that Maternal Grandmother was severely shocked by what the villager recounted thoughtlessly the other day. It may be that the images of variously disfigured corpses went in and out of the guest quarter of our house all night long and disturbed the dreams of an unhappy old woman. It is certainly possible that they did. Maternal Grandmother was praying that her only son had met his death in battle in as neat and peaceful a posture as restful slumber. She prayed ardently that Satan's bullet had struck him in a vital spot, so that he crossed the boundary between this world and the next instantly, not only without bodily pain but also without feeling sorrow at leaving his old, widowed mother sonless in this sorry world. Maternal Grandmother murmured stubbornly that her son died with all the parts of his body intact, and that he could never have met the fate of those ghosts in ancient tales who had to linger in this world wandering over hills and plains in search of their scattered body parts.

But the voice was weakening perceptively. Aunt's coughs, on the other hand, became more high-pitched. Grandmother's murmurs were becoming more and more subdued under the continuously invading boise of the rain.

5

The day appointed by the blind fortune-teller was inexorably approaching. The rain poured on, and everyone was tired. With the exception of Paternal Grandmother, everyone was really completely exhausted. Worn out by waiting, and by the rain.

The stepping stones in the river that served as a bridge between our village and the next were sunk under the rising water long ago. After that, a thick rope had been tied across the stream, so that grown-ups forded the river against the rapid current coming up to the waist holding on to the rope, and children were carried across pick-a-back on the grown-ups' shoulders. But, as the water was now deeper than a grown-up's height, it had become utterly impossible to cross the river. Thus, traffic to town had as good as closed down. There were people who averred they saw things like pigs, oxen and uprooted pine trees being washed down the river from upstream, but Father brushed off such rumours as nonsense. According to Father, our village was located on the upstream shore of the Somjingang River, so that such things could not happen unless there was a great flood. But it was true that this year's rainy spell was unusually long and severe, and as a consequence traffic to and from the village was tied up, which gave Paternal Grandmother grave worry.

"He's certain to be coming by the road from the town. What bother it is that the river's so swollen!"

There was a toad that had taken up abode in the dirt verandah of our house for many days, despite my manifold persecutions. It seemed to deem itself lucky to have found a shelter at all after having its cave wrecked by the long rain. Pitiable as it was, it aroused my mischievousness by the absurd sight it presented as it dragged its clumsy body around under the wooden floor or on the dirt verandah. On the third day, I turned it bellyside up and, inserting a barley straw in its anus, blew into the straw until its belly was puffed up like a rubber ball. After that it disappeared for an afternoon. But the next morning it was back on the dirt verandah, claiming its right of residence. Squatting on the stepping stone, it gazed vacantly with its protrouding eyes at the water dripping from the eaves.

On one of those days, trouble was discovered in the barn. It was not the kind of trouble that broke out suddenly one morning, but rather a gradual development over many days, but because no one had noticed the development we were all aghast at the discovery. The discovery was made possible by the mist that rose from the bags of barley that had been stored in the barn as soon as they were reaped. As the peas had done some time ago, the grain was now sending up pale yellow sprouts. It was lucky that Father made the discovery when he went in to set mousetraps; otherwise, all the family would have had simply to starve until harvest in the autumn. Suddenly the entire family went around busily, as in the peak farming season. To store the barley bags so as to prevent further damage was a big problem. We installed a storage platform of wooden bars in the barn to provide ventilation space between the floor and the barley bags, and spread the steaming barley on all the level places in the house to let it dry. Wherever I went—bedrooms, kitchen, everywhere— there was barley. I detested barley, and not only because it felt rough in the mouth and gave tummyaches. Whenever I saw the slit in the barley grain I recalled a legend told me by Paternal Grandmother.

Once upon a time there lived a boy whose father was ill with a fatal disease. The boy consulted a doctor, who prescribed a concoction made out of live people's livers. The boy therefore killed three people he met on his way home—a scholar, a monk and a madman—and made a broth with their livers, upon drinking which the father's disease was entirely cured. The boy buried the corpses in a sunny place. The next year, a strange plant was seen growing on the tomb, and its grain was what we now call barley. The slit in the barley grain is thus the slit the boy made in the bodies of the men for the purpose of taking out their livers.

It was truly unpleasant to live in the house with floors covered all over by such an unpleasant grain. I felt cornered and bound. But Paternal Grandmother was a woman of truly amazing determination. Even in the midst of such ado, she simply went on with her plans. First, she ordered Mother to take out of the chest her treasured silk cloth and sew a

Korean-style outfit for Uncle. In her opinion a Korean suit is the most dignified and comfortable garment for indoors. And she made Mother prepare Uncle's favourite dish—fried squash slices—in mountainous heaps, despite Mother's protest that it would get spoiled and become inedible in two days. She seasoned the fern fronds herself, and complained that because the times were hard plants didn't grow as they ought to. All the dishes that were liable to become spoiled were heavily salted or deep fried to prevent deterioration. At last the preparations were almost complete. There was food enough to give an ordinary village-scale feast for country people like us. Grandmother's face, as she looked around the kitchen, lit up with the pride of one who has accomplished an important task. Now there was only one worry still left for her.

"He's sure to be coming by the road from town. What bother it is that the river's so swollen!"

"What's there to worry about in that? Even if the river's swollen a bit, how could it hinder his coming, if he's destined to come? He knows traffic often gets tied up in rainy seasons, so he'll take the stone bridge and come by the circular road." Father brushed aside Grandmother's worry, to put her at ease. But Grandmother shook her head.

"Of course he'll take the circular road. But that's four miles longer. Four miles sounds pretty short, but think of walking four more miles in this rain. And his feet frostbitten, too!"

Paternal Aunt came the day before the appointed day. As soon as she arrived she inspected the cupboards and shelves in the kitchen, and complimented Mother and Paternal Grandmother for their thoroughness. She seemed quite satisfied with the preparations that had been made. Aunt showed as complete a faith in the homecoming of my uncle as had Paternal Grandmother. It was this aunt who had introduced grandmother to the blind fortune-teller. As she was thus the one who induced my grandmother's complete faith in the fortune-teller, it was understandable that she held as firm a belief in Uncle's homecoming as had Grandmother. But her idea of a fit welcome for the returning uncle was so perfectly identical with Paternal Grandmother's that even my mother, who was chary of complaints against her in-laws, marvelled secretly to Maternal Grandmother and Maternal Aunt on the resemblance of taste between her mother-in-law and sister-in-law. It was not as if Mother was not hoping for Uncle's return. Even Maternal Aunt, who hardly ever spoke in those days, and Maternal Grandmother, who had once invoked curses upon communist partisans, silently wished for the happy reunion of the relations as they watched the heated preparations. But wishing and believing are two different things. I also ardently wished for my uncle's return. But even in my childish judgment it did not seem very likely that an event like that could occur as easily as predicted. If Uncle were to come, in what status and by which road would he be coming?

I had chanced to overhear Father talking to Mother in the kitchen. Father said that such a thing was impossible. If one detached oneself even a little from Paternal Grandmother's touching faith—and it was a complete, unshakable faith—and examined the matter with any objectivity at all, the impossibility of the prediction being fulfilled was so evident that it made our hearts ache. As a last resort, Father thought of the possibility of Uncle's having surrendered himself to the police somewhere. But he quickly denied the likelihood himself. Had that been the case, we would have had by now some notice or interrogation from the police. Father knew better than anybody else that our family was under surveillance. There was a man who could be seen sauntering up and down along our twig fence at times and casting suspicious glances into the house. Though outwardly we had freedom of movement, we were like fish securely cooped inside the net drawn by that man. I knew from long before that the man sometimes dropped in at our neighbour Jinku's to gather information about what was going on in my house, and that once or twice he even called my father out to a tavern for a talk.

It was I who shuddered most of all when the man came into view. His appearance had dreadful meaning to me. It always awakened anew my guilty conscience, which I was trying to lull to sleep. The sight of him always made me recall Paternal Grandmother's voice as she called me a butcher of men who sold his uncle for a sweet. Father should have struck me dead that night with the wooden pillow. It gave me unendurable pain to behold Father's face as he returned from a talk with that man.

The only way I had of escaping from my paternal grandmother's censure that kept reviving in my memory was to imagine myself dying in the most pitiful shape. That was the only way of comforting myself out of the tormenting consciousness of guilt. I pictured to myself the scene in which the whole family, especially my paternal grandmother, shed tears without end in front of the dead youth. The greater Paternal Grandmother's sorrow and regret, the more sweetly consoling it was to me. But when I woke up from the daydream I always found myself as impudently alive as ever, and I could not but dread meeting Paternal Uncle face to face. It was because of this guilt that, while ardently wishing for my uncle's return, I also secretly harboured the horrible wish that I might never have to face Uncle again—that Uncle had died long ago in some steep, deserted valley and would never be discovered by anybody. Really, the anticipated day, which was just one day ahead now, filled me with mortal dread. I was so terrified that I prayed today would never end.

But I think my terror and anxiety were nothing compared with the pain my father endured. I had heard Father pleading in the kitchen with Mother, who was complaining about Paternal Grandmother's excessive vigilance.

"I feel the same as you do. It's a hundred to one that he won't come. And even if he does by some extraordinary chance, it won't be an event of the kind Mother plans it to be. That I know better than you do. But what can I say to Mother? It's best simply to do everything that she bids us. That's better than making her think we're trying to thwart her joy and giving her a grievance. Don't you think so?"

Father was appealing to Mother by telling her of his own agony at having to follow his old mother's lead, even having to seem assiduous in following it, while knowing the waited-for event to be an impossibility. Even though Paternal Grandmother's faith, nourished by her boundless motherly love, moved our hearts at first and made us pray for the fulfillment of her expectation, we were far from having the same faith at any time. We were only hoping and waiting with her because

we did not want to disappoint the old lady on any account.
Father had already prognosticated the despair that would
follow Grandmother's disappointed expectations, and the
terrible aftermath of that despair. But there was nothing any
of us could do except try our best not to cross the old lady.
It was a pity that the blind fortune-teller, reputed to be
divinely inspired, had not told Grandmother which road
Uncle would be taking for his homecoming.

It was already night. The rain, which thinned down from
around dusk, was now a mere misty drizzle. Into the hazy
halo of the lamp hung on the gatepost the rain descended
in sprinkles of powdery drops, as if it, too, was quite exhausted. Even though ever since the beginning of the war the
whole village was in the habit of extinguishing all light after
supper-time, without any express order, we had hung out a
lamp tonight, letting it keep vigil through the night like a
lonely sentinel. It was, of course, at Paternal Grandmother's
insistence. Who knows, she said, even though Uncle was due
to arrive from around eight to ten o'clock tomorrow morning,
he might be coming in the middle of the night due to some
sudden change of plan. Grandmother did not want it to look
as if the family was unprepared for his return.

"It was for an occasion like this that we saved up the
expensive kerosene."

She ordered one more lamp to be hung from the eaves
and warned us not to let the lamp die out in any of the
rooms. She explained very succinctly the reason we had to
keep the house as bright as day.

"We have to keep the lamps burning bright so he can spot
the house from far, far away and run all the way home,
knowing his mother's waiting for him with wide-open eyes all
through the night."

The night deepened. Even so, nobody seemed to be thinking of going to bed. No one in the family had the guts to
spread out bedding when Paternal Grandmother was tensely
surveying the house all over. The weather also seemed to be
flattering my grandmother. The long, fierce rain had changed
to a drizzle in the evening, and then by degrees withdrew out
of sight and out of hearing, so that as the night deepened
even the dripping from the eaves ceased. And the cool wind

that carries away humidity began to blow. Well, the rainy spell had persisted long enough, and it was time for the rain front to retreat. But Grandmother quickly related the change in the weather to the forthcoming happy event of the morrow, to her great satisfaction.

It must have been long past midnight. I had left the inner room to come to the guest room and lie down beside Maternal Grandmother. Neither my maternal aunt nor my maternal grandmother was asleep. With all the tense excitement in the inner quarters they couldn't fall asleep, I suppose. Aunt was lying still on her back, facing the ceiling, and Grandmother was seated leaning on the wall, facing the door. My eyes were tracing the flickering shadow of the lamp's sooty flame on the ceiling. My ears were wide open, and were listening to the songs of the night in the distant grass beyond the darkness outside the door.

All around was quiet. The house couldn't be quieter, even had everyone been asleep. It was so perfectly still that the stillness rather hampered my listening to the sound of darkness. It was as if my auditory organs were being paralysed under the pressure of the stillness that weighed all around. So much so that I sometimes suspected that the sounds that came to my ears were not sounds that actually existed in the world but rather some illusion created by my bewitched brain. But collecting myself and listening again, I seemed to be hearing some wakeful being besides myself patiently filing away in the darkness at the edge of the vast stillness with a sharp file. For a long time I had been concentrating on distinguishing amid the whisper of the wind the chirp of the crickets from the chirp of the katydids, and was relishing the sweet and sour tastes of the sounds. Suddenly, there sank into the midst of the murmur of insects an unfamiliar sound, and its strangeness made me tense. But the sound ceased as unexpectedly as it began. As it fled away, just as I was about to grasp the tail end of it, I felt again darkly that I might have been bewitched by something. But the sound came again after a pause. It was very distinct this time. It was not loud, but it was distinctive among the many hushed sounds of the night. It was like the sound made when children blow into the mouth of an empty bottle, or like the siren of a ship on a distant sea. It was, at any rate, a faint but pregnant sound. It was also a very obscure sound, and I was completely at a loss to discern its direction. It seemed now to be coming from somewhere around the river's shore outside the village, or from the kitchen garden of our house, right outside the door. The strange, secretive sound that stole through the stillness of the night—I lay bewitched by it. Like a boy chasing fox-fire in the graveyard, my consciousness was already rushing to the river's shore, drawn by the mysterious strain of the eerie sound.

"It's the whisper of the king snake," Maternal Grandmother said. Her words, which fell upon me like a huge, dark shadow, almost made me scream.

"It's the king snake calling up the snakes."

Grandmother's words coiled round my body like a huge snake darting out its forked tongue, and I could hardly breathe. It was my beloved maternal aunt who chased away the chilly feel of the snake against my body. I had a protector. I was infinitely thankful that I was not the only one to have heard the sound. My aunt was already sitting up beside me and staring at the door. Maternal Grandmother twitched her lips, preparatory to saying something more. Aunt put her hand on my shoulder and gave Grandmother a sideway stare.

"Don't!"

But Grandmother kept twitching her lips. Had not Aunt subdued her once more, Grandmother would surely have said something.

"Please don't!"

Aunt pulled me under her quilt. Buried snugly under Aunt's armpit, I heard the sound once more. The sound like a ship's siren from a distant sea once more scattered chill all over the room. This time, too, it was indistinguishable whether the sound was coming from the river's shore or from the kitchen garden of our house. Then there was a long interval. The snake's call sounded for the third time, and then came no more. But the aftertaste of the sound lingered in the room for a long time and kept our mouths shut. Maternal Grandmother was still sitting in an awkward posture, stooping forward toward the door. Waves of emotion crossed her face. Sometimes she looked vacantly into space, like a person hit hard on the head, but the next moment she looked out beyond the door with narrowed eyes, like someone trying to work out a very complicated problem. At last she turned towards me and Aunt.

"Dongman," she called. "Dongman, my dear."

But when my eyes met hers she furtively averted her face. After some hesitation, she slowly opened her mouth.

"Do you think so, too?" she asked, apropos of nothing, and again hesitated for a long while.

"Do you also think that what happened to your uncle happened because of me?"

I decided to answer the question. The voice asking the question was so urgent that I thought I had to say something in response. But I realised the next moment that no answer was necessary. She was not looking at me, nor was she paying any attention to me. She was completely absorbed in her own thoughts. She would not have heard me even if I had said anything in response.

"No! What happened that night was none of my willing. I'd no thought of spying on anybody. I'd been to the out-house and saw the light in the inner room and heard whispering voices, so I just went nearer to see what was going on. Who'd have known it'd bring about such consequences? A team of horses couldn't have led me there if I'd known such a thing were going to happen. I'm not saying I did well to be so curious. I know I shouldn't have done it, but it's wrong to think it's because of me that things ended that way. Even if it hadn't been for me, your uncle would've returned to where he came from, as he was fated to do. That was his lot."

Aunt hugged me tightly. With my face buried snugly between Aunt's breasts, I heard Grandmother's murmurs in dreamy cosiness. Then, my whole body loosened up like after a heavy flogging and violent weeping, and drowsiness utterly overwhelmed me. Even in my dreamy exhaustion I vowed to myself that I would marry my aunt for sure when I grew up, and my ears grew inattentive to Grandmother's murmurings.

6

I woke up, before I was sufficiently refreshed, to the sound of Paternal Grandmother's furious reproaches uttered just inside the gate. Although the sky was brightening, it was still early dawn. Summer nights are short, and, as I had gone to sleep long past midnight, to wake up in early dawn meant I had as good as skipped sleeping that night. I felt a numbing pain inside my head, and my eyelids kept sliding down. But my condition was vigour itself compared with the rest of the family's. Because of many days' fatigue and tension, Father's face was swollen and yellow as in jaundice, and Mother had become gaunt as a mummy. Maternal Grandmother and Maternal Aunt were not much better. But Paternal Grandmother was energetically imperious, loudly scolding the wearied family from early dawn. She was giving an awesome bawling-out to Mother and Father.

The lamp hung on the gatepost had died out. The wind must have blown out the flame—the oil can was more than half full, and the glass shade was wet with drops of water. The blown-out lamp had infuriated Paternal Grandmother. She took it as a test God had put on Father's and Mother's devotion. Grandmother's ire was not soothed by giving Father and Mother a severe scolding. She declared that this proved to her that Father and Mother were not fit to be trusted with looking after Uncle's welfare, and announced her resolution to take charge of the keys to the barn and the safety cabinet until she saw signs of amendment.

"I won't say anything more this morning, because a woman shouldn't raise her voice on the morning of festivity. I'll leave the rest up to you. I won't move a finger, but just entertain myself with watching what you do." Then she clicked her tongue in self-pity as she turned around to head for the inner quarters. "Lucky woman I am, to have such a thoughtful elder son!" She strode across the yard toward the inner room. "What sins am I expiating, to be blessed with a son and a daughter-in-law such as those?" she grumbled to herself as she passed in front of the guest room, loud enough to be heard by neighbours.

Paternal Grandmother was as good as her word. She really

did not move a finger. After she went into her room, slamming the door shut, she did not utter a single comment on what was going on outside. Instead, she kept a keen watch over what was happening in the yard through the glass pane of the small window, and did not remove from her face a disapproving, discontented look. All of us in the family came out with brooms or other utensils and, with a keen consciousness of supervisory eyes upon us, swept the yard, scrubbed the floor, cleaned cobwebs, and tidied the house. Paternal Aunt and Maternal Aunt also joined in, and the house regained the neat appearance it had had before the long rain. Maternal Aunt and Paternal Aunt went into the kitchen with Mother to help with the breakfast, and Father and I dug a deep ditch between the footpath leading from the gate to the yard and the kitchen garden, sweating profusely, to drain the water from the yard.

The sky was still cloudy. We had hoped to see the sun for the first time in a long while, but the sky did not look cheerfully disposed. Nevertheless, a corner of the western sky was clear, and there was a cool wind that drove away the clouds. There was no sign anywhere of a renewal of rain. Even that much beneficence was a blessing to us. Not only my family but everybody felt the same. Village people who dropped in on us from early morning began their greetings by talking of the weather. Then they talked of Uncle. The men accosted Father very smoothly, beginning with comments on the weather, and the women kept going in and out of the kitchen. My house teemed with village people like on a feast day, and the members of the family were kept busy responding to inquisitive neighbours. What the neighbours were most curious about was to what extent the members of our family believed in the prophecy. Of course they did not use words like "superstition". Although they expressed wonder at the fact that one word of a fortune-teller could lead to such large-scale preparations, they were polite enough not to treat it as a mere foolishness, at least in our hearing. They tended rather to be sympathetic, and commented encouragingly that the devotion of the family, if nothing else, would bring back Uncle. Father simply smiled. Father saw, in the attitude of some of the people who spoke thus, that they were amusing themselves with what was going on in our house. Some of them were talking exactly in the attitude of a doctor who tells his dying patient he'll be well in a few days. As it drew near the appointed hour, more and more people gathered in the house, so that our yard teemed with people like on a village festival day. It looked as if everyone in the village who could walk on his own legs had drifted into my house. I could see the stranger smoking a cigarette, sitting on the porch of Jinku's house. My house was bustling like a market-place, and the family had still not had breakfast. Grand-mother had forbidden us to eat, as all of us were to eat together when Uncle came. It wasn't as if we were starving for want of food, so I resolved to be patient, but my stomach howled very pitifully.

At last it was eight o'clock, the beginning of the period[2] appointed by the fortune-teller. Time raced past, amid the tense excitement of everyone. Soon it was nine o'clock, and then it was approaching ten o'clock. But the long-awaited Uncle did not show up.

After the villagers had all dispersed we sat down to a late, late breakfast. Only the village head ahd Jinku's family remained and tried to console us. Paternal Grandmother remained in the inner room, and the rest of the family sat around the table set in the side room. The spoons moved slowly, although the table was luxuriously laden with colour-ful dishes. Paternal Grandmother refused to eat breakfast, even though she told the family to go ahead and eat. Her spirit was not sunken, even though the time appointed by the blind seer was quite past and gone. Well, she still *looked* spirited, anyway. She said that from the first she had not thought the hour was all that important. What was important, according to her, was the day, not the hour. She said that there could be accidental errors even in events supervised by Heaven; and man often cannot move exactly to schedule. She insisted one must make allowances for slight errors even in the prophecy of divine seers. For Grandmother, the day

2. The fortune-teller had predicted that the uncle would return in Chinsi, the hour of the dragon, wh..h is from eight to ten o'clock in the morning.

was still only just begun. She said that, since he could not fail to come that day, she would wait a little longer and have her first meal of the day with her son. She did not betray any tiredness.

Our dog Wolly, who had been peering in at the rooms, standing with his forefeet on the edge of the living-room floor and smacking his lips, suddenly stepped down to the dirt verandah. We heard Wolly bark, turning to the gate. Then we heard a shout of children. Father's spoon stopped still in the air, and all of us instantly ceased all movement. Children's exclamations were rapidly approaching our house. Flinging the spoon away, I ran outside. The noise instantly surrounded our gate. I was hit by the shouts of the children in the middle of the yard. The first thing that came into my view was a pack of children with gaping mouths. All of them had rocks or sticks of wood in their hands. The children hesitated a little before the gate, not daring to rush into the house, and raised their weapons threateningly. One of the boys threw his rock forcibly. Where the rock fell I beheld the thing.

There was a lengthy object sliding into the house. It was a huge snake, longer than a man's height. My whole body constricted the moment I saw its horrible bulk with its yellowish scales glittering dazzlingly as it slid, reviving in my memory the eerie whisper of the night before. But I was a boy, and a snake meant an adventure. Horror had a moment's grip on me, but the next moment I was as excited as any of the other boys who kept screaming and throwing rocks. I could not control the aggressive destructive urge that all male children instinctively feel towards all reptiles. I ran over to the barn and fetched the big wooden staff that Father used when carrying heavy things on a pannier. I raised both hands high in the air, ready to strike the snake dead if it moved an inch nearer me. But a hand grabbed my arm with rough force. I looked around to see that it was Maternal Grandmother. At the same moment, there arose a piercing scream from behind me.

"Aaaack!"

With that, Paternal Grandmother fell on the floor as limply as a piece of worn-out clothing. Maternal Grandmother twisted the staff from my grasp. Her eyes glared at me in silent reprimand.

The unexpected appearance of the huge snake threw the whole house into utter confusion. The most urgent problem was Paternal Grandmother, who had fainted. The family gathered in the inner room to massage her limbs and spray cold water on her face in an effort to bring her around. The village people, who had dispersed, gathered in the house once more, and talked and exclaimed so noisily that it was like sitting in the middle of a whirlwind. It was only Maternal Grandmother who did not lose her calm in the midst of the noise and confusion. As if she were simply carrying out pre-scheduled procedures, she put things in order one by one with a truly amazing composure. First of all, she drove away the people. With the help of the village head and Jinku's father, she drove out all the village people who came for the show, and locked the gates fast. The children and grown-ups who had been driven out of the gates came round to the part of the twig fence next to which stood a persimmon tree. The huge snake, taking advantage of the heated confusion, had slid down the kitchen garden through the grown mallows and lettuces, and had already coiled itself around the upper branches of the persimmon tree. Its yellow body wound around the persimmon bough, it kept darting its wiry tongue in and out. It must have suffered a deadly blow, for its tail was more than half cut from the body and dangled precariously. The tireless children had followed it up to the persimmon tree and were still throwing rocks and sticks.

"Who's that throwing rocks?"

Maternal Grandmother's reprimand was sharp as a sword.[3] All throwing ceased. Then Maternal Grandmother began slowly walking to the persimmon tree. Nothing happened, even when Maternal Grandmother stood upright right below the persimmon tree with the coiled snake, and sighs of relief escaped from the people who had been watching with

3. The giant snake was believed to have supernatural properties and powers. It was believed that spirits of the dead could enter it to visit people in this world. It behoved people, therefore, not to hurt it but to conciliate it by all means. The giant snake is venomless.

breathless suspense. Maternal Grandmother did not waver a bit, even though the snake's fiery dots of eyes gleamed in all directions and it raised and lowered its head threateningly. Grandmother slowly lifted both hands and clasped them palm to palm on her bosom.

"My poor boy, have you come all this way to see how things are doing in the house?" Grandmother whispered quietly, in the tone of one singing a lullaby to a fretful baby. Somebody giggled. Instantly, Grandmother's eyes grew sharply triangular.

"What mongrel is it sniggering there? Come up here at once! I'll wring your neck!"

Everybody hushed still as death at Grandmother's fiery rebuke. Grandmother turned to the snake again.

"As you can see, your mother's still in good health and everybody's doing all right. So put your mind at ease and make haste on your own way."

The snake did not stir a muscle. It only darted its wiry tongue in and out, and raised its head a couple of times.

"You mustn't linger here crouching like this any more when you have such a long way to go. You shouldn't, you know, if you don't want to grieve your family over-much. I know how you feel, but you must consider others' feelings, too. What would your mother feel if she knew you were lingering here like this?"

Maternal Grandmother was earnestly entreating, as if the snake had been a real live human being. But, however ardent-ly she pleaded, the snake did not show any inclination to move away. A neighbourhood woman then told Grand-mother the method for expelling snakes. The woman, whose body was hidden from view and whose voice only could be heard, said that you could chase away snakes with the smell of burning hair. At Maternal Grandmother's bidding I hurried into the inner room to get some of Paternal Grandmother's hair.

Paternal Grandmother was lying under a quilt stiff as a corpse. Although she was breathing, she was still unconscious. I urgently demanded some of Paternal Grandmother's hair of the family members sitting around the unconscious form with ashen-grey faces, waiting for the arrival of the doctor.

My demand must have sounded preposterous. It took quite a long time to explain what use Grandmother's hair would be. It took a longer while for Paternal Aunt to collect a handful of Paternal Grandmother's hair by combing the unconscious old lady's hair with a fine-toothed bamboo comb. The hair collected from repeated combing was given me at last. When I came out to the yard, Maternal Grandmother had in the meanwhile prepared a small tray of a few dishes. On the round tray were Uncle's favourite dishes of fried squash slices and seasoned fern, and there was also a large bowl full of cold water. After taking the knot of hair from me and putting it on the ground, Maternal Grandmother slowly raised her head and looked up at the persimmon tree.

"These are what your mother has prepared for you for many days. Even though you can't taste them, take a good look at them at least. They're all proofs of your mother's devotion. It's not that I'm trying to get rid of you. You must understand that. Please don't blame me too much for the bad smell. It's just to hurry you along on the long way you have to go. Put your worries at rest about your family, and just take good care of yourself on the long way ahead of you."

As she finished talking, she turned up the live coal in the tinder bowl. When she placed the knot of hair on it, it burned with a sizzling sound. The smell of burning protein quickly spread all around. What happened next drew an exclamation of astonishment from everyone. The huge snake, which had till then been immobile as a rock despite all Grandmother's entreaties, slowly began to move. Its body, which had been coiled round and round the persimmon tree, smoothly unwound itself and the snake dropped to the ground. After hesitating a little, the snake slowly and waveringly crept towards Grandmother. Grandmother stepped aside to make way. She followed its tail as it slid away and kept chasing it, making a swishing sound with her lips. Like chasing away sparrows from the fields, Grandmother swished and even clapped her hands. The snake crawled over the ground noiselessly, twitching its gleaming scales. All the members of the family also spilled out to the living-room floor and fearfully watched the snake sliding across the yard. Wolly, whose tail clung to his inner thighs, dutifully barked with a fear-strained voice from beneath the living-room floor. The snake slowly coursed its way through the empty space between the barn and the kitchen, its half-detached tail shakily trailing behind.

"Swish! Swish!"

Spurred on from behind by Maternal Grandmother's hoarse voice, it had already slid past the well and crossed the backyard. Before it now was the bamboo grove, densely overgrown.

"Thank you, dear. Just trust your brother to take care of all the household, and think only of keeping your body whole for your long, long journey. Don't worry at all about what you're leaving behind here, but take good care of yourself. That's a good boy. Thank you, dear."

Maternal Grandmother saw the snake off with earnest entreaties, standing beside the well, until it completely disappeared through the bamboo trees and the bamboo shoots which had sprouted thickly during the long rain.

Jinku's father arrived with a doctor from a neighbouring village. Paternal Grandmother regained weak consciousness several hours after she had fainted. On waking up from her stupor of a few hours, she looked round the room like one who had been on a few months' trip to a faraway place.

"Is it gone?" were her first words after regaining consciousness. Paternal Aunt quickly understood and nodded. Paternal Grandmother lowered her eyelids, as if to say that was all that mattered. Paternal Aunt quickly recounted all that had happened after Paternal Grandmother had fainted away. She related how Maternal Grandmother chased away the neighbours and reasoned with the snake under the persimmon tree and made it come down from the tree by burning Paternal Grandmother's hair, and saw it off every step of the way until it disappeared through the bamboo grove. Mother occasionally added details to Paternal Aunt's account. Paternal Grandmother was quietly weeping. Tears gushed endlessly from her eyes, flowed down her sunken cheeks and wetted the pillow case. After she had heard all, she told Father to go and ask Maternal Grandmother into the inner room. Maternal

Grandmother, who had been resting in the guest room, followed Father into the inner room. It was the first time Maternal Grandmother had stepped into the inner room since the unhappy day of the clash between the two in-laws.

"Thank you," Paternal Grandmother said huskily, raising her sunken and lustreless eyes to Maternal Grandmother.

"You're welcome." Maternal Grandmother's voice was also tearfully husky.

"I heard it all from my daughter. You did for me what I should've done. What a hard and fearsome thing you did for me."

"It's all past now. Don't exert yourself any more with talking, but try to collect your strength."

"Thank you. Thank you so very much." Paternal Grandmother held out her hand. Maternal Grandmother took it. The two grandmothers just held hands for a while, and could not speak. Then Paternal Grandmother expressed her remaining worry.

"I wonder if it went on its way all right."

"Don't worry. It must have found a comfortable place by now, and be keeping a protective eye on this house."

Even that brief conversation drained Paternal Grandmother's strength, and she panted. Everyone sat around her till she fell asleep with difficulty and then, leaving only Paternal Aunt to watch over her, we all came out of the inner room to breathe a little.

Paternal Grandmother fainted again that night. She vomited back the few spoonfuls of broth and herb medicine we had spooned into her mouth. From the next day, it was as if her consciousness was playing hide-and-seek in and out of her body like a playful urchin, and there was not a moment's ease for anyone in the house.

Grandmother struggled on for a week, though she had lost control of her body. On the last night of the seventh day, the old lady who always thought more of the son away from the house than the son at home closed her eyes softly, like a spent candle flame quietly subsiding. It may be that in Grandmother's long life the happiest and proudest times were the few days she commanded and scolded the family with amazing vigour, without sleeping and without eating, in rapturous expectation of her younger son's return—like the last radiant soaring of the candle flame before quite sinking down. On her deathbed Grandmother held my hand and forgave me all my misdeeds. I also in my heart forgave her everything.

It was a long, wearying rainy spell indeed.

Park Wan-so

Born in 1931, Park Wan-so made her literary debut as late as 1970, after her fifth and last child began school and left her time for writing. Her mastery of the medium of fiction surprised readers from the first, and she has been a prolific writer since her late beginning.

She has a sharp, unerring penetration into her characters' mentality that lets escape no hypocrisy, attitudinising, or self-deception. The subject of most of her stories is the everyday life of everyday people in the modern world. With surgical precision, she exposes the vacuity of prosperous middle-class existence, the enormous cost of maintaining mistaken values, and the unintentional cruelty of people towards themselves and towards one another. In her stories, the delight of the critic to expose coexists with the humanitarian's pity and horror at the discovery. She has treated a wide variety of themes in her stories, important among them the meaning of the Korean War experience. 'A Pasque-Flower on that Bleak Day' (1973) cannot be called a characteristic story of this author, but the bold succinctness of the conlcusion bears the stamp of her directness and force.

A Pasque-flower
on that Bleak Day

Park Wan-so

Dallae was a village of innocent farmers.
I say "innocent" because they always earned their living by diligently tilling the land, and abided by those laws that all who call themselves human beings must abide by, regardless of whether anyone notices or not.

But even to this innocent village, which neses cosily in the lap of mountains, came the roaring of cannon.

Considering that there was a violent clash in the adjacent town, the damage to this village was very small.

The village itself had never become a battleground, and it had escaped bombing. The village people only knew by hearsay how houses collapsed into dust within the blinking of an eye and frolicking children instantly turned to pieces of torn flesh.

The village people firmly believed that such a fortunate escape from injury was due to the grace of the mountain spirits of Dallaebong Mountain, to whom they offered sacrifices every year on the first of the tenth month by the lunar calendar.

But the number of war victims in the village was not much smaller than that of the neighbouring village which had been a battleground and which had suffered bombing. There was a

---

1. A Pasque-flower is called in Korean an "old woman flower", because it has very little attraction of any kind. The name of the flower, therefore is often used as a simile for old women who have lost all attraction as women.

massacre each time the occupying government changed according to the fluctuation of the battle front.

Besides, early in the war young men joined the Republic's army as volunteers or were conscripted by the communist army; there were people who fled south as refugees, and some people were kidnapped to the north by the communists. The village population had shrunk by more than half. Well, those who left the village, for whatever reason, were all men, and in the village now remained only women. There were widows and there were grass widows; there were maidens and there were old women. Except for suckling babies there was not a single male in the village. All males who could walk had been sent away with fathers, uncles, or any distant relatives fleeing south for refuge.

Men were sacred beings who were entrusted with continuing the family line, and it was the women's duty to safeguard such sacred beings.

Even though all duty and morality were disregarded and despised, this duty of women had become more urgent and inviolable.

From the time there remained only women in this village the informing ceased, and consequently the slaughter ceased also. The command for slaughter had come from the elementary school building at the entrance of the village. According to whether the Republic's army or the communist army occupied the elementary school building, accusations were made against neighbours as communists or as reactionaries, and slaughter ensued.

But the women were not interested in who occupied the elementary school building. Whichever side occupied the building now, there were no more men to be killed off or conscripted, and no more property to be requisitioned. And of course they knew there were no benefits to be derived, whichever side the occupying army might represent.

Their only concern was how to remain alive until peace came and the men returned.

Spring was still far away, and barns were empty in every house. Administration was in a vacuum in this village, even though the elementary school building was still occupied by some army.

One day, there spread a rumour in the village that the occupying army at the elementary school was now neither the Republic's nor the communists', but that of the "big-nosed Americans".

Soon, big-nosed Americans began to saunter around the village, noisily chewing gum and peering into houses.

"Saxi have yes?[2] Saxi have yes?"

Whenever they spotted women they accosted them with such words, making lurid gestures. The horrified women hid deep in their houses. They trembled. The naked carnality that glowed on the faces of these big-nosed foreigners made them shudder.

The big-nosed men seemed to be looking for professional foreigners' prostitutes, but there could be no such prostitutes in this rustic village.

Terror engulfed the village. After dark, the women were too scared to remain alone in their houses, and so they gathered one after another in the biggest house in the village.

That house was not only the biggest in the village but it was also the house of the village matriarch. Although in troubled times the villagers might make accusations that led to the deaths of their neighbours, still this, like many other country villages, was a tribal community.

As night deepened, the big-nosed men's cry of "Saxi have yes? Saxi have yes?" took on an urgent and threatening tone, like the wailing of beasts in heat.

The young wives and maids, sitting in a circle around the matriarch, stayed awake all night trembling. Even the next day the big-nosed men did not show any sign of moving elsewhere.

It was night again. The big-nosed Americans went around,

2. "Saxi", in Korean, is a young or relatively young woman—in her twenties or thirties, or even early forties. The term is applied to any young or youngish woman who is or looks married. (In the old days, married and unmarried women were told apart by their hairstyle.) However, the word is sometimes used to designate "prostitute", really short for "tavern saxi". "Saxi have yes?" is the literal translation into English of the Korean for "Do you have a saxi?" or "Is there a saxi?" The Korean word order is preserved, no doubt to make it easier for Koreans to understand.

knocking on the gates, urgently wailing "Saxi have yes? Saxi have yes?"

"I'm afraid we can't spend tonight in peace," the matriarch said in a parched voice.

"I'd bite my tongue and die first, rather than suffer defilement." A young bride who saw the outbreak of the war a few days after her marriage and lost her husband to the volunteer army a few days after the outbreak of the war spoke decisively, putting strength into her lean shoulderblades.

"I'd die, too, by hanging myself from the beam."

"I would, too, even if I had to jump into the well."

All the women declared they'd die. They declared it heatedly, lest they be suspected of harbouring secret wishes for rape by the big-nosed Americans.

The matriarch smiled weakly. "That's enough talk of dying, for young women who've got many decades ahead."

The wailing of "Hello, saxi have yes? saxi have yes?" approached nearer.

"I suppose I'll have to play saxi to the big-nosed men tonight," the matriarch said slowly in a parched voice.

"You?"

The maidens and young wives who had vowed to preserve their chastity even if they had to give up their lives, with faces solemn as stone monuments, instantly writhed, giggling.

"Come, Okhee, fetch your cosmetics." The matriarch did not giggle but commanded sternly. Okhee was the old woman's granddaughter, a bride-to-be, whose fiancé was at the front now.

"Are you growing senile?' Okhee was embarrassed, and gave her grandmother a jabbing and sideways stare.

"I'm not senile yet. Go and fetch your cosmetics." There was an irrefutable authority in her voice.

In peaceful times, the biggest festival in this village was the day of sacrificial offering to the mountain gods. On that day the men killed a sow and the women baked rice cakes. The women's work was always supervised by this matriarch.

The matriarch always spotted at one glance the women who were menstruating or who had had intercourse the night before, and excluded them from the preparations. At those times her entire body gave off irrefutable authority, as if the safety and welfare of the whole village for the year ahead depended on her.

The young women now sitting around her saw the matriarch giving off the same authority as on the days of the village festival. That threw the room into solemn silence.

An elderly woman, however, dared object. "Ma'am, that's very generous of you to try to protect these young girls. But take a moment to think. The big-nosed Americans aren't blind. Cosmetics can't hide all your wrinkles."

The woman broke into giggles in the midst of her words, and the other women also stifled their giggles.

"Don't waste any more words, but bring the cosmetics case quickly," the old woman's parched voice calmly commanded again, silencing the murmurs.

Okhee at last brought her cosmetics case, and the women's eyes by degrees lit up with curiosity.

As the cosmetics had been purchased for use on Okhee's wedding day, there was a complete set, although not of the most expensive brand.

"Now put make-up on my face," the matriarch commanded, pushing the cosmetics case towards a young woman who used to be well-to-do and wear very elaborate make-up on her pretty face before the war.

"Oh, what an absurd idea!" The young woman hesitated embarrassedly.

"Are you interested yourself?" the old woman interrogated maliciously.

"You *are* getting senile, aren't you?" the young woman protested hastily, and began to put make-up on the old woman's face with experienced movements.

The wailing of "Saxi have yes?" became more insistent. The lamplight grew dimmer as the oil can was drained. The old woman, leaving her face to the young woman's disposal, murmured as if to herself,

"We can't tell the big-nosed people's age by looking at them, can we? It must be the same with them regarding us. Different races age differently. And that thing is bound to be done in the dark, anywhere or any time. Oh, yes, it's done in the dark." The old woman spoke thus more to assure herself than for anybody to hear.

The make-up job was completed. The old woman looked at herself in the mirror and smiled contentedly. Well, it was not so much a smile as a forced coquettish twitching of the mouth, and it cast a horror on all the women gathered there.

The scream of "Saxi have yes?" now reached the gate of this big house. The big-nosed men seemed to have perceived stirring of people inside, and they shook the gate like mad.

"Okhee, lend me your clothes, too."

The old woman changed into Okhee's flowing red skirt and yellow blouse. Then she wrapped her head with a colourful striped muffler.

The "Saxi have yes?" had become a violent scream, and their kicking almost knocked the gates down.

"I'm ready now, so open the gate and give me away," the old woman said sharply and dryly.

Someone slid aside the crossbar of the gates. The gates opened wide. The other women shook with thrill and shame, as when releasing water they could hold no more, and hid away in dark corners.

There stood the only saxi in the lamplight. A huge big-nosed soldier stepped in and lifted the saxi in his arms. But perhaps perceiving human presence in every dark corner of the house, he did not lay her down on the spot but strode out of the gates with her in his arms.

"Come on."

The other big-nosed soldiers who came in after him also went out of the gates. A jeep was parked not far from there. All through the trip the saxi sat submissively on the big-nosed soldier's lap, as light and yielding as a baby.

It was a short ride to the elementary school. The building was completely dark. But as the soldiers opened the glass window-door and the plank door, an incredibly strong light fell on the old woman. Simultaneously, there arose a shout of glee. The old woman crouched herself in the shape of a shrimp in the big-nosed soldier's arms and covered her face with both hands.

The old woman was soon thrown on the bed. She collected herself by force of will and looked around the room through the fingers hiding her face. She wanted to see how many big-nosed soldiers she would have to entertain that night. Fortunately, there didn't seem to be more than five or six.

The huge soldier who had brought her in in his arms began to undress her. The old woman was in despair. She knew that the Westerners were barbarians who did not observe the Confucian and Mencian rules of decorum, but she had never imagined that any human being could do that thing under a light brighter than day. The old woman and her late husband had been a fond couple till they were in their sixties and had no less than seven children, but they had never done that thing even under lamplight. The most light they had had was moonlight shining through the paper-panelled window.

The old woman desperately held on to her blouse ribbons and skirt strings. She thought no more of what her face looked like.

But the old woman was as powerless as a fretting baby to stay the huge soldier's fingers. The big-nosed soldier stripped off her garments one by one as easily as he would corn husks. The old woman had desperately thought to herself that surely these men would turn off the light when taking off her undergarments. But alas! The old woman's shrivelled body was revealed under the light stronger than daylight.

Her breasts, which had nursed seven children, were pasted to the ribs, and her belly, cracked and wrinkled through repeated pregnancies and deliveries, was like a dried-up canal. These now were exposed under a light brighter than the midday sun's.

The old woman gave up struggling and, hiding her face behind both hands, began to cry weakly.

Well, even though the old woman had stopped struggling, the grey flannel knickers, the last item of her undergarments, clung to her hipbones, which were as lean as barren hills, and did not go down any further.

The old woman thought, crying, that she had no choice but to bite her tongue and take her own life if that also came off and her private parts were revealed under the bright light, and thought how difficult a thing it is to take one's own life.

She hoped that the big-nosed soldiers would kill her with a

bullet, without bothering to strip off that last item, as they must have discovered by now that they had been duped.

Suddenly, there arose a noise of merry laughter. In her miserable and desperate state, the old woman thought she had never in her life heard such heartily merry laughter.

Before the war, there had been many unfortunate events in the village, but also many happy events. The young people of the village often got angry, but they also often laughed. But however pleasant the occasion, in her compatriots' laughter there seemed to be some sediment of stale sorrow at the bottom of it, and the aftertaste of the laughter was very much like the aftertaste of sighs. To her knowledge, only babies could laugh such hearty, merry laughter as these foreign soldiers were laughing now.

Even in her miserable state, the old woman began to steal glances at the big-nosed soldiers through the fingers of her hands covering her face. The big-nosed soldiers had all rolled off their chairs and were roaring with laughter, rolling on the floor and squeezing their sides.

Well, in the room there were only herself flung on the bed and the soldiers; the room was bleak and there was no amusing sight whatever. But the laughter was so merry that the old woman raised her crying voice, so as not to laugh along with the soldiers.

The laughter ceased at long last, and one of the soldiers pulled her up from the bed and put her clothes on her one by one.

When the old woman had all her clothes back on, the soldiers led her out into the dark. The old woman's heart contracted, as she thought that they were leading her outdoors to shoot her.

But the soldiers put her in the jeep. And they loaded some heavy boxes on the jeep, too. They brought the old woman down in front of the big house they had taken her from, and unloaded all the boxes as well.

To the old woman, who stared in bewilderment, the big-nosed soldiers smacked their lips, repeatedly carrying their hands to their mouths in simulation of eating, and pointed to the boxes.

"Mama chow chow, okay? Mama chow chow, okay?"

The big-nosed soldiers got in the jeep again and drove off toward the elementary school.

On hearing the departure of the car, all the women in the house rushed out at once. The old woman quickly summoned her dignity and ordered the women to carry the boxes the big-nosed soldiers had left there into the house.

There was food in every box. There were canned fruits, canned meat, sweet preserves, fruits, milk, sweet and sour and fragrant powders, chocolates wrapped in silver foil, sweets, jelly, crisp biscuits inside colourful boxes. The old and young women looked at them ecstatically, and hardly dared to breathe.

It was the old woman who, befitting her age, first recovered composure. She calmly recounted her adventure of that night and concluded thus:

"It was thanks to their being Yankees that I returned alive and even received presents. If they had been Japanese, they'd have shot me dead the moment they found out they were deceived. Oh, yes, they'd have killed me a hundred times over. And if they had been Russians they'd have raped me nonetheless, regardless of my age. Oh, yes, I'd have died crushed under their weight, and there'd have been no need for them to shoot me with a gun."

All the women gathered there completely agreed with her and shuddered.

Of course, neither the old woman nor any other woman in the village had ever set foot outside of this country, and none of them had ever seen or become acquainted with any foreigners, whether Yankees or Russians. This was their first contact with any foreigner at all.

Nevertheless, the old woman pronounced such a confident dictum with a hundred per cent certainty, and all the other women were unanimously of the same opinion. That much intuition into national characters is simply basic knowledge to anyone born in this land.